"Gradually it was disclosed to me that the line separating good and evil passes not through states, nor between classes, nor between political parties, either—but right through every human heart.

—Alexsandr Solzhenitsyn
The Gulag Archipelago

"Anybody who has ever built a 'new heaven' only mustered the power he needed through his *own hell*."

—Friedrich Nietzsche
The Genealogy of Morals

Explore more of the world of *The Two Riders*
and the Forbidden Minds series at:

ArmondBoudreaux.com

Publisher's Note:
If you enjoy this novel, please leave a positive Rating and/or review on Goodreads, Amazon, or other similar websites to let other readers know. Reviews work!

FORBIDDEN MINDS | BOOK TWO

THE TWO RIDERS

ARMOND BOUDREAUX

Uproar Books

1419 PLYMOUTH DRIVE, NASHVILLE, TN 37027

THE TWO RIDERS

Published by Uproar Books, LLC.

Edited by Rick Lewis.

Cover illustration by Edouard Noisette.

ISBN: 978-1-949671-26-1

First paperback edition.

FSC
www.fsc.org
MIX
Paper from responsible sources
FSC® C005010

For my sister Yvette

Author's Note

The ideas that became Forbidden Minds first took shape for me in 2016, and I wrote *The Way Out* in 2017. I point this out because the series has turned out to be far more topical than I anticipated or intended. When I began writing this story about a dangerous virus and the totalitarian regime that resulted from it, I had no idea what 2020 had in store.

Whatever your values and political preferences are, I hope that you come away from this book asking yourself difficult questions about what it means to be human, genetic engineering, reproduction, civil disobedience, technology, and a whole host of other issues. These questions can't help touching on the conflicts, fears, and conspiracy theories of our current moment, but they also transcend them.

--Armond Boudreaux, September 8, 2021

PART ONE

1

Jessica

Soaring at three hundred miles per hour over the treetops outside of Atlanta, Jessica thought that Val made it all look too easy. Flying. Fighting. Being a hero. Being strong and courageous. As a child, Jessica had often compared herself unfavorably to her sister. Val was strong. A fighter. But Jessica could be strong in her own way, too, and she reminded herself that in the last twenty-four hours, she'd been just as courageous as Val had been. In fact, Jessica had probably shown more courage than most people ever do in their whole lives.

And the time for courage wasn't over yet.

"We're here," Val said. She pushed a lever forward, and Jessica's head and insides lurched. The Dragonfly's airspeed, indicated by red digits on the instrument console, plummeted to less than one hundred miles per hour in seconds.

Jessica had been the one to insist they launch a rescue mission to protect the eight-month-old infant Taylor from being seized by government agents who had uncovered her budding telepathic abilities. So why was it that Val was the one who seemed completely focused and unfazed by the danger? With Jessica's stomach in knots and her heart in her throat, Val's apparent calm was starting to piss her off.

Below them, the trees opened up to reveal a wide clearing and, about a mile ahead, the Artemis building. As they approached, Jessica was surprised to see police barricades scattered about in seemingly random triangles. Only then did she remember the deadly riot that had happened here when she had come to interview Dr. Hayden. Less than seventy-two hours ago, but it felt like it had been months.

Those must mark where the bodies fell, she thought. *We're lucky there's not still an army of police and DHS investigators on the scene.*

But it was still an hour before dawn. The cops and TV reporters would doubtlessly be back in a few hours to continue their work.

The Dragonfly's heads-up display outlined the four-story building in light blue. Long and rectangular with its name emblazoned in large red letters, Artemis Advanced Reproduction reminded Jessica of the aeronautics facility that she'd once visited when she was young. Another testament of humankind's technological aspirations—the aeronautics facility representing our desire to fly higher and faster, Artemis our need to master nature.

"I'll land right in front of the doors," said Val, guiding the Dragonfly closer to the ground. "If anybody's home, that should get their attention pretty quick."

Jessica wasn't thrilled about making themselves so visible, but she also didn't have any better ideas. They'd lost their cell phones at the Singer Institute in North Carolina, so there was no way to contact Dr. Hayden.

"I want to do this as fast as we can," said Val. "Find Hayden and get out of here. No dicking around. We have to make it back before dawn."

All night Jessica had been thinking about saving the baby from being taken to some place like the research facility where they'd just escaped with Val's eleven-year-old son. She hadn't thought much about seeing Dr. Hayden again, but now that she *was* thinking about it, her heart felt a little too big for her chest. Maybe Merida's jealousy wasn't just paranoia, after all?

Have to be careful about thoughts like that from now on, she told herself.

What a world she lived in now. Telepaths. Viral pandemics created in labs and deliberately released. Far-reaching conspiracies to control human reproduction and prevent the births of telepaths. Jessica and Val, rebels on the run from government agencies.

Val killed the Dragonfly's propulsion engines and settled into a hover just in front of Artemis's metal and glass entrance. She switched off the HUD and turned on the vehicle's floodlights, which glinted off of the glass. Jessica squinted as her eyes adjusted.

"What now?" she said, suddenly feeling silly. How did they get the attention of somebody in an underground bunker in the middle of the night? "Shouldn't we be getting swarmed by security?"

"What's a couple of rent-a-cops going to do against a Dragonfly?" said Val, pulling the pilot's joystick to one side and turning the aircraft so that the rear loading ramp faced the building. "I imagine security is talking it over right now, and it's just a matter of time before they call up Hayden to ask him how to proceed."

"What if they go straight to the police first? Or Homeland Security?"

"If he's hiding an illegal child in an underground bunker here, there's no way he doesn't have security report everything to him first. The last thing he wants is to get the government involved."

Val landed the Dragonfly. Again, Jessica felt awe—maybe a little envy—at how competent her sister was. The landing was barely noticeable beyond a soft *thump* and a pneumatic *hiss* from the landing gear.

The two of them unbuckled their safety harnesses and moved from the cockpit to the cargo hold. Motors and pneumatic pushrods whined as the loading ramp in the back opened.

"You do the talking, but I'm taking no chances here," said Val. "First sign of trouble, and I'm out of here—with or without you."

"I get it," said Jessica.

Getting Val to leave her son and husband behind had been no easy feat. They'd only just been reunited after three days of absolute hell. Jessica had no doubt Val would abandon the mission—and her—in a heartbeat rather than risk losing them again. Jessica didn't know what it was like to love someone that much. The detached, objective attitude of a journalist had been her vocation, and most of the time she thought that it was the best way to live. Baby Taylor had awakened something in her, though—a ferocious drive to protect the small, the innocent, the voiceless.

They descended the loading ramp to the sidewalk. The smell of humid night air and the feeling of solid concrete under her feet came almost as a relief to Jessica after spending much of the night in the Dragonfly, which smelled like guns and cold metal.

The inside of the atrium was completely dark except for a single light that dimly illuminated the reception desk.

"Kind of looks like nobody's home," said Val. "Maybe he got wind of what happened in North Carolina and ran."

Or maybe someone's already been here and taken them, Jessica thought. After all, the bastards who had shown up at Jessica's apartment two nights ago had known that she'd met with Hayden that day—and that she'd gotten that damned computer from his nurse.

"Shit," she said. "They've already—"

"Jessica? *Val*?"

The voice came from Jessica's right. She turned to look, and there stood Hayden several yards away on the sidewalk. He must have come out a side exit rather than the front door. Instead of the lab coat he'd worn when Jessica had interviewed him, he now wore jeans and a T-shirt. If anything, the street clothes made him more attractive. Jessica scolded herself for thinking that way.

"Dr. Hayden," said Jessica, her heart lurching. "I'm so sorry, but you and the baby are in danger. You have to come with us. Now."

Hayden frowned. "An agent came here asking about you and the computer. I don't know how they knew, but..." He trailed off, looking up. Jessica heard it, too. A distant whining noise.

"Fuck," said Val. "That's them. We have to—"

But another sound cut her off—a rapid *putputput* and *crackcrackcrack* as bullets struck dirt and concrete. Jessica watched Hayden turn toward the sounds, then heard herself scream as the bullets struck him. Blooms of blood and bright red flesh burst open from his back, legs, and shoulders as his body tumbled backwards onto the concrete.

2

Merida

Merida and Celina crouched between two dumpsters in the alley behind Merida's restaurant. Combined with her nerves, the stench of the trash made Merida feel queasy. From here, she could see the back door. She had expected someone to be guarding it, but the alley looked deserted. All she had to do was get inside, get the computer, and get out. Easy. Right?

"Well, let's get it over with, I guess," she said.

Celina grabbed her forearm. "No, wait."

"What?"

Celina closed her eyes. After a few seconds, her voice spoke in Merida's mind: *Two guards. Watching the door. From that window across from the restaurant.*

"I'll never get used to you doing that," whispered Merida.

Well, said Celina's thought-voice, *give it time. You've only known that telepaths exist for a day or so. And I thought you* liked *the idea of being in somebody else's head. I thought it was sexy to be able to know what somebody wants without them having to say it.*

"Being able to do it, yeah," admitted Merida. "I don't want somebody else in *my* head, though."

Celina grinned, and her thought-voice became even more sultry. *Just imagine what it's like to be with someone who knows every little secret desire you have.*

Merida shifted from a crouch to her knees and peeked around the corner of the dumpster. Even if she found Celina's flirting sexy—and as much as she hated to admit it, sometimes it was—the smell of trash was too overpowering to be turned on by much of anything. And more importantly, she couldn't let Jessica down. They had to get the computer and dump its contents onto the internet. It was their only hope of saving themselves now. Hopefully, when everything was out there, the world wouldn't stand by while Jessica and Merida and the rest of them were taken by government agents and killed. Right?

Merida pushed aside the thought that this was all ridiculous, the skeptical voice saying that they were all going to die no matter what happened. She tried to bury the fear that she couldn't trust the average person to stand up to the government any more than she could trust Celina to stay out of her head. Tried to disregard the nagging thought that even if they managed to release the information, a lot of people would dismiss it as just another conspiracy theory.

"The guards?" she said. "How can we get past them?"

Celina's eyebrows lifted slightly. *Oh, I can take care of them.*

She paused, and for a few seconds, Merida wondered if she had trailed off on some weird sexual fantasy. Finally, her voice spoke in Merida's head again.

There we go. You can get to the door now.

"What? Won't they see m—"

But Celina leaned forward suddenly and kissed her. Before she understood what was happening, Merida's lips parted—almost on instinct. But then she planted her hands on Celina's shoulders and pushed her back.

"Why did you...?" she said, wiping her mouth with the back of her arm.

I just wanted to see what you'd do, said Celina's voice. She shrugged. *You get so worked up over Jessica and whether or not she's really into you, I wondered how quick you'd forget about her*. She smiled and caught her lower lip between her teeth. *You taste good.*

Merida's hands shook with anger. "You fucking..."

But the triumphant look on Celina's face faltered, and her eyes dropped a little.

Sorry, she said finally. *I can't help it sometimes.*

"You can always fucking help it," Merida said through gritted teeth. "We didn't have to rescue you from that research facility. We could have taken Val's kid and left the rest of you there to rot."

Celina changed suddenly. Her shoulders slumped slightly. Her wide eyes—always ready to take in everything about the world around her—narrowed. Her lips, normally full of mirth and perpetually seductive, curved into a slight frown. It was almost like looking at a different person.

You don't understand, said her thought-voice. *You don't know what it's like to—*

"*Talk* to me," said Merida, still trembling.

Celina winced like a frightened animal. It made her look younger. Sometimes it was easy to forget that she was barely in her twenties, at least ten years younger than Merida. It made the kiss that much more infuriating.

"The guards won't be a problem," she said, not looking at Merida.

"Why not? There's no hiding from that window."

Slowly, Celina's mouth stretched into a sad smile. *Life's too short to pout, I guess. Those guards are a little occupied right now.*

Merida looked up at the window and then back at Celina. "Are they still there?"

Celina grinned. *Let's say that two manly men are discovering something new and unexplored in their sexuality.*

An image flashed in Merida's mind. A dark room lit only by the dim city light coming through a window. Two men, both wearing SWAT gear, were kissing.

Merida shook her head, trying to clear her mind. "That's what they're doing right now?"

Celina's smile widened. *I thought that might keep them busy for a while. They're going to really freak out when they're done, though. Better get moving.*

Setting aside what she wanted to say to Celina, Merida stood slowly, glancing both ways down the alley.

There's nobody else, said Celina's voice. *The alley's deserted, and there's nobody in the restaurant. Just two dudes getting friendly upstairs.*

Clenching her fists, Merida started toward the door. Suddenly she needed to be as far from Celina as she could get. She could still taste the girl's mouth, and the mixture of embarrassment, shame, revulsion and—she had to admit it—*arousal* that Celina had caused in her was enough to make her feel almost sick. And those two men in the floral shop—was she *raping* them? Was that what it was? What other word was there for what she had done?

If it makes you feel any better, said Celina's voice in her head, *at least one of those guys was hoping to feel us up tonight. Well, he hoped to feel up Jessica, anyway. He figured she'd be the one going after the computer. Their big plan was to wait for us to grab the device, then put us down with sedative darts. And he figured, hey, when you've got a hot chick on your hands, unconscious...*

Fine, thought Merida. *Now stay out of my head.*

Sorry.

It sounded like she meant it.

3

Val

Braden, Kim... Val thought, as if Braden were close by and could hear what she was thinking, as if he wasn't back at her cousin's farm, hiding in the darkness of an old barn. *I'm sorry I left you.*

Cursing herself for letting Jessica talk her into trying to save the baby, Val grabbed her sister's arm and dragged her up the loading ramp into the Dragonfly.

"Get strapped in," she said, pushing Jessica toward one of the passenger seats that lined the cargo bay.

But something seemed to awaken in Jessica. Her eyes flashed. "No, I'm going to get the baby," she said. "She's still—"

Suddenly, the air filled with heat, light, and a roaring noise as if the night itself had begun to burn. The Dragonfly rocked, sending Val staggering and Jessica falling flat onto the floor.

"Too late for that," shouted Val, though she couldn't hear her own voice.

She closed the loading ramp and ran to the pilot's seat. Two other aircraft registered on the sensors. A pair of UAD-9 Dragonflies. Through the windshield, she could see them hovering in the darkness about two hundred yards ahead, their canopies reflecting firelight that must have been coming from the building. They were targeting the facility, and any second, one of them would target this craft, too.

"I can't leave her!" shouted Jessica, who now stood in the doorway behind her.

"She's already gone," said Val. "Get strapped in *now*."

Never should have left them, she thought again as she powered up the Dragonfly. She remembered the expression on Braden's face when she'd left him at the barn with Kim. It had almost looked like distrust. And Val thought that she knew why. Hugging her son, she had thought briefly about a moment at the creek two nights before. Just a flash of memory and a stab of guilt.

Not long after she and Braden had fled their home, they'd been pinned down by a pair of Dragonflies. Braden had been unconscious because of a sedative dart, and Val had thought then that all was lost. For a second—just a second—she had thought about shooting Braden to keep him from falling into government hands.

Had Braden read her memory? Was that the reason for the strange look on his face? Would he understand? Would she die tonight without getting a chance to explain to him what had gone through her mind in her desperation?

But now was not the time to think about it. She buried those questions in the problem of the moment. There was no way she was getting the Dragonfly off the ground without being shot to pieces, but she didn't need to lift off in order to strike first. She trained the targeting computer onto the two UADs.

Two beeps signaled that she had a lock.

"Have some of this," she said, firing the Dragonfly's nose-mounted miniguns at the other two craft. As the cannons lit up the night, she pulled back on the joystick and got the Dragonfly into the air. The UADs veered away from the hail of bullets, which gave Val time to fire the propulsion engines and push forward.

Jessica fell into the co-pilot's seat beside her. Val barely registered that she was saying something about the baby, but she had no time to respond. As they passed between the UADs, one of them turned to follow. A shriek from the dashboard signaled that it had radar lock on her, and Val heard the sound of its cannons firing as if from somewhere far off.

Bullets struck the fuselage somewhere behind them—*rattatatta*—and Jessica screamed. Damage alarms sounded. Through it all, she heard explosions somewhere behind them. Val banked left, pulling out of the stream of bullets, and spun around to face the UAD.

Jessica gasped. "Oh, my God."

Val had fought in war. She had killed. She had seen soldiers killed. She'd seen guerrilla fighters blow up entire city blocks and hold children hostage. But right now, she couldn't help gasping along with her sister. While the one UAD had been firing on them, the other had been launching missiles at the Artemis facility.

The roof of the building's center section had caved in, leaving only a tower of fire where once there had been glass and metal. The rest of the facility's concrete structure was riddled with holes that belched flame. An icy hand closed around Val's heart at the thought of the people trapped inside. The unborn babies that had been sleeping and dreaming of color in their artificial uteruses. The telepathic girl they'd come here to save. The medical staff who had probably been struggling to stay awake through the night shift.

Before she could react, the first UAD was firing at them again. Bullets spattered the front of the Dragonfly, and Val veered wildly away from it. They had her on her heels, and one good punch would knock her down permanently.

Why aren't they firing missiles? she thought.

But then she understood. The agents didn't know that Braden wasn't with them; they probably hoped to bring the Dragonfly down without killing everybody inside. And so far, she'd stayed too close to them for them to fire EMP rockets.

"Fucking hell," she said, easing the joystick back and to the left. Then she punched the accelerator, passed directly under the UAD, and headed toward the woods.

The UAD was a faster model than Val's transport Dragonfly—too quick to lose for long. Before she could turn and re-engage, the radar-lock alarm sounded and more bullets struck them.

"*Dammit,*" hissed Val.

Time for something desperate. She killed the propulsion and the rear lift engines.

"Don't throw up!" she shouted at Jessica. Jerking the stick backwards, she maxed out the front lift engines, and the Dragonfly's nose lifted. The craft flipped over, and Val's stomach seemed to flatten into her pelvis.

"Hang on!" she screamed.

As the world turned upside down, the UAD came into view. The targeting system beeped for lock, and Val pulled the trigger to fire two missiles. Alarms screamed at the insane maneuver as the Dragonfly's nose turned toward the ground. For half a second, they were looking at the ground, and then at trees, and then at the dark horizon. They'd done a complete 360-degree flip.

"Holy shit," groaned Jessica.

A pair of loud *booms* and a concussion rocked the Dragonfly—and Val knew the missiles had hit their target. One UAD down. She fired the rear lift engines again and turned the craft to face Artemis.

Jessica let out a sob. "No!"

The building was an inferno. Fire gushed from gaping holes in the outside walls. Smoke rose high into the air. The middle of the structure, which had been a large vestibule made entirely of glass and metal, was just a column of flame now. But the other UAD was nowhere in sight.

Val glanced at the radar screen, and as she did, a hail of gunfire showered the troop carrier. She jerked the control to the right, sending them careening out of the spray, and then throttled up to full.

The acceleration rocked her head back against her seat, and the Dragonfly rocketed toward Artemis. More gunfire erupted somewhere behind her, so she banked left and circled around to the front of the building. As she passed over a parking lot, she barely registered people running across the asphalt.

Some of them survived, she thought, but then she heard the sound of the UAD's miniguns. Had the bastard shot at them?

Before she could look at her rearview monitor to find out, though, a *ping* sounded from the dash, alerting her that the UAD had her in radar lock. A shrill alarm sounded. A rocket.

Please, God, let this work, she thought. She killed the thrust engines and swung to the left, heading straight into the column of flame that rose from the middle of the building. In an instant, the temperature inside the cockpit rose, and all Val could see was a swirl of red and black.

"What the hell are you doing?" Jessica yelled.

Several alarms sounded from the dash, and the whining noise of the lift engines slowed to a dull *whir*. With a loud *bang*, the top of the Dragonfly struck something solid, probably part of the building's structure, and Val's heart rose into her throat as the craft plummeted a few meters. She hit the accelerator, and again the carrier rocketed forward, the engines starting to scream. Somewhere behind her, the missile exploded as it struck the building.

"Come on," Val groaned, pulling back on the control stick. Red and orange whirled around the windshield for a second, and then everything turned black as they cleared the flames.

She glanced at the dash. The UAD was at her eleven o'clock high. Another *ping* meant that it had a lock on her again.

Acting entirely on instinct, Val killed the accelerator and spun the Dragonfly around. The UAD was hovering high above her, next to the tower of smoke. As she pulled back on the stick to turn her nose up toward it, the alarm sounded again. Another rocket.

At the same time, Val fired guns. The UAD reeled, the back end of its fuselage bursting into flames. Then Val jerked the control, and the Dragonfly rolled to the left.

The missile blazed past them, hit the ground, and exploded. The close blast sent them into a spin, the whole craft shuddering. Val's stomach rolled, and the blood rushed to her head as everything became a blur.

Several images rose in her mind as the world swirled like a maelstrom around her: two girls, ten and twelve, running through a pecan grove during midsummer; Kim cradling her face in his palms while he kissed her; Braden climbing the old hickory that stood in their front yard; Kim handing a newborn Braden to her as she lay on their bed, panting and dripping with sweat from labor; the girl in Iran who had spit on Val for saving her life. And then the ground rushed up to meet her, the darkness swallowing up everything—noise, heat, fire, life.

James Watts: *The New York Times*

State officials in California, Oregon, and Washington have officially set a date for an interstate summit to discuss the possibility of secession from the United States and the formation of a new union of states, sparking outrage from the White House.

The summit, called "seditious" and "treasonous" by the President, will be hosted September 19 in Portland. In direct contrast to session conventions planned in Georgia, Alabama, and New Hampshire in the coming weeks, the Pacific coast states are rallying behind SRP protections and enforcement rather than against them. California Governor Lisa Verner specifically cited her concerns about the conservative-dominated Supreme Court...

Carlo Moyers: American News Site

Governor Alex Vincent of Florida just came out in favor of a state referendum on the question of whether or not to leave the United States. Speaking at a rally in Boca Raton, the governor finally broke his neutrality on the issue and urged the state legislature to let voters have their say as early as this November...

4

Kim

Kim's whole body ached from exhaustion, but he couldn't sleep. He had tried for a few hours, but between his fear for the others, the discomfort of the cot, and the aching in his injured shoulder, he couldn't drift off. So he had climbed the stairs to the hayloft and sat in the loft door at the gable end of the roof, letting his feet dangle over the edge. He tried to set aside his worry, to feel content watching the stillness of the night and listening to the sounds of crickets chirping.

He was grateful for the scent of warm, humid air and old barn wood. He'd had trouble shaking the smell of the Paul Singer Institute since they'd left it two nights ago. There was nothing particularly unpleasant about that smell in itself, which had reminded him of the colleges he'd attended and of the hospitals and clinics where he'd worked over the years. But now, the memory of that place's smells made him realize how much he loved the way that he and Val had lived since he'd removed Val's implant. The quiet, rural life surrounded by trees, grass, dirt. Kim had spent most of his early life almost completely removed from the natural world and surrounded by artificial things. Plastic, vinyl, linoleum, drywall, brick, metal. Now he couldn't bear the thought of going back to that kind of life.

Are they going to be home soon? came Braden's voice in his head.

Kim smiled in spite of his fear. "Home?"

I mean, are they going to be back soon? Braden corrected himself.

I'm up in the loft, Kim thought. *You can come up if you want to.*

Downstairs, he heard rustling and then creaking as Braden climbed the rickety wooden stairs onto the loft. Soft footsteps crossed the platform toward him. Because Braden was so mature for his age, it was easy to forget that he was still just a kid, that he hadn't quite shaken off childhood yet.

"I don't know when they'll be back, but I hope soon," said Kim. "You know your mother. She's probably kicking some ass or blowing something up right now."

The boy sat down next to him in the loft door and let his legs swing forward and backward in the night air, his heels bumping lightly against the outside wall of the barn.

"Yeah," he said, not very enthusiastically. His face looked a little puffy, the eyes especially. The lack of sleep was getting to him.

"You okay?" said Kim.

It was a stupid thing to ask a kid who had just been held prisoner in an underground cell, but Kim didn't know what else to say.

"I'm fine," said Braden. "I hope they save that baby."

"Me, too. And if Merida succeeds with the computer, maybe our lives can return to normal again. Maybe *better* than normal."

"What do you mean?"

Kim leaned his head against the side of the loft door. "Well, if the world finds out the truth about the virus and the real reasons behind artificial reproduction, the laws will probably change.

They'll have to. People won't accept such an invasion of their privacy and freedom based on a lie."

Braden looked skeptical. "Do you really think so? Those men at the Institute, the ones who went around killing everybody. You don't think they'll do whatever it takes to protect the secret?"

"Do you think people like that can stop your mom?" said Kim, putting on a confident smile. "Could they stop a father protecting his son? Do you think they could stop *us*?"

Braden looked out at the night. "What if you're wrong about people? What if they want the lie, because they like what it led to? What if they don't want to believe what that computer says?"

Accustomed to having all the answers, Kim opened his mouth to speak, but then he shut it again. That was the thing about having kids: they asked easy questions when they were young, but the older they got, the more difficult the questions became. The same questions had been in the back of his mind since the Institute. Would the truth about the Samford Virus change people's minds about SRP? Or would they prefer the easy choice to the hard one?

"And what about people like me?" said Braden. "Do you think they'll accept us?"

"Some might not," said Kim, "but I think most people will come around."

You're not really sure about that.

Kim sighed. "No, I guess not. But look." He shifted and pressed his back against the door frame so that he was facing Braden with one leg dangling from the edge. "When I was in college, some people didn't want me to succeed. They didn't like Japanese people coming to this country and doing so well for themselves. They hated me for the fact that I was a good student. They assumed it came easy for me because I'm Asian. They didn't care that I grew up poor or that I'd worked hard all my life. They just thought that people from Asia had an unfair advantage in life, and they couldn't stand me for it. I know it's not the same as what you'll face. You're going to meet a different type of prejudice, and it'll come in different forms and from different people. But that's what life is like. We all have our own advantages and disadvantages. There's no getting around it. What my experience taught me is that some people will always dislike you no matter what."

"Why?"

Kim shrugged. "I don't know. Human nature, I guess? Evolution? It's in our nature to stick to our tribe and see outsiders as our enemy."

Braden's eyes fell. He seemed troubled, more troubled than the conversation warranted. They'd talked about this issue before—it wasn't news to Braden that the world was always full of people who regarded you with suspicion or wanted to hold you back. Was it simply that the events of the last two days had finally caught up to him?

I'm fine, Braden said.

Are you sure? It's okay if you're not okay.

Holding on to the edge of the floor, Braden leaned forward so that he could look down at the ground below them. *I'm just tired, I guess.*

"Hey, be careful," said Kim. He reached out and gently pushed the boy's upper body backwards so that he wasn't leaning so far out. "I'm a good doctor, but I'm not sure if I'm up to patching up broken bones with one good arm and no medical tools."

Braden pulled both his legs up onto the floor and hugged his knees to his chest. "Sorry."

Kim patted the boy's leg and ruffled his hair. "I know it's been a hard few days on you."

Braden looked at him and offered a forced half-smile. "On *me*? You're the one who got shot."

"And you got kidnapped."

"I guess we've both had a shitty couple of days."

Kim laughed at this. Hard. The laughter sent shocks of pain radiating out from his shoulder. Still, he kept laughing—and wincing.

"Any other time," he said, grimacing, "I'd scold you for the language. But I needed that laugh."

Even in the dark, he could see Braden's face turning red.

"You and Mom cuss all the time," he said. He shrugged his shoulders and lowered his head as if trying to hide it in a shell.

Kim straightened his back in a mock haughty expression. "No, we don't!"

Braden looked up at him, one eyebrow raised and his mouth stretching into a bright but incredulous smile.

"Well," said Kim. "We don't curse a lot *out loud*..."

"Yeah," said Braden. "The truth comes out."

"It always does. Your mom, your aunt, and the others are making sure of that."

At this, Braden's bright expression faded. For a while, the two of them just watched the night and listened to crickets chirping. Eventually, Kim started to feel like he could go to sleep.

"Why don't we try to get..." he began, but he trailed off and looked out into the darkness.

There was a droning sound coming through the woods. A gas-powered engine. Headed toward them. Before long, Kim could see headlights moving along the dirt trail that cut through the woods.

"What do we do?" said Braden.

5

Theresa

Her body ached from walking, but she pressed on, her legs almost carrying her of their own accord. She didn't even know for sure where she was going to go, but she knew that she had to get as far from the Institute as possible.

She'd been walking all night, sticking close to the narrow road that cut through the mountains, but far enough away that no one would see her as they drove. Cars came and went, their engines whining or roaring as the drivers hurried to respond to the carnage that had happened when Bowen let her out of her room.

She had killed. Not just killed—she had murdered. Slaughtered.

She'd made the soldiers, or whatever they were, shoot people—and then themselves. She'd forced some Very Important People to smash their skulls against concrete until they were dead. She could still hear the sounds—a dull, wet *thud*; a hollow *crack*.

She'd made Bowen shoot his friend.

Bowen, who had thought such horrible things about her...

He'd deserved what she had done to him, right? A man who did the things that Bowen did, who thought the things that Bowen thought—that man had deserved to be hurt and killed. Didn't he?

They had *all* deserved it, but Bowen especially. She'd seen what had occupied his mind. She'd been his obsession in life. Well, she and Celina.

He'd had such ugly thoughts about Celina, about doing disgusting, horrible things with her. His thoughts about Theresa had been... well, he'd thought of those fantasies as sweet, as tender, as *loving* in some sense.

But it all amounted to the same thing. He had wanted Theresa and Celina as playthings. And he'd imagined Theresa saying to him, "It's okay. You can have me." As if her permission made every disgusting fantasy in his head okay.

Was that what most men were like? Did they all imagine having women and young girls as playthings? Her father hadn't been that kind of man. He had thought of his love for her mother as a kind of formal dance in which each partner acted and responded gently and carefully to the moves of the other.

But her father was dead. And even when he'd been alive, Theresa had thought that he was a rare man. An old-fashioned one, at least. He and Theresa's mother had been so old-fashioned that they'd conceived Theresa illegally and birthed her at home because they rejected government regulation of reproduction.

Were there any good men left besides her father?

She'd made it all of the way down the mountain and had started to climb the gentle slope at the bottom of the next when she heard the noise. A buzzing sound that she knew all too well. She'd come to expect it at certain times of the day, like when Institute doctors and nurses had taken her to the lab for tests.

A drone.

Even though she knew that it was nonsensical, her first instinct was to run. Suddenly, she didn't feel tired or achy at all, and her legs picked up the pace automatically. She charged between trees in the dark, limbs pawing at her face and spider webs clinging to her hair. But she barely noticed these things. She only knew that a drone meant she was caught. That she would hear the whistle of a sedative dart and then wake up restrained in a cell with bright lights and a glass wall.

No matter how hard she ran, the buzzing got steadily closer, and before long, her legs were beginning to shake and burn beneath her. She reached out with her mind, hoping to find whoever was controlling the drone and force them to leave her alone, but it was no use. They were far away.

"Theresa, wait." The voice sounded small and tinny. It was coming from the drone.

She pushed on, her pace slowing as the slope became steeper. Her heart pounded. Her head felt light. Pretty soon she'd hear the *pop* of the drone firing a dart, and then she'd sleep. Everything she'd done at the Institute had all been for nothing. Bowen, Simmons, all the death and pain she'd caused.

Finally, her knees buckled beneath her, and she fell onto cool, wet leaves.

Her head swimming, she waited for the sedative dart. Or maybe they'd just kill her and end the whole thing. That would be better. Then she could see her parents again and leave all of this behind.

If I don't go to Hell for killing all those people.

She pushed the idea away. Surely, God wouldn't send her to Hell for killing people as awful as Bowen? People who deserved it? People who were evil?

"Theresa," said the voice again, and a light fell on her from above. Wind from the drone's propellers washed over her, rippling her clothes and whipping her hair against her face. "Please. I'm not going to hurt you, and I'm not going to send you back to the Institute."

The voice was almost... kind. Sympathetic, even. But she knew better than to think that mattered. Bowen, the other doctors, the nurses, and all the technicians had sounded sympathetic, too. Emotions could be faked in voices. And sometimes people could *feel* sympathy even as they violated you and hurt you. It was all in the service of some "greater good," after all. People could do so much evil out of a desire to do good.

The blinding lights dimmed to a blue glow, and the drone fell into a hover just a few feet above the ground. This was a different kind of machine than the ones that had guarded and escorted her at the Institute. Bigger. Black and silver and bulky, with a projector lens on top.

"Please give me a chance to show you that you can trust me," said the voice.

The projector lens lit up, and the translucent image of a man's head and upper chest appeared like a ghost above the drone. He wore a dress shirt with the collar unbuttoned and a tie loosened around his neck. Middle-aged. Probably a little younger than her father had been before he died. In other circumstances, she might have thought that his eyes looked kind. Trustworthy. Appearances were usually deceiving, though.

"I want to help you," said the man, the image flickering slightly as if the device were struggling to hang on to data signal. "I want to make sure that you never have to run or be afraid again."

"You're lying," said Theresa, trying to hold the words back even as her lips spoke them. She'd hoped that at a moment like this, she could be stoic. That she could show them she wasn't afraid, but her will wasn't strong enough.

"Let me show you something," said the man. His hands appeared in the image. He was holding a small touchscreen device like a phone or a tablet. "The lower compartment of the drone is about to open. Don't let that frighten you."

A whirring sound, and a pair of doors swung open from the underside of the drone. *This is it,* Theresa thought. A barrel was about to appear and fire the dart at her. She could try to get up and run, but it wouldn't make any difference. So she just watched.

"I'm giving this to you so that you know you can trust me," the man said.

Two black objects dropped onto the leaf-covered ground. Then the drone backed away and shone its spotlight on the earth. A pistol and a small cardboard box.

"Pick it up," said the man. "It's yours."

Theresa didn't move. Before she could stop herself, she said, "It's a trick."

"I promise you, it's not," said the man. "This drone isn't even equipped with weapons. It's for deliveries and communication only. And with your gifts, you can tell there's nobody nearby. Nobody waiting to spring a trap on you."

Theresa's heart pounded. The gun was a revolver, and she could see that it was loaded. She'd never handled a gun in her life, but she knew the principle from movies. You cocked it and pulled the trigger. And since she was at close range, she might even hit the drone. Then she could run before another drone came.

When she tried to move, though, she found that she couldn't. It was like the nightmares she'd had as a child where the monster was coming closer but her body was paralyzed.

"Who are you?" she said.

The man smiled. Again, he looked kind, but this was more unnerving than comforting. Bad guys were supposed to wear black suits and carry guns. They definitely weren't supposed to be kind and drop guns on the ground for their victims to pick up.

"I'm someone who wants to keep you safe from people like the ones at the Singer Institute," he said. "I'm someone who wants to help you build a better world for yourself and people like you. My name is Daniel Cartwright, and I'm a U.S. senator from the great state of West Virginia."

6

Merida

Merida removed the metal panel from the oven to reveal the computer she'd hidden on the night she and Jessica got caught. She slid her hand over the laptop's surface, thinking about the first time she'd seen it and the fight that she'd started with Jessica over it. Her insides squirmed at the thought of Jessica, who was probably charging into worse danger than she was.

But that wasn't the only thing, was it?

She was worried about Jessica, but she was also worried about *them*—their relationship.

Celina's voice spoke in her head. *Better hurry.*

What do you think I'm doing?

But something washed over Merida like a hot breeze. Was it fear? She was already afraid. This was different—like she was feeling someone else's fear.

You'd better hurry more*, then. They're coming. From all sides of us.*

"Dammit," said Merida through clenched teeth. She slid the computer into her backpack and headed out the back door. Cool night air helped push away whatever feeling had come over her in the kitchen. Now only her own fear was left.

Upstairs in the building across the alley, the two men were yelling at each other. Apparently, whatever trick Celina had played on them had worn off. Now they sounded pissed at one another.

"Time to move," whispered Celina, who met Merida at the door.

For the first time since she'd met the girl, Merida saw fear in Celina's face. It looked odd, like it didn't belong there. To Merida, she had seemed completely beyond fear.

I just don't want to go back, Celina said. *I like being free. I like working with you.*

Merida gestured at the window and men arguing. "You gonna do something about that?"

Celina shook her head as if trying to get rid of a distraction.

Sorry.

Suddenly, the two men went silent.

They're headed out the front of the building now. Shouldn't be a problem for a while.

Merida sighed. She wished Celina had just done that to begin with instead of... whatever you called what she *had* done. But for now, she pushed those thoughts aside. They jogged down the alley toward the car that they'd stolen when Jessica and Val had dropped them off outside Atlanta.

"How far is your reach?" Merida said. "You can't reach as far as Jessica and Val, can you?"

Definitely not that far. Sorry.

Merida knew better, but she couldn't help asking.

"Stop right there!"

The voice came from behind them. Merida's instinct was to run as hard as she could, but before she could move, Celina grabbed her shirt and dragged her between the two dumpsters. Merida peeked out to see a half-dozen men move into position at the end of the alley, rifles in hand.

"Didn't expect you to be here, Celina," yelled the voice.

Now Merida recognized it. Marcus of the Big Ass Gun. Captain Tinycock. Commander Compensator Pistol. So he'd survived the massacre at the Institute. Probably by being a coward and hiding. Or maybe he'd already left before the bad stuff really started. Merida preferred to think that he was a coward, though.

More footsteps sounded from the other end of the alley. They'd blocked off both sides. No way out.

Merida swung the backpack off her shoulder and pulled out the guns that Val had given them. She held one out to Celina, who shook her head.

"You don't want me to have one of those," she said. *I don't need it, anyway.*

Merida wasn't sure she knew what the hell to do with hers. Val had shown her how to cock it, aim, and fire, but she'd never even held a gun in her life before tonight. She'd always hated the idea of guns, had been completely baffled by the rednecks who seemed to worship them even more than they worshipped Jesus.

"It's a tool," Val had said, trying to calm Merida's nerves. "Like a hammer, a car, or a computer. It can be good or bad. You're the one who chooses what to do with it."

Like *that* helped.

Merida was so nervous right now she was likely to shoot herself in the foot. Still, she put Celina's pistol back in the backpack and held her own as Val had shown her. Both hands on the grip, the left cupping the right for control. Finger off the trigger until she was ready to shoot. Never point it at anything she wasn't willing to destroy. Always treat it as if it's loaded (even when it wasn't). She remembered everything that Val had told her. The question was whether or not she could shoot accurately.

"This is your one chance to cooperate, Celina," Marcus called down the alley. "If you make this easy, it could be really good for you. You'll be able to have all the fun you could ask—"

But Celina's thought-voice blocked him out. *He wants to have sex with you, you know. You and Jessica both, at the same time.*

Merida looked at the girl, who met her gaze with a grin. It was as if there had never been any fear in her at all, as if the immediate threat of Marcus and his men had driven away all the dread she'd felt. The fear of being taken back to that crazy place in North Carolina—it was gone, as far as Merida could tell.

"That's..." Merida began, but she shook her head. The last thing she needed right now was to get distracted. "What are we going to do?"

Marcus shouted down the alley again. "Give up the lesbian and the computer, and I guarantee you'll love the job we're offering you."

"'The lesbian?'" said Merida, her hand tightening on the gun's grip.

Celina's smile widened. *I'm telling you, he wants you. Bad. He just covers it up by acting like you and Jessica are beneath him. He's got this one fantasy where—*

"Can you shut up and do something about this asshole?"

Celina rubbed her lip with one finger as if considering the problem. *If I take them all down at once, I'll probably knock you out, too. I can't carry you out of here.*

"So one at a time, then!" snarled Merida. The gun almost seemed to vibrate in her hand. And it occurred to her that she wasn't so much afraid of what *it* was capable of doing, but what *she* was capable of doing with it. And right now, she thought that she could kill anybody who stood in their way.

They're sending drones, said Celina. *Even if we escape from here...*

Just shut these guys down. One problem at a time, please.

Tell that to them.

Celina closed her eyes to concentrate, and there was a commotion from down the alleyway. Feet shuffling. Grunts. The click of several guns being cocked.

"Wait, wait," said one of the men. "*Wait!*"

Gunshots rang out from both ends of the alley, some of them ricocheting off the walls. Thuds. Screams.

Merida chanced a peek around the dumpster. Several men lay on the ground—but not all of them. Two were aiming rifles at Marcus.

More gunfire.

One of the two men with rifles dropped. Then Marcus dove to one side, did some sort of crazy roll into a crouching position, and shot the last of his men in the face with his big-ass handgun of overcompensation.

"*You fucking bitch!*" screamed Marcus toward the garbage dumpsters.

Celina closed her eyes again. Another gunshot.

This time, Merida didn't dare look. She had no desire to see what Marcus's stupid, fucking long-barreled pistol had done to his own stupid, fucking head.

"Problem solved," said Celina.

Looking at her, Merida's chest hitched. A tear had fallen down the girl's cheek, its trail glistening in the light of the streetlamps that illuminated the alleyway.

Celina dried her eyes with the sleeve of her jumpsuit, then rubbed her temples with her fingertips. "Too much of this kind of stuff plays hell on my brain. My head is killing me."

"Let's move," Merida said. But now that the alley was quiet, she could hear the *buzz* of drone engines coming from somewhere nearby.

What Nobody Will Acknowledge about SRP and Rape Culture

By Vivian Muirren

During an interview with Steve Cravey in Friday's *The New York Times: Video Edition*, Madelyne Zehr described in horrific detail the sexual assault committed against her by Michael Crist when they were both college students at Yale two decades ago. The two of them met in a political science class, hit it off, and agreed to go out that night for dinner and a movie. Afterward, Crist went to Zehr's apartment. He soon began pressuring Zehr to have sex with him.

"He kept saying that there was no reason for me not to give in because I couldn't get pregnant," Zehr said in the *NYT* interview. "He kept saying, 'You've got an implant, so there's no reason for us not to' [have sex]."

When Zehr refused, Crist raped her.

"It wasn't violent," she said. "But it was rape. He pushed me down onto my bed, and I just let him do what he wanted. I think he thought that he was being assertive in a sexy way. And I kept telling myself that it was just sex. There weren't any consequences, so it was just sex."

While Crist's office has issued a statement denying Zehr's allegation, the story of their encounter echoes stories told over and over by women: men expecting sex from them because they can't get pregnant.

Slowly but surely, stories like Zehr's are finally beginning to force policy makers, medical professionals, and social scientists to confront a disturbing social side-effect of the Safe Reproductive Practices policies that have been in place for the better part of this century: the data shows that rates of both date rape and violent sexual assault rose dramatically and stayed high after the implementation of SRP. And the stories from women who buckle under the tremendous pressure to "put out" are far too common.

READ MORE
VIEW COMMENTS

7

Jessica

Something warm on her face. In her eye. A low rumble like distant thunder. The steady *beep* of an alarm.

A woman's voice. Urgent.

Another voice. Cold. Electronic.

"Wake up!" someone said, but it sounded far off.

Something shook her body. She opened her eyes. Flickering lights. Orange and yellow. Blue and red also.

"Jessica!"

A blurry face, slowly coming clearer. Val. Her sister. The Dragonflies. The fight. Explosions. All those babies.

"*System failure,*" said the Dragonfly's AI voice. "*Lift engine A3 obstructed.*"

"Oh, my God," Jessica said, but it came out as a whisper. Her head seemed to split open when she spoke. "What...?"

"I knocked those other two bastards out of the sky," said Val, "but we hit the dirt. I think the plane's okay, but I've got to check some things out before we try to take off."

"Hayden..." said Jessica, fumbling at the buckles of her harness. "Artemis."

She wiped her eyes with her shirt sleeve. It came away with blood from a gash in her head.

As her eyes adjusted, Val came into clearer view. And in the face of her war-hardened sister, she saw sympathy. Sorrow. She could hardly believe it, but there were tears in the eyes of the libertarian veteran who just wanted the world to leave her alone—stubborn tears that wouldn't fall, but tears just the same.

"I'm sorry I couldn't save them," Val said, her voice flat. Almost a whisper. "Sorry I couldn't save *her*."

Jessica let the harness fall off of her shoulders and got to her feet. Pain radiated from her head down through her spine. She had to support herself on the back of the seat and the Dragonfly's instrument panel.

"Not your fault," she croaked, putting her arms around Val.

Val's silence said more than her words might. Jessica didn't have to be a mind reader to know that Val absolutely blamed herself for all of this. If only she'd been faster in the air. If she'd used some other dogfighting tactic. If she had just done a better job of hiding her son.

Or maybe... if she hadn't broken the law at all...

"Not your fault," Jessica said again. She let go and looked at Val's face.

"He was our friend, once. Hayden, I mean," said Val. "When I came home from the war, I thought I was done seeing the people I was close to getting killed."

For a second, Jessica thought that her sister was about to break down. This was the last straw, the thing that would break her. But almost as if she'd flipped some switch inside herself, Val wiped the tears from her eyes, and that unearthly determination that was so at home in her expression returned.

"Right now, we've got the others to think about. Are you okay?" She leaned closer to look at the gash on Jessica's forehead.

"I'm fine," Jessica said, though she still felt like she had a bad hangover.

Jessica looked around the cockpit. Her eyes seemed to have completely cleared now. She could read the writing on the dash, the information on all the screens, and the readouts displayed on the HUD. She still felt a little off-balance, though, and as she looked through the windshield to the grassy field outside, she realized that the Dragonfly wasn't sitting level. It leaned to the right slightly.

"I might need your help," said Val. She stepped through the doorway into the cargo area, and Jessica followed.

"Can we fly?" asked Jessica. "I bet we don't have long until they send more agents after us. Or before the police show up."

"The AI is saying that all the engines are functional," said Val, "but there's something obstructing the rotor blades on one of the lift props."

She opened a locker that was built into the fuselage and took out a rifle with a long magazine.

"Same principle as a pistol," she said, holding the rifle out to Jessica. "But this gun is full auto and has a holographic sight. Just put the red dot on the bad guys, squeeze the trigger, and mow them down. It's gonna kick like a mule, so hold it steady. Shoulder-width stance. One foot in back, like the fighting stance in *hapkido*."

Jessica stared at the gun before taking it. It was lighter than she'd expected it to be. "How do I know the 'bad guys?'"

Val rolled her eyes. "Don't give me that." She took another rifle from the locker for herself. "You know who the enemy is. The safety's off, so keep your finger off the trigger unless you're ready to fire. Don't point it at anything you aren't willing to shoot. And hopefully you won't need to use it at all." She walked to the back of the Dragonfly and put her hand on the button to lower the cargo ramp. "Ready?"

Jessica wiped blood from her eyebrow. Suddenly, more than anything else in the world, she needed to get back to Merida. She needed to see her. Put her hands on her. Know that she was alive and safe. "Let's just hurry and get out of here."

Val pressed the button. The hydraulic motors whirred to life and squealed a little louder than they had before now.

"You cover me while I clear the prop," said Val. "Then we should be able to take off."

As the ramp lowered, light and heat poured through the opening. Jessica groaned and shielded her face with one hand. When the ramp reached the ground, her insides lurched—a figure stood at the bottom of the ramp, a woman silhouetted by the flames that had completely engulfed the Artemis building. She had a pistol aimed at Val.

Val moved faster than Jessica. She raised her rifle and aimed it at the woman. "Drop the gun now!"

To Jessica's surprise, the woman lowered her gun—but didn't drop it.

"Valerie Hara?" she said, taking slow steps toward the ramp. "Jessica?"

Jessica knew that voice. Relief surged through her, making her limbs feel numb and weak. "Havana?"

She let the rifle drop to her side and stumbled forward, her heart swelling. Hot tears poured down her cheeks as she saw Havana's tattoos and scrubs and recognized her face in the light. "Did you get her out? Did you—"

"All those babies," Havana said, her eyes dazed. Her face twitched a little. "Hayden."

Jessica grabbed the woman's shoulders and shook. "*Did you get her out?*"

"We got out," said Havana, her eyes focusing on Jessica's. "I can't believe..." But she trailed off, her body starting to shake. She couldn't bring herself to say it.

Suddenly, she dropped to her knees and screamed. Veins and tendons stood out in her neck and throat. When she couldn't scream any more, she looked at the flames. "Deshawn. Elizabeth. Esther. Antonio. Jaxon. Renee. Anastasia. Ricardo. Da'Montre. I remember their names. They had *names*."

"I'm sorry," Jessica began, but her words trailed off in a whisper. How did you say "sorry" for something like this? How could words say anything about so much death and pain?

She fell to her knees and put one arm around Havana, whose body shuddered and hitched. Together they slumped and wept, two defeated women shouldering the weight of so many lives, the hopes of so many parents.

"Look," said Jessica, staring at the fire reflected in Havana's eyes. "We can still fly. Val just needs to get one of the engines cleared. Go get the baby and..."

Sirens. Even over the roar of the burning building, she could hear them. Then came the whine of car motors running at high speed.

Val came running from in front of the Dragonfly.

"Time to take off!" she yelled. "Now!"

"Taylor's alive!" said Jessica. She grabbed her sister's arm, which was hot from the fire and slick with sweat.

"Too late," said Val. "They'll take us out with darts or cut us down with—"

"*Down on the ground now!*" boomed a voice through a loudspeaker. "*You have to the count of five to comply!*"

Dozens of cars and police hoverbikes were racing into position around them, setting up a perimeter about thirty yards away. As the first cars came to a skidding stop, officers leapt out, took up positions behind car doors, and aimed pistols at them.

"*Five!*"

"Val, please," said Jessica, her heart hammering. Her head felt light, like she was in danger of passing out. "We can't leave her."

"Jess," said Val, "we might not be leaving here at all."

Something in Val's voice turned Jessica's stomach. Was it blame? Did she think that they weren't going to make it back to her husband and son, and she blamed Jessica for it?

"*Four!*"

Hoverbikes, similar to the ones yoked in the Dragonfly's cargo area, were moving to form a semicircle around them, closing them in against the burning building. Their big, enclosed propellers made a low, throbbing sound as they moved. Then, with that familiar *buzz* that reminded Jessica of angry bees, drones detached from the bikes' bellies and glided forward. Each drone had three red lights that glared at the women like insectile eyes.

Havana drew up close to Val and Jessica. "Even if we make it to the woods without getting shot, all we'd do is draw their attention to where she's hiding."

"When he gets to 'two,' run up the ramp," said Val. "I'm sorry about the girl, Jess. But there's no saving her in this situation."

"*Three!*"

Jessica's knees shook. She wasn't sure that she could move her legs at all, much less run.

Taylor. Merida. Taylor. Merida. The names repeated in her head like the words of a liturgy, but all she could see in her mind's eye was the face of that baby. Helpless. Probably afraid. At least

Merida had Celina with her. That was probably better protection than guns or a Dragonfly.

"*Two!*"

8

Merida

Running down the alley toward the car they'd stolen, Merida tried not to look at the bodies of the agents lying in heaps on the ground. But as they passed the corpses, she made herself lean down and grab a rifle from one of them. Just in case. It was a lot heavier than she had expected, and the metal felt cool, even on a warm and humid night like tonight.

Do you know how to use that? said Celina's thought-voice.

"Not a clue," said Merida.

The *buzz* of the drones had grown louder, echoing off the high-rise buildings that surrounded them, but Merida still couldn't tell where the things were. If she and Celina could just make it to the car before getting shot by a sedative dart, though, they should be able to outrun the drones. How many minutes before the police showed up? That gunfire had been *loud.* It was bound to draw a lot of attention their way very soon.

When they reached the car, she passed the computer and rifle off to Celina and fumbled in her pocket for the keys. Pulled them out. Dropped them.

"Shit," she said, bending over to pick them up.

As she did, something whistled over her head, and the night air exploded with a burst of gunfire. She dove toward the car for cover, landing face-down on the pavement next to one of the wheels and scraping her elbows.

"It's alright," said Celina. "Get in the car."

"What—?" said Merida.

She turned and looked at Celina. A thin wisp of smoke rose from the rifle's barrel. A few yards away, a pair of smoking heaps lay on the asphalt several feet apart from one another. Celina had taken down a pair of drones.

"Can we go now?" said Celina. "This thing kicks pretty hard. I don't want to have to use it again."

Merida got to her feet. Blood dripped from her skinned elbows. "Holy shit. That was a hell of a shot."

Celina shrugged. *Well, this thing fires like a million bullets a second or something, so...*

Merida laughed. With a dozen dead bodies behind her and probably the whole U.S. government about to descend upon them, it felt strange. But truly she hadn't felt this good—this *free*—in a long time. A stab of guilt pricked her heart at the thought, and not just because they were leaving dead people in their wake.

"Let's get the hell out of here," she said.

Celina put the rifle in the back seat while Merida cranked the car, an old gas-burner Ford from the '20s or '30s. It was ancient, but it ran, and they'd chosen it because there shouldn't be any technology on it that would allow for tracking. Celina had made the owner hand them the keys and then go for a long walk in the woods.

Merida put the car into gear and pulled onto the street. "It's so weird driving a car this—dammit!"

Blue lights in her rearview mirror. Two—no, three police cruisers.

Merida floored the gas. The old four-cylinder groaned and then screamed, but the car accelerated. "This thing isn't fast enough to outrun them."

"Head for downtown," Celina said. "We're going to have to lose them and ditch the car."

Downtown Atlanta. A maze of streets all named Peachtree. No grid, just a bunch of random intersections and alleyways. Could they really lose the cops there?

"We'll have to do it fast before the Dragonflies show—"

Celina cut her off. "Well, hello there."

She turned to look out the passenger window. Something was moving alongside them, its engines making a loud *whirring* sound. A police hoverbike. It dropped low so that the officer, a man in a black leather suit with form-fitted armor plates, could look through their window. With one hand, he pointed at the side of the road.

"Shit," said Merida. "We can't outrun fucking hoverbikes."

A loud voice projected from the bike: "*Pull over now!*"

Not really thinking about what she was doing, Merida braked and jerked the wheel left at the intersection. Celina's head slammed into her window with a *bang*. The car's tires squealed in protest, and for a second, Merida thought that either the car would flip over or they'd skid into one of the light poles that lined the sidewalk on Victory Avenue.

"Ouch," said Celina.

"Sorry about that."

The hoverbike was back again, this time on the driver's side. Merida chanced a glance over at it. The driver had something in his hand that looked like a grenade.

"Sorry about this, dude," Merida said. She swerved toward the bike, trying to knock it off course—hopefully without killing the cop. The man pulled back on the handlebars, though, and the bike rose up above the roof of the car.

"Watch this," said Celina.

Suddenly, the bike dove and slammed into the ground, metal squealing and sparks flying everywhere. In the rearview mirror, Merida saw the officer get flung from the tumbling bike and skid down the road with both arms tight across the visor of his helmet. He had clearly been trained to handle wrecks on that thing.

"He'll be alright," said Celina. "Look at—*oh!*"

Two of the cop cars swerved to avoid the downed officer, but the third plowed right over him. Merida let out a yelp.

"I didn't mean for that to..." said Celina. "Um, oops?"

"Fuck!" screamed Merida. "I didn't sign up for killing cops!"

"Just keep moving," said Celina. "Focus on the road."

Merida swerved right onto Jameson Road, hoping that some of the cops would miss the turn, but two followed with barely a screech of their tires. The third was nowhere to be seen—no doubt checking on the hoverbike officer he'd hit. There was more traffic in this part of town—self-driving cars, mostly—but Jameson was four lanes wide in each direction, so Merida zigzagged between the other vehicles easily. Her pulse pounded in her temples.

A squeal and a crash behind them. Weaving between cars, Merida couldn't look back to see what had happened.

"That's one more down," said Celina.

Not dead, I hope, thought Merida.

Ahead was an exit onto Delaware Avenue. Merida waited until the last minute and then swerved onto the ramp, hoping again that the cops would miss the turn. No dice. Heart pounding, Merida floored the gas pedal and broke past three vehicles that were coming down Delaware and weren't moving over for her to merge.

Nice driving, said Celina's thought-voice.

Merida didn't answer. She squeezed between a pair of self-driving semis and swerved toward another exit, which took them onto Abrams Street. One of the semis blasted a warning sound that consisted of an air horn and a series of loud beeps. Behind her, she could see the cop car, its blue lights flashing and spinning.

"Can you get the last one?" said Merida. She glanced at Celina, who smiled like someone who'd been asked to eat a bowl of ice cream.

I'm useful to have around, huh?

Merida looked into the rearview mirror in time to see the cop car swerve suddenly and plow right into the Jersey wall that lined each side of the ramp. Sparks flew as the car scrubbed against the concrete barrier.

"Hell yes!" said Merida, slapping the car dash with her hands. She felt light-headed. Almost giddy. Conscience be damned.

She pressed the gas pedal to the floor and sped down the long ramp toward Abrams Street. The light was green, and there was no traffic. If she kept going, they could be out of sight of any cops and ditch the car.

"I'm not responsible for assholes who help to hunt down people like us," said Merida. She looked at Celina. "They *choose* to work in a corrupt system. Right?"

"Corrupt system?" said Celina. Her voice sounded strange. "Oh, girl. You're so cute. It's *people* who are corrupt. The 'system' can't do anything good or bad without—*look out!*"

But Merida looked back at the road too late.

9

Jessica

Jessica was ready to run, but the scream of rockets and a blast of machine gun fire filled up the night, drowning out every other sound.

The cops all turned their attention toward the noise, but too late. With a concussion that sent Jessica, Val, and Havana backwards onto their butts, several police cars exploded and bullets cut the officers down like so many weeds. Sprays of blood flew. In a few cases, limbs went flying, severed from their bodies.

"Get on board!" screamed Val, who was already crawling toward the loading ramp.

All around them, gunfire erupted—surviving officers returning fire as three Dragonflies appeared in the air above them. Their long wings formed dark X-shapes against the sky. More insect-like than any Dragonfly Jessica had seen before. And instead of the usual flat-black paint, these had a dark blue and green finish.

For a wild second, Jessica wondered if they were from some other country, or maybe some kind of paramilitary group? Were they here to help Jessica and the others?

"Jess!" screamed Val. "*Now!*"

Jessica thought of Merida, who was probably—hopefully—trying to make her way safely out of Atlanta right now with the computer. Then she thought of Baby Taylor, probably held close in Beck's arms, huddled against some tree in the woods nearby.

Please let Merida be okay, she thought.

Then she grabbed Havana by the arm. "Which way to Taylor?"

The other woman nodded toward the east, through the flaming ring of cop cars.

Jessica picked up the rifle that Val had given her.

As they ran toward the woods, Val screamed something after them, but Jessica couldn't hear the words. She had come to save the baby. She couldn't fly a Dragonfly or gun down enemy aircraft. But she could do *this*.

Bits of grass and dirt showered Jessica as she ran, and blasts of hot air washed over her in waves. From behind her came more screams and the whine of lift engines as Val took off.

"This way!" yelled Havana. She tugged Jessica's arm toward a spot at the edge of the woods directly behind Artemis.

Something was coming from behind them. Instinctively, Jessica ducked, pulling Havana down with her. As she did, a riderless hoverbike flew over their heads in a flat spin before crashing twenty yards ahead.

"Holy fuck," said Havana. "Thanks."

"*Stop right there!*" screamed someone behind them.

Without thinking, Jessica wheeled around, raised the rifle to her shoulder, and placed the holographic crosshairs on the chest of an officer running toward them. The moment he started to raise his gun, Jessica squeezed the trigger. With a short burst, the gun shook against her and put half a dozen bullets into the officer's torso. A dark plume of blood spurted from his throat, and he went down like a doll. She had just killed a man—a man who had just been doing his job. A man who had believed that she was a terrorist.

"Good shooting," said Havana, pulling Jessica's shirt. "Now let's move. You can feel bad about it later."

Her stomach threatening to vomit up bile and her legs feeling numb, Jessica followed after Havana. A Dragonfly raced directly overhead, so close she felt the hot blast of air from its propellers sting her face. Not one of the new ones, she realized. It had the broad belly of a troop carrier.

Val.

The Dragonfly turned suddenly and spun so that the nose was facing them, then settled into a hover about fifty feet off the ground. Gunfire erupted from either side of the cockpit, and Jessica fell to the ground almost involuntarily. She could hear the bullets whistling through the night just feet above her.

Havana was on the ground beside her, covering her ears against the roar of the gunfire. Val's Dragonfly hovered almost motionless, unleashing hell at—

At what?

Jessica looked back and saw nothing. She rose to her feet, which took no small amount of willpower as the hail of bullets continued. Sprays of dirt were flying up from the ground where bullets struck, and beyond them, more than dozen police officers were pinned down by the gunfire, unable to move forward.

"She's protecting us!" screamed Jessica, grabbing Havana by the back of her scrubs. "Get moving!"

Keeping her head low, Jessica dragged Havana toward the woods. The rational part of her mind knew what Val was doing, but the bullets felt damn close as they whistled through the air.

As they passed beneath the Dragonfly, the wind from its engines whipped Jessica's clothes so hard she thought her shirt might come right off. Then they reached the woods. Limbs and pine needles slapped Jessica's face as they moved between the trees. After they had gone a short distance, Havana held up a hand for Jessica to halt.

"Beck?" she called. "It's me. Jessica Brantley's with me."

"Over here," said another voice. A small white light flashed somewhere ahead and then died.

Havana waved for Jessica to follow. "This way."

They made their way between pines and oaks. Leaves, pine straw, and sticks crunched under their feet. Even with the noise of fighting behind her, Jessica's breathing seemed as loud in her own ears as the explosions that had destroyed the cop cars. As they came closer to the place where the light had flashed, Jessica began to sense a familiar tingle in the air. The night seemed almost to *crackle* with energy. They were close to her.

Beck stepped out from behind a thick oak, clutching Baby Taylor against her chest. Behind her were two men that Jessica had never seen before. All of their faces were shadowed, but Jessica could see well enough to tell that Beck was as cold and determined as she had been when Jessica first met her, while the two men looked terrified and confused. Baby Taylor was cooing nervously, her soft voice letting out little panicked noises every time an explosion went off or a Dragonfly screamed over their heads.

"What do we do now?" said Beck, then shushed the baby in her arms with a gentleness that seemed foreign in the angry woman.

"Look," said one of the men, who wore light blue scrubs. He stepped toward Beck, his hands out at his sides in a gesture that said, *Let's be reasonable here.* "I appreciate you getting us out of the building, but I don't know what is going on here and—"

"Shut up," said Beck.

The man stopped and stood statue-like for a few seconds, his arms frozen in that appeal to reason, before backing up and stuffing his hands in his pockets.

"We make it to the safe house," said Havana, "take the car, and follow through with the rest of Hayden's plan. Only now we have *that*—" She pointed at the rifle in Jessica's hands. "—to clear the path if necessary."

Staring at the baby in Beck's arms, Jessica had almost forgotten about the gun. She straightened her back and lifted the rifle to a ready position.

Beck leveled her gaze on Jessica. "You're coming with us?"

"I—" she began.

But she didn't know what she was going to do.

In choosing to follow Havana over boarding the Dragonfly with Val, she might have just given up any chance at ever seeing Merida or Val again. But now the choice was made. With a twinge in her chest, she realized that helping get Taylor to safety was the most important thing. Maybe even more important than getting the truth out.

But what about Merida? What about their life—whatever was left of it—when this was all over?

"I'm just here to get you to safety," she said. "After that, I'm on my own. How far is it to your getaway car?"

"Safe house is three miles west of here," said Havana. "If you're not coming with us, I'm not telling you more than that."

For a second, Jessica felt herself bristling. But she understood, so she nodded.

Two Dragonflies howled over their heads, the wind from their lift engines making the tall pine trees sway. Taylor let out a little squeal of terror, and a sick feeling rolled Jessica's stomach.

"Let's move," said Beck. "While those bastards are distracted. If she gets too excited..."

"Didn't you give her the sedative?" asked Havana.

"I forgot to fucking grab the kit, okay?" growled Beck. "I was too worried about the bombs bringing the fucking building down on our heads."

At this, Taylor let out another cry, and Jessica's head began to spin.

"Okay, okay," said Havana, her voice artificially light. "I was just asking. Don't upset her."

Beck stroked Taylor's cheek with the backs of her fingers, like a mother, and shushed her. "It's okay, sweetie. I'm sorry."

"We can get something for her at the house before we head out," said Havana. "Now let's—"

Before she could finish, a sharp sound—*whip*—rang through the air.

"Oh," said Beck, almost in a whisper. "God."

Instinctively, Jessica ducked, and something whistled through the air above her, striking a tree to her left. Two thuds in the dark. Three. People were dropping to the ground.

Taylor started crying—really *wailing* now. Jessica threw herself forward, landing flat on her stomach, and used her legs to push herself in Taylor's direction. She groped wildly in the dark, trying to put her hands on the baby. Suddenly, a sharp pain like a migraine threatened to split her skull from one temple to the other. She felt herself curling into a fetal position, her hands covering her ears. It did no good, though. The baby's power couldn't be kept out by physical barriers.

She was screaming something. Or was that Havana? Maybe it was both.

Fear gripped her, both her own fear and the baby's. Just when she thought that she was about to pass out, something else—a sound, a vibration, faint but high-pitched, like a dog whistle—began to overpower the force that was radiating out from the baby. It almost seemed to shake the ground, and yet it was so faint that you might miss it, like a gnat buzzing close to your ear. This was a *real* sound, not a telepathic force. Something nearby.

Then Jessica heard the footsteps.

There was something strange about them. They were heavy. Metallic, maybe. Machine-like. *Thud. Thud.*

The baby had stopped crying—as far as Jessica could tell, anyway—but Jessica could feel her presence. Fear. Confusion. A need to be close to bare skin. To nurse. A little comfort would help. Just a little. It was enough to make tears well up in Jessica's eyes even now. The helplessness. The need for a mother.

White pain drove all these thoughts away. A sting like a pinprick in Jessica's neck.

No, not Jessica's.

Taylor's.

And then the baby's presence was gone. Cut off like a holocall that had been abruptly ended. They had sedated her.

More of those heavy, metallic footsteps. *Thud. Thud.* And as they moved away, the sound that vibrated like a dog-whistle grew fainter. And then there were other footsteps, normal ones this time, and the sound of something being dragged away.

Oh, God, thought Jessica.

10

Theresa

The drone backed farther away as she approached the spot where it had dropped the pistol. She crouched and touched the metal of the barrel. Cold. Her fingertips slid across the steel toward the cylinder, tracing the grooves. She slipped her fingers around the rubber-coated grip and picked it up. The weight felt reassuring.

"That's so you can feel safe," said Senator Cartwright. "So you can protect yourself. It's an old gun. No tracker. No fingerprint lock. No safety. Even if you reject what I have to say, it's yours, and nobody will be able to trace it to you or use it to track you."

Theresa raised the pistol and pointed it at the drone. Cartwright stared back at her, unmoved.

"I know your first instinct is to shoot the drone and run," he said. "I know you have every reason to distrust me and everyone else. You've been told lies about your future. You've been told lies about your gifts. You've been drugged and imprisoned and manipulated."

Theresa put her thumb on the pistol's hammer and forced it back. It took more effort than she had expected, and the gun was starting to shake in her trembling hands.

"You can do whatever you think is best, Theresa," said

Cartwright. "I can't do a thing to stop you. And if you choose to run away, I absolutely will not follow you. I could send more drones. I could even send a team of U.S. Special Forces. But I won't do any of those things. I promise."

He paused. Somewhere in the woods, an owl hooted.

"If you want to go, I won't stop you." He gestured with his hands as if to urge her on.

Theresa stared down the barrel of the gun at the drone, working out how to aim it. A small pin with a white dot stuck out of the top of the front of the barrel, and it lined up with a pair of white dots on either side of a groove on the back of the gun. You lined up the dots, put the center one where you wanted the bullet to go. Click. Bang.

Something about the man hovering like a ghost over the drone's projector lens made her pause, though. Why would he have given her a gun if he were like the others? Like Bowen, that disgusting man?

"What do you want?" she said.

Cartwright crossed his arms and touched his chin almost absent-mindedly. "First, I want you to know that you aren't alone. There are others like you. Bright, beautiful, powerful people just like you. Goddesses and gods. People who have joined me in the fight to make the world better. People who are going to take humanity into the future. Remarkable people who are waiting to take their rightful place as the shepherds of humanity."

Theresa felt the urge of the trigger against her finger. Another centimeter back, maybe less, and it would fire. Things seemed simpler, easier, with one of these in her hands.

"That's what *they* told me," she said. "They said I was going to help them make the world better."

"I know," said Cartwright. "They wanted you to be part of

Project Eris. They wanted you to go into foreign countries and 'advance America's interests,' which really meant advancing *their* interests."

His expression—a faint smile, his brow furrowed, his eyes narrow—said that he felt sorry for her. Theresa wished that she could look into his mind. People were very good at faking their emotions. They put on masks of sympathy because it was polite or expected, when they didn't actually care about you at all. Sympathy, love, compassion—most of the time those were just a cover.

"My organization doesn't serve 'America's interests,'" Cartwright continued. "We serve the *people* of this country, especially people like you."

"Telepaths," said Theresa.

Cartwright smiled, *really* smiled, and nodded. "That's right. People like you are the future of the human race. Instead of fearing what you can do, we should embrace it, welcome it. That's what I want for you, Theresa—to be 'a Goddess among Gods, ador'd and serv'd by Angels numberless, thy daily train.'"

Is that a quote from the Bible or something? Theresa thought. She'd never heard anyone talk the way this man did. Was he sincere? Manipulative? Crazy?

"I'm here," continued Cartwright, "because unlike the people who worked for the Singer Institute, I value you for who you are, not for what you can do for me. And one day, the whole world will, too."

The gun had grown heavy in Theresa's arms, which began to shake. She lowered it so that the barrel pointed at the dirt and leaves on the ground, but she kept her arms straight and her fingers tight around the pistol's grip.

"People in power, people like Richard Bowen and Nancy Jones-

McMartin, want to use you for their purposes," said Cartwright. "I want to help you use your powers—to serve your own interests."

"And what are those?" said Theresa. No doubt whatever he thought "her interests" were, they conveniently matched his interests.

"The number of telepaths in this country is small. Still a tiny percentage of the population. But you are a powerful force in the world. Unchecked, that force will be like Noah's flood, come to wipe the whole world clean. I want to help direct the waters so that they leave what works and cleanse what doesn't. Sort of like making sure that we have two of every species on the Ark. My organization is changing America from the ins..."

But Cartwright paused and trailed off, his eyes narrowing.

"Theresa, the drone's sensors are picking up another person nearby."

Theresa didn't need the drone's sensors to tell her that, though. She could feel his mind touching her own.

CNN

Lawmakers Flipping Sides: What's Going On?

By Addie Winston

Kenny Cooke is right: there *is* something happening in Washington. But where Cooke and his fellow conspiracy theorists think that a vast cabal of blackmailers is manipulating U.S. politics, I think that a much more mundane theory is correct: we are witnessing a renaissance of cooperation and compromise in a body that has for decades been paralyzed by polarization and partisanship.

On Monday, Senator James Bush reversed course and joined several of his Constitution Party colleagues in voting for the Wall of Separation Act, a controversial law that will require clergy and ministers to be licensed by the government before they can serve in churches, mosques, synagogues, and other houses of worship. In voting for the Wall of Separation Act, Bush joins several senators in defecting from the official positions of their parties. Now the bill will return to the House, which is expected to pass the Senate's modified form of the bill by the end of the week.

That wasn't the last of the week's political shockers, though. On Tuesday, Senator Grace Bacall told reporters that she would vote in favor of the B.O.R.D.E.R.S. Act, a law that critics say will reduce immigration to the U.S. by as much as eighty percent, dropping total annual immigration by roughly...

READ THE FULL ARTICLE
VIEW COMMENTS

AlanB: I'm always impressed with politicians who can break with their parties, but this? I don't know about the WSA, and I'm DEFINITELY not a fan of the B.O.R.D.E.R.S Act.

DesPurc: This is weird. Somebody has something on Bush. I wonder if those rumors about him and Rick Thompson are true. Not sure about Bacall, though. She seems pretty boring. Hard to imagine somebody having any kind of dirt on her.

TheRonster: There HAS to be some kind of blackmail going on here.

Christian K: I can't get over the irony in calling it the "Wall of Separation Act."

MondarJeshop: So long, freedom of religion. You had a good run.

CarlosC: I'm not at all in favor of that horrible B.O.R.D.E.R.S. Act. But lawmakers crossing the aisle? Not letting their parties dictate how they vote? I say ABOUT DAMN TIME!

CheFan68: Listen to all you fukin whiners. Go cry and suck your thumbs babies! Wall of Separation, BORDERS, all of it. Bring it the fuk on.

SWColextor1138: govmnt man who come to my church and asks

my preacher for his license better have an army with him cuz I defend my first amendment rights with my second amendment rights

11

Kim

Kim grabbed Braden's arm and pulled him away from the loft door. The two of them scrambled into the darkness of the barn and crouched next to an old bale of hay. From here, they could see the tree branches illuminated in yellow by the vehicle's headlights.

"Can you tell me anything about them?" said Kim. He put his arm around Braden's shoulders and felt the boy trembling.

I'm listening now, said Braden. *They're nervous. Angry, too. I can't tell who they are, though.*

I already know who they are, thought Kim.

Braden drew away from his embrace and looked at Kim, his eyes shadowed in the glow of the headlights.

Your mom's cousin Evan, Kim thought.

From the glow of the headlights, Kim could tell that the vehicle had stopped right in front of the barn door. The engine fell silent, but the lights stayed on. The *clack* of old door latches. Worn-out hinges groaning. Footsteps in the dirt. Low voices.

I've never met Evan, Kim thought. *No idea what kind of man he is, except that he and his family keep to themselves. Pretty conservative, I think. Hate the government.*

Do you blame them?

Kim had never *hated* the government, even after the Susan Wade Act and Safe Reproductive Practices. At least, not until the last year or so, when Braden's nightmares forced him and Val to confront the enormity of what they had done in defying the law. And when they had come into his home to arrest them for the crime of having a son.

No, I guess I can't blame them.

"If there's anybody out here, come on out and let us see your hands up high," said a deep, masculine voice. Evan, presumably. He wasn't shouting, but the sound carried just the same. It was the voice of a man that you did not screw around with.

Braden closed his eyes and leaned slightly in the direction of the loft door. *He thinks... He thinks we're here to... take his land? I don't understand. He thinks we're here to scare him and force him to give up his land?*

Stay here, thought Kim. *Wait here for me.*

"No," hissed Braden. He gripped Kim's shirt sleeve and tugged. *They've got bows and arrows. They're... they're willing to shoot if they think it's necessary. They heard the Dragonfly leave, and they think the government sent somebody here to scare them.*

They won't shoot me, and—

I should just knock them out. I can do it from here.

And then what? We can't run until your mother gets back, and we can't just keep them unconscious for hours and hours hoping no one comes looking for them. Our best chance is to explain ourselves quickly.

"I'm going to say this again," said Evan. "If there's anybody here, you'd better come out now. I don't tolerate people trespassing on my land. If you want to avoid trouble for yourself, just come on out."

Kim stood slowly, the boards beneath him creaking. Braden stared up at his face, terrified.

I can make you stop, his voice said. *I can make you hide with me.*

"Do you trust me, Braden?" said Kim. He put his hand on his son's cheek.

I do trust you, but—

"I know I'm not a former Marine," he said. "I know I'm just a doctor. But I would move mountains to save you. And I'm doing this right now to keep you safe."

Braden's lower lip trembled.

She almost shot me to keep me out of their hands. When we were in the creek and the Dragonflies found us. She thought about killing me.

For a second, Kim forgot about the people standing outside the barn with their bows aimed and simply stared at his son. "I don't understand. What...?"

Mom. She almost killed me. I saw it in her head before she left to go and save that baby. She's terrified that I'll see it and hate her. And now you're about to leave me.

Son, you can't... You know better than anybody that everyone thinks things in desperate moments that they'd never think at any other time. I know it's hard, but if she thought that, you can't blame her for it. What matters is the choices people make. And she saved you. She—

"Last warning," said Evan. "Come out or we come in."

Kim looked toward the opening. "I'm here, Evan. I'm about to come out."

His heart pounding so hard that it seemed to fill up his chest, throat, and head, Kim crouched and put his good arm around Braden.

"We can't do this now," he whispered into Braden's ear. "Please trust me. And trust your mother. We can talk more later. I promise I'll listen, if you'll promise to hear me out, too, okay?"

Will you promise that you aren't going to get shot again?

Kim let go and stood up. "They don't want to shoot anybody unless they have to, and I'm not going to make them have to. They're not our enemy, Brayden. They just want to protect their land."

Braden's eyes narrowed with anger. *Promise me.*

"I promise," said Kim. "I love you. Now get behind there." He pointed to the space between the bale of hay and the outside wall of the barn.

At first, the boy looked like he would refuse, but the cold, angry expression on his face melted and left simple fear where it had been. He crawled behind the bale and peeked out at Kim.

Everything is going to be alright, thought Kim. He turned toward the car lights and raised his voice. "I'm walking toward you now, Evan. Look up toward the loft door."

12

Merida

The other car came out of nowhere. Merida saw only a green blur before there was a crash, a jolt, and the car began to spin sideways. And then they were falling. Everything turned upside down. Another crash. And then silence for a while.

Merida opened her eyes. She was hanging upside down, held up by her seat belt. Celina was beside her, right side up. No, upside down. She'd come out of her seat and was crouching on the roof of the car. So, yeah, right side up. Her lips moved, but there was only a muffled sound.

"—ot to get moving before..."

But she stopped and shook her head.

Can you understand me? said her voice in Merida's mind.

Merida tried to nod. All the blood had gone to her brain, and she felt on the verge of passing out again. Or popping like a squeezed cherry tomato.

I'm going to unbuckle you, said Celina.

"Wait," Merida groaned, groping with her hands. She wasn't sure what she was groping for, though.

Celina reached out. Click. Merida fell and crashed into the ceiling of the car.

She managed to soften her fall a little with her hands, but she still banged her head hard and her body tried to crumple in half. The steering wheel caught her legs, so she awkwardly maneuvered and twisted until she ended up on her back with her legs sticking out the shattered side window and her head in Celina's lap.

"Come on," Celina said. She turned and squeezed through the passenger side window. *Still some glass on the ground. Be careful.* "Ouch!"

Merida flipped over and got on her hands and knees. She ducked under the car door, placing her hands carefully to avoid shards of glass. Most of the glass must have ended up somewhere else as they rolled, but tiny fragments still dug through her jeans into her legs as she crawled.

Still trying not to swoon and faint from the blood rush to her brain, Merida used the car for support as she stood. Her head was killing her now.

"We've got to keep moving," said Celina. She reached into the car and dragged out the rifle and the bag. "More cops will be here soon."

Merida rubbed her temples and looked around. The car had fallen down an embankment into an empty lot that lay in a deep depression beside the street. A construction site. Cement mixers and heavy equipment were parked nearby, and a crane towered above them, a generator dangling from its boom so that no one could steal it.

"Are you okay?" called a voice from above.

Merida turned. A man stood on the road at the top of the embankment, his hands on his hips.

"You came barreling off that ramp," he said. "I couldn't do nothing to..."

But he trailed off. For a second, he looked dazed, and then he shook his head like someone trying to wake up.

"My car's up here," he said. "The key's still in it."

"Well, *that's* nice of him," said Celina, elbowing Merida gently in the ribs. "He's offering us his car."

"Yeah," said Merida, unable to make herself feel the least bit guilty about stealing yet another vehicle. "Very nice of him."

The man worked his way down the embankment, stumbling a little halfway down but not falling. He wore an EMT's uniform. Thick, barrel chest and strong arms. He was about to be late for work. Or late getting home.

"I..." stammered Merida. "Thank you."

Stupid, she thought. She took the bag from Celina, leaving the gun in her more competent hands, and slung the strap over her shoulder. The two of them climbed the embankment to the street and found a green Chevy in the middle of the lane, the driver's door open and the emergency lights flashing.

Neither woman spoke as they got in. Merida turned off the car's self-driving mode, put it in Drive, and started down the street. She drove fast to get away from the accident scene, but she didn't floor it as she had before. They weren't being pursued, and driving like a maniac now would only draw attention.

"Now we figure out how to get this stuff onto the internet," said Celina.

"Now we get the hell out of town and back to Jessica's cousin's place, somehow," said Merida. "We can figure out how to—"

I can't help thinking that we'd better get the information dumped now.

Merida checked the mirror for flashing lights. Stopping here in town to upload the laptop's data to the internet was crazy, right? Any second now, Dragonflies and hoverbikes and the whole damn police department would be swarming every inch of the city to find them. Celina's telepathy was one hell of an advantage, but the numbers weren't on their side. All it took was one bullet to kill Celina, and then the game was over.

But getting the truth out there was the real mission. More important than not getting caught. More important than not getting killed.

"Dammit," she said. "Dammit to hell."

She turned left off Abrams Avenue. Then she made three more turns before taking a ramp onto I-75 South.

"Look around," she said. "See if you can find this guy's—"

But Celina was already handing her a phone. *Way ahead of you. And I got the passcode before we even left.*

Merida merged into the interstate traffic and glanced down at the phone. Celina had already unlocked it, so a picture of the man with a wife and two kids stared back at her.

"Here," said Merida, handing the phone back to Celina. "Let's not risk any more accidents, okay? I need you to find an address for me."

13

Val

She was getting too old for this shit.

After Jessica and Havana made it to cover, Val turned and flew south over the woods. The new arrivals were fast, though. One of them was tailing her in seconds.

"Get the hell off of my ass," she said, yanking the steering yoke backwards and to the left.

With a whine of protest from the lift engines, the Dragonfly went into a drift. The craft tilted to one side, and the back end swung around like a car whose rear wheels had broken free on loose gravel. The G-force pulled Val's body down into her seat, and she let out a groan as all her inner organs threatened to squeeze down between her hips.

If her sister hadn't run off to the woods, they might have been able to get away while the three new aircraft were engaged with the police. Now she was going to have to take down three bogeys *and* find Jessica before she could head back to her son and husband.

Damn you, Jessica.

As she swung the Dragonfly around in a wide arc, the UAD that had been chasing her roared past, the scream of its propulsion engines reverberating in the cargo bay behind her. She pressed the button to make radar lock, but the bogey was too quick. It turned, ducked, and passed right under her before she could target the missiles.

Shit.

These pilots were better than the others. Quicker. Not federal agents who'd never faced off against another aircraft before, but trained military pilots who knew what to do in a dogfight. Their planes were different, too. Some kind of newer model that looked more insectile than other Dragonflies.

Her radar sounded an alert. Two bogeys were coming up behind her—fast.

Shit shit shit.

Val banked to the right, throttling down the propulsion engine and throttling up the forward lift engines. This sent the troop carrier into another drift—even tighter this time. Her head swam, and for a second, she thought she might pass out. But she fought through it and brought the Dragonfly around to face the two bogeys.

Beep. Targeting lock on both UADs.

She hesitated before firing.

"What are you up to?" she said.

Instead of pressing the attack, the two UADs had settled into a hover, one at two o'clock high and the other at ten. From here, Val could put missiles into each of their bellies, easily. Was it a trick? A trap?

Val pulled the trigger.

A pair of missiles launched. Just as they cleared the launch tubes, the two bogeys sent countermeasure flares hurtling toward the ground. The missiles' guidance systems took the bait, following the glowing flares into the dirt instead of their targets.

"What the hell?" said Val.

Those countermeasures had been impossibly fast. Had to be AI. No pilot had that kind of response time.

"Fine," said Val, switching to guns.

She pulled back on the control stick to raise the troop carrier's nose toward the two Dragonflies. But again, she hesitated. The rear portions of the bogeys' bodies, which resembled an insect's thorax, began to tilt downward, apparently attached to the front fuselage by a giant hinge. The effect was so much like a huge insect preparing to sting that Val felt the hair on the back of her neck stand on end.

"Valerie Hara," said a female voice over the communicator. "Stand down and land your Dragonfly in the field next to the Artemis facility immediately. If you fail to comply, we will force you down."

So they're still trying to avoid killing me, Val thought. *That's all I need.*

"Computer, highlight targets," she said. "Identify."

The HUD outlined the two bogeys in blue, highlighting weapons in red. Miniguns on either side of the cockpit, missile launch tubes just behind the canopy, and something else that the computer labeled a "Stinger" on the underside of the thorax.

"What is...?" said Val, leaning closer to the HUD.

"*Targets identified,*" said the AI voice. "*U.S. Department of Homeland Security aircraft designation: UAW-1 Wasp. Urban Enforcement and Anti-Aircraft vehicle. Weapons include—*"

As the computer spoke, small doors opened on the underside of the planes' thoraxes, revealing some kind of gun. Probably the "Stinger," whatever that meant. Val wasn't going to wait to find out.

She pulled the trigger, and a hail of bullets from her miniguns sent the two bogeys—called "Wasps," apparently—careening to either side. Then she switched to missiles again. Before she could fire them, though, something struck the back of the Dragonfly with a loud *clang*.

Glancing at the radar screen, Val saw that the third Wasp had taken up position just behind her. Had it fired a weapon? If so, it hadn't done any damage. Then two more *clangs* came, this time on either side of the cockpit. The impacts sent tremors through the Dragonfly, making Val's jaw clench.

Through the windshield, Val could see a pair of thick, gray cables that extended from either side of her Dragonfly to the underside of the Wasps. A shudder ran through the troop carrier as the Wasps moved backwards and pulled the cables taut.

So, the Stinger is just a tow cable? Val wondered. *Fine, let's see them drag me down to the ground and dodge missiles at the same time.*

As if in answer, words appeared on the Dragonfly's HUD in bold letters.

WARNING. SYSTEM BREACH DETECTED.

"Oh, shit," said Val, her heart skipping a beat.

The cockpit lights flickered, and for a second, all of the HUD graphics scrambled. Then a new message appeared.

SYSTEM SHUTDOWN INITIATED. GOODBYE.

"Computer, cancel shutdown!" yelled Val, tugging the control yoke to one side. If she could break loose from the cables...

Before the Dragonfly could respond, all interior lights and instruments went dark—and the lift engines shut down.

Val's stomach lurched and rose toward her throat as the Dragonfly began to fall.

14

Merida

Can he do it? thought Merida.

They'd driven to Brookhaven, a suburb of Atlanta, to the home of Wallace—Coleman Wallace, but he'd introduced himself as "Wallace" when Merida first met him—an IT guy who worked at American News Site with Jessica. Merida had met him a few times at company parties. Clone. Yellowish orange hair. Eyes the same bright green as spring grass. An uneven bluish tint to his skin from the early days of cloning when the geneticists hadn't yet perfected altered skin colors. Awkward personality. Maybe a little bit creepy. Sometimes he told mildly offensive jokes at ANS parties, so Merida didn't feel completely terrible about what they were forcing him into.

They sat in the living room of Wallace's house—Merida on an old, comfortable recliner; Celina and Wallace on the couch. Celina was staring at Wallace while he pecked away at the laptop's keyboard. He'd run a cord from it to a computer that sat on his coffee table. A holographic screen hovered over the table, displaying lists of files and a pair of progress bars, each creeping their way toward one hundred percent.

Merida had to read them backwards because she was looking at the screen from the back side.

MOVING 48%
BACKING UP 67%

Looking at the setup, Merida couldn't help worrying that someone in some remote location would detect the laptop through the network and that at any moment Dragonflies and police vehicles would surround the house.

His skin is really creeping me out, said Celina's thought-voice. *Why can't people just have kids the normal way?*

Well, that's not didunophobic at all, thought Merida.

Just look at those eyes, though. You aren't creeped out?

Merida had to admit that the combination of colors—the yellow-orange hair, green eyes, and pale blue skin—was off-putting. Wallace was clearly the product of the early days of designer children. But Merida scolded herself. Wasn't it bigoted to think those kinds of things? And anyway, it wasn't as if Wallace had chosen his skin color. His parents—or parent, you didn't need two for a clone—had chosen it for him.

Still, if the lights were turned off so I couldn't see his eyes, I'd let him... you know... Celina grinned at Merida.

Oh, for fuck's sake, thought Merida. *Do you* ever *think about anything else? Now answer my question: can he do it?*

Yes, replied Celina. She rolled her eyes at Merida but went on grinning. *He can do it. The funny thing is, I think we could have just asked him. He likes you and Jessica a lot. I think he would have been happy to help.*

Ugh, thought Merida, remembering what Celina had said about Captain Tinycock, about him wanting Jessica and Merida together.

She took a gulp of the coffee that Wallace had given her when they'd arrived. French press. Lots of caffeine, and even though she was sweating and hot, the warmth of the drink felt reassuring. It was the same kind of coffee she served in her restaurant.

"This computer is *old,* man," said Wallace, his voice bright like a child with a new toy. "I know you can't leave it with me, but I wish I could keep it. I like antiques."

Not because he wants to get you in the sack, said Celina in her head. *He thinks you and Jessica are pretty, but he's not fantasizing about you or anything. He just likes you. Well, I won't lie. He probably would sleep with one of us if we were willing. But he doesn't think we ever would, and he wouldn't ever try. Not in a million years. He just wants to ask if you like movies, tabletop games, video games, that kind of stuff.*

In that case, Merida *did* feel bad for what they were doing to him. As soon as the files on the laptop hit the web, the government would pinpoint their source and converge on his house. His life was about to become a living hell. They might already be on their way.

Celina went on. *I think... he's got nobody. No family. No friends, really. Just the people he works with, and I bet none of them like him very much.*

They don't, added Merida.

He's... I feel pretty bad for this guy. Even if he's a little creepy-looking. He's smart and has a good job, but he's got nothing to live for. I think he'd help us just to have something new to think about.

Merida looked around the room at Wallace's taste in decoration. He clearly did like antiques. Movie posters from the twentieth century—*The Terminator, Star Wars, Batman, Mad Max, Leviathan, Citizen Kane, Conan the Barbarian, The Big Sleep,* and a few others—covered the walls. There were statues of characters from cartoons or comic books that Merida didn't recognize. *Star Trek* and *The Twilight Zone* memorabilia. An old phonograph sat on a table in the corner along with a stack of vinyl records. A pair of bookshelves flanked the fireplace, and Merida could hardly believe that the shelves were full of books—real, printed books. The titles all sounded like sci-fi and fantasy novels. Yes, she could see Wallace being the type to ask her if she wanted to play video or tabletop games with him.

"Just a few more..." said Wallace, squinting through his glasses at the laptop screen and then glancing up at the hologram over the coffee table. "Yep. All done."

"It's out there?" said Merida, her stomach turning over.

"Well, no. I copied all of the files to my device," Wallace said, his eyes bright and his smile sincere. "Few more things to do before I send it out into the world. This is crazy stuff. I just glanced at a little bit of it while it was copying, and holy shit—is it all true?"

"So you can put it on the web now, right?" said Merida, moving forward to sit on the edge of the couch. "Not to be pushy, but we need it out there as soon as possible."

"Just a few minutes," said Wallace. He took a big gulp of his coffee. "I want to make sure we go wide. Agora. WorldShare. WikiLeaks. You name it. I don't want any government agency to be able to isolate and eliminate the data before it's everywhere. I'm even going to set it to dump from Jessica's username on the ANS website." He grinned at Merida, looking proud of himself, but then a nervous expression took over his face. "I have to have access to everybody's user accounts. Not just Jessica's because I... I mean..."

"It's okay," said Merida.

Wallace blushed but moved on.

"Plus, I'm planting a few bombs," he said, lowering his voice.

"I'm going to set the information to get squirreled away on a couple of private places on the web. They'll wait there for a day, and then they'll start releasing one by one for the next week. That way, if anybody tries to shut down the initial information dumps, there are backups. That's just a redundancy, though. The world is going to pick this stuff up and run with it. There won't be any stopping it. For once, the conspiracy theories turn out to be true, huh?"

Wallace's body quivered with excitement. Celina smiled at him serenely, but there was something in her face. Her eyes seemed to be drooping a little, and her face had gone slack.

"This thing is getting out there," Wallace said. "I haven't been this excited since the Golden Waltz leak brought down President Evans. Our names are going to be up there with Mark Felt, Edward Snowden, Janet Hoyt, and Trevor Prince."

"Thank you, Wallace," Merida said, though she felt silly saying it. With Celina sitting right next to him and using her influence on him, it made no sense to thank him, especially when it probably meant that he was going to jail. Or worse.

Still sitting on the couch and holding the laptop, Wallace made a kind of a bow and put his hand on his heart. "It is my pleasure, ma'am."

He looked from Merida to Celina.

"I know you think that you're forcing me to do this," he said. "But you're not."

"I stopped trying to force you five minutes ago," said Celina, rubbing her temples. "And it's a good thing, too. I'm exhausted."

"*Telepaths*, man," Wallace said, whispering almost reverently. He turned to Merida. "I still can't get my head around it."

"I don't understand," said Merida.

"I told you that I thought he would help willingly," said Celina.

"I could..." Wallace looked around as if trying to spot the right words somewhere on the posters in the room. "I could feel her in my head. It was kind of..." Here he blushed and looked down. "Kind of..."

He shook his head, giving up on the thought. Merida thought that she knew what it was, anyway. *It was kind of sexy*. She understood.

"Anyway, I could tell," Wallace said. "And it's not forcing me if I would do it anyway, right?"

Here he paused and looked at Celina again. A look of confusion crossed his face, and then recognition. Celina smiled, and he smiled back. Merida couldn't "hear" it, but she could tell that Celina was communicating with him telepathically.

"That's *so cool*," he said. "No, wait—" He squinted as if concentrating on sending a thought to Celina. Then he laughed and slapped the sides of his thighs. "Telepaths, man!"

Merida forced a laugh. "Yes, it's very cool. But listen, the clock is running." She pointed at the window, where the darkness was beginning to turn grayish blue. It wouldn't be long until sunrise.

Wallace tore his gaze from Celina and set the laptop on the table next to his own computer. "Right. Sorry."

15

Kim

He stepped toward the loft door slowly, his right hand held high.

"Hands up!" shouted a voice. A young man. Probably one of Evan's sons.

"I've been shot in the shoulder," said Kim, trying to remain as calm as he could. "My left arm is in a sling."

The lights of the vehicle, which he now could see was a gas-powered truck, silhouetted four figures. They stood in front of the barn with their bows raised. Two were teenage boys with the lean frames of youth. Evan was clearly distinguishable as a big man with a bushy beard, broad shoulders, and a barrel chest. The other must be Tasia, Evan's wife. All of them were aiming arrows up at the loft door.

"Who else is up there?" said Evan.

"Just my son," said Kim, his heart racing. He felt a little ashamed at how nervous he sounded. "He's eleven. We don't mean any harm here. We're—"

"Tell him to come on out, too," said Evan.

I'm here, said Braden's voice in Kim's head. The boy appeared next to him, his hands by his sides.

Put your hands up, Kim thought.

Braden raised his hands over his head.

"Anybody else?" said Evan.

"Just us right now," Kim said. "My wife and three others are gone, but they'll be back in a few hours—we hope."

"We heard something big like a helicopter or a Dragonfly flying off," said Evan. "My son saw lights. Was that you?"

"My wife, Val," said Kim.

Evan stared up at them for a moment without speaking.

It's going to be okay, thought Kim. *Evan is a good man. Mom says he is, anyway.*

"How bad is your injury?" Evan said.

"Better now," said Kim. "Still sore, but I'm healing."

Evan lowered his bow and turned to say something to the others. Then he looked up at Kim and Braden again. "Stay right there. I'm coming up."

He put down his bow and disappeared through the barn door below them. Then Kim heard the big man climbing the rickety ladder and the floor of the loft vibrating with his steps. He was behind them now.

"Kimiya?" said Evan, his booming voice softened. "Kimiya Hara? You're Valerie's husband?"

Kim's heart felt heavy with relief. "I'm surprised you know my name."

"Valerie and me ain't never been real close," said Evan. "But I keep up with family. I was glad to see that she came home from the war and found some happiness. Lot of folks didn't. Where's she gone? Why are you here? They're saying some bad stuff about her in the news."

Kim lowered his hands and turned to face his wife's cousin.

A massive man. Kim wasn't short, but Evan was almost a head taller. Not anyone to mess around with. Thick neck and shoulders. Arms bulging in the sleeves of his T-shirt. He had short, bright ginger hair on his head, but his beard, which fell to his chest, was deep red. Almost auburn. Evan had very much inherited his looks from the Irish side of Val's family.

He looks like a Viking, came Braden's thought-voice. *But he isn't going to hurt us. He's... good. I guess you know that already. He doesn't know if he can trust us yet, though.*

"It's a long story," said Kim. "We needed a place to lay low for a few days."

"It's okay, Tasia," Evan said, directing his voice past Kim. "All good up here."

"We hoped you wouldn't notice us in this part of the property," said Kim, again his voice quavering. Evan's sheer presence commanded fear, even when his words and tone were compassionate. Kim chided himself for this.

"Why didn't you come to me for help?" he said. "Valerie's my cousin. You didn't think we'd turn you over or something, did you?"

"We didn't want to put your family in danger," Kim said. "And with what's going on, it's hard to know who we can trust."

Evan's eyes narrowed. "I saw on the news that Valerie was at that place in North Carolina."

"Yes," said Kim. "What are they saying about that?"

"Nothing good."

"It's not true. None of it."

"Tell me what *did* happen, then," said Evan.

Kim nodded and looked at Braden.

I'll do it, said his thought-voice. *If you want me to. It's the only way he's going to believe the whole story. If you... want him to know the whole story, I mean.*

"It's a long story," said Kim again, not taking his eyes off Braden. "I'd better let my son tell it."

16

Theresa

"You're her," said a voice from the woods. Male, but high-pitched. Scared. "The one who killed everybody."

Theresa turned and reached out with her mind. She found his easily, a consciousness just beyond the reach of the light cast by the drone and the holograph.

But this mind felt different than the ones she was used to reading.

With most people, she imagined her own mind like a swelling tide that overwhelmed a coastal city. The water would reach into every side street, every alleyway, and eventually every room and basement of every building. The city had no dikes, no protective walls. Given enough time, nothing was out of her reach, and nothing resisted her. But *this* mind felt like another huge wave rising to meet hers. They crashed together and caused a kind of reflection. The wave of her mind reverberated back at her.

"Not everybody," she said.

"You killed the senator," said the voice, now distraught. He stepped into the blue light of the holograph. Like Theresa, he wore a jumpsuit. His eyes were dark as if he hadn't slept in days, though the effect might have been exaggerated by shadows. "She was my only hope of seeing my mother again."

Theresa stepped toward him, wondering if getting closer might let her overpower his telepathic strength with her own. For a few seconds, it felt like this might work, but then the boy pushed back. A sudden pain rang out like a bell in Theresa's head, radiating from a single sharp pinprick behind her right temple. A roaring like wind crescendoed in her ears.

"Stop pushing me," said the boy, biting out the words through gritted teeth. But he continued to push against Theresa with his own mind. It felt as if the two of them were in a shoving match on a tightrope. If either of them gave up, they'd fall.

So Theresa closed her eyes and pushed harder, spreading her stance and squaring her shoulders into a fighting posture, as if this had some effect on her ability. But it was no use. There was no question that the boy was about to overpower her. She'd used up too much strength in controlling all of those people at the Institute and then walking all night through the woods. The pain in her head was steadily increasing, and the pinprick grew into a tiny sun burning inside her skull. Her body began to slacken, giving in.

"Theresa, Francis, stop!" shouted a voice from behind her. Cartwright. "I want to help you—*both of you*."

Slowly, the boy—his name was Francis?—began to pull back. The tiny sun in her skull began to shrink. Or maybe *recede* was the better word. She pulled back herself. The energy behind the two opposing tidal waves was dissipating and spreading out into the ocean.

"You can't waste your energy—your power, your gifts—fighting each other," said Cartwright. "You need to work together. To make the world better for people like you."

Francis's shoulders slumped with defeat. "They're going to kill my mother. Because of what you did." His head drooped, and he covered his face with his hands.

Theresa's knees trembled and threatened to buckle beneath her, and her head swam. Everything seemed like a dream. Had all this been a fantasy? Was she still in her cell, imagining her revenge on the people who held her captive in an underground cell? Wishing that she could punish Bowen for his disgusting thoughts about her? But the way that the fabric of her jumpsuit clung to her clammy skin told her otherwise. She was here, now.

"I'm sorry about your mother," said Cartwright. "I can try to help her. I have connections that might be able to extract her and keep her safe."

Francis let out an almost inaudible sob. His body trembled.

"The important thing right now is for you two to realize that you're allies in the same cause," said Cartwright. "If you join me in the—"

Theresa stopped listening, though. She knelt on the ground, sat back on her heels, and put one hand over her eyes. But the pain in her head was gone. Quietly, carefully, slowly, she allowed her consciousness to reach out. Not moving too fast. Just letting the water trickle and seep into crevasses and crannies. Perhaps if she moved slowly enough, Francis wouldn't realize what she was doing. She began to hear fragments of Francis's thoughts.

dead

your fault

HER fault

freak

kill

mother

it's all your fault

baby

But where she heard most people's thoughts like voices through a thin wall, slightly muffled and softer, Francis's thoughts sounded tinny. It was as if she were listening to someone from the opposite end of a long tunnel. There was distance and distortion... but the anguish in his thoughts told Theresa everything that she needed to know. He was about to explode like a—

Suddenly his voice erupted in her skull.

Get the fuck out of my mind!

Theresa felt as if she'd been struck in the head by something heavy, and she fell backwards onto the dead leaves and moss. Cartwright was shouting something, his volume and urgency distorting the drone's speakers.

"I don't want help!" Francis shouted, spittle flying from his mouth. "I don't want allies! I just want my fucking life back! And there's not a thing you can do to give it to me. She *let* them take me! They paid her money for me!"

Theresa struggled to her feet. She expected to feel his mind press against hers at any moment, the small sun to erupt and burn again. She steeled herself for it, pushing outward with her own mind to meet whatever force he had left to assault her with. But she met no resistance this time, only a strange feeling. A vibrating energy, high-pitched. Like feedback when a microphone got too close to a speaker.

Just kill me, came Francis's voice over the *buzzing* noise. *Okay? If I'm dead, maybe they'll leave her alone. And I don't have to live with this anymore.*

His face tightened and strained as if he were about to crack. His teeth ground against one another so hard that his whole head shook, and his eyes almost bulged in their sockets.

Do it!

The *buzz* in the air rose steadily, threatening to drown out everything else. Though she knew better, Theresa could swear that she was vibrating with the energy.

I'm sorry, she thought, raising the gun and putting the sights on Francis's chest. *None of us deserve what they've done to us. You didn't deserve what your mother did. Maybe she did it because she thought she had no other choice?*

She thought of her own parents, who had done such a good job of protecting her. Had loved her into being. Had kept her safe. But they hadn't been able to keep her safe from their own deaths. She didn't blame them. Didn't *want* to blame them. There had to be some good in the world. Their goodness was all she could hang on to. Maybe if Francis had had that, too...

Don't you get it? his voice screamed in her head. *She was glad to give me up!*

Behind her, Cartwright was shouting something that Theresa couldn't understand.

I'm sorry, she thought. She pulled back the gun's hammer. It locked into place with a heavy *click.*

Buzzing. Fever pitch now. Her skin began to tingle. She would punish the whole world for this if she could. Everyone who looked at people like her and Francis and said "freak" or "monster." Everyone who would treat them with suspicion and fear.

Thank y—

The sound of the gun wiped out everything else. The buzzing in her skull. The energy that filled the air around her. Cartwright's shouted pleas. Even the barely audible noises of the woods. Bang, muzzle flash, and silence.

A dark stain opened up in Francis's chest. His strained face slackened. Wild eyes turned sleepy. And then he fell forward onto his face.

Theresa lowered the gun and stepped toward the body. He wasn't dead yet. No doubt his heart had exploded as the bullet passed through it, but energy still radiated from his mind. Faint. Faint. A fleeting image of a woman with stone-gray hair. Faint. Almost nothing.

She crouched and touched the back of his head, her hand shaking. Laced her fingers into his hair. Closed her fist and felt the locks slip through her fingers.

Make... it... right, his voice whispered in her mind.

Silence.

She stood, wobbling a little with dizziness, and turned to face the drone. Cartwright's image hovered there, his arms crossed and a look of sympathy on his face.

"I'm sorry you had to do that," he said. "Francis was clearly deeply trou—"

But Theresa cut him off. "Tell me what you do. Tell me why I should help you."

Cartwright's eyebrows lifted slightly in surprise. Then he smiled sadly. "It's more like this: let me tell you how I can help *you*."

"Then tell me *that*," said Theresa, her chest tightening.

"That's something better explained in person," said Cartwright. "But I think you already know that my goals are not the same as those people who held you at the Institute. I don't want to study you scientifically. I don't want you to serve military intelligence or the CIA or anything like that. I don't want to serve anyone at all, except other people like you."

"How?" said Theresa.

"Like I said, it would be better to meet and—"

"Then come and get me."

17

Merida

Merida peeked through Wallace's blinds at the driveway, yard, and street outside. The stars were fading as sunrise approached. A couple of cars drove past, their passengers unaware that the world was about to change. One car slowed in front of the house and came nearly to a stop, and Merida's insides squirmed. But then it moved on.

She turned to Celina and Wallace, who still sat next to each other on the couch. "As soon as it's done, we go. We're going to be moving in daylight no matter what, but we'd better not stick around too long."

Celina smiled and leaned back on the couch. *Maybe we have a little time before we go...* Her eyes cut over at Wallace, who still sat on the edge of his seat, making swipes and gestures on his holograph screen. *I guarantee he would be happy to play along.*

Merida scowled at her.

I'm kidding, said Celina. She slid onto her side and stretched out on the couch next to Wallace. *To be honest, my head is killing me. Side effect of all the manipulation I've done tonight. The last time I had this much trouble was...*

She trailed off, a dark expression crossing her face. Her eyes darted to Merida and then away into space again. After a moment, whatever it was seemed to pass—as if Celina had simply decided not to think about it.

I wouldn't have gotten through this without you, Merida thought. *Thank you.*

Celina stretched, her body lean and sinuous like a cat, and closed her eyes.

Damn skippy. I think maybe you owe me some head when this is all over with.

I think we'll find somebody else to do that, Merida thought. *I might talk a good promiscuous game, but I've only got eyes for one woman.*

Not opening her eyes, Celina smiled faintly. She was almost asleep. *I don't know. I'm pretty irresistible. I might make you an offer you can't refuse.*

Trying not to think about what that meant coming from a telepath who could control people, Merida looked at Wallace. The hologram, which hovered between them, made his face glow blue. *Bluer, rather.* Four new progress bars had appeared.

SENDING 11%
SENDING 7%
SENDING 11.5%
SENDING 3%

"I..." Merida said, struggling against the words. How would Jessica and Val respond to her inviting Wallace into their group? "I feel terrible for putting you through this. You... if you want to, you can come with us. Once it's done." She felt like a kid about to bring home a stray dog.

Celina opened her eyes and grinned. *That's an idea.* She winked. *We can keep him like a pet and take him out to play any time we—*

Shut up.

Wallace crossed his arms and slumped over. The bright face that he'd worn since Merida and Celina had arrived dissolved. He reached out to the hologram and touched a button. "That's cool of you. But I'd better not. I've still got a job."

"I understand," said Merida. She moved around the coffee table and sat in the chair. "I just hate to think of you... if they found out..."

She couldn't even bring herself to say it. It didn't matter that Wallace said he would've helped them without being coerced. They'd forced him into this, and his life might be over because of it.

But Wallace shook his head. "I got recruited for a job at the CIA when I was younger, right out of college. It was so cool to go on those interviews... to visit their computer labs and meet with real, live CIA agents. Like being in a movie. They offered me the job, but I just couldn't do it. I didn't want to live in that world. At the time, I didn't know exactly why I felt that way. I guess it was just the lefty in me. I wanted to fight for the little guy, not the powers-that-be. But maybe I was just a coward, you know? Afraid to join the fight on either side."

He rubbed his face with his hands.

SENDING 21%
SENDING 19%
SENDING 23%
SENDING 34%

"Anyway, I'm going to stay here. I'm good at what I do. They won't know it was me. You don't have to feel bad."

Celina sat up, moving slowly as if her body were stiff, and patted him on the back. Wallace started at the gesture, then glanced at Celina and smiled.

"You seem like a good—"

But before he could finish, Celina had reached out, grasped his chin with her fingers, and kissed him softly on the mouth. At first, Wallace just stared back at her, his eyes wide with astonishment. But soon he closed his eyes and kissed her back.

This isn't for me, said Celina's voice in Merida's head. *It's for him.*

Merida shook her head. She wanted to argue with Celina that it was gross, that she shouldn't offer herself to men as a "thank you," even just a kiss. But her stomach was twisted so tight from watching the slow movement of the numbers on the holographic display that she couldn't bring herself to argue.

After a moment, Wallace drew back and hugged his arms to his chest, struggling against the huge grin that threatened to take over his face.

"It's embarrassing, sitting next to somebody I can't hide my thoughts from," he said. "You know that I'm..." He blushed, the effect turning his blue-tinted skin a faint shade of violet. He looked at Merida and then down at the floor. "Celina knows that I'd really love to go with you. I'm tired of the same damn thing over and over again. It would be cool to have a different kind of life. To do something that matters. Not just program. Not just design pages that trick people into scrolling and scrolling. And I... I've always liked being around you and Jessica because you didn't treat me like I was different."

Merida's face felt hot. She might not have treated him that way, but she had seen him as different. He *was* different. And not just because of his exotic appearance. To be honest, most people just thought that he was *weird*. But he was different in other ways, too—ways that Merida was only now beginning to see. What had she done to make him think that she wasn't like everyone else? She'd just been better at hiding it, she supposed.

SENDING 80%
SENDING 72%
SENDING 79%
SENDING 68.7%

"Sometimes I hate my parents for making me look like this," Wallace said.

He held out his arms as if to remind Merida and Celina of his skin color. Then he gestured at his hair.

"Not just sometimes. Always, to be honest. I haven't spoken to them in years. It's like..." He looked around at the room's nerdy decorations. "It's like I was this weird mix of political activism and fashion statement to them. If they'd let nature do its thing, I would've had dark brown skin like my father because my base DNA is his. I look just like him except for..." He sighed. "But my mother was into bright colors. She was the one who decided that I'd be blue. There was something else besides *looks,* though. It took me a long time to figure this out, but she wanted people to know that I was an edited clone, that I was *different.* She wanted to be able to say, 'My child isn't like your ch—'"

A *ping* from the computer cut him off.

SENDING 98%
SENDING 98%
SENDING 97.9%
SENDING 98%

"Almost ready," Wallace said, moving forward in his seat. "Those hit one hundred percent, then *bam!* The whole world will—"

But the screech of brakes outside cut him off. The living room windows lit up with bright white and flashing blue.

SENDING 99%
SENDING 99%
SENDING 99%
SENDING 99%

"Oh, fucking—" Merida began, but a loud *buzz* that seemed to vibrate the whole house cut her off. Every light in the house flickered and went dark, and both the laptop and Wallace's computer made loud *pops* before going dead, too.

The New York Times

Didunophobia Remains a Problem

By Shelley Fish

This week, the House Subcommittee on Cloning and Genetic Engineering has heard testimony from human cloning experts, social media leaders, bioethicists, and sociologists about the public's evolving attitude toward cloned persons. While some positive news came out of the proceedings, the overall picture was sobering. In short, Americans remain suspicious of cloning and still see people of alternative conception as different from individuals who were conceived through the union of sperm and egg...

The Wall Street Journal

While Geneticists Play God, Shelley Fish Fears "Didunophobia"

By Courtney Clark

Over at *The New York Times* opinion page, Shelley Fish is worried about didunophobia. Not surprisingly, she conflates two related—but different—issues. First, there is the question of how "naturally conceived" people treat clones. Second, there is the ethical question of whether or not we should be engaged in human cloning at all.

Fish seems to think that if you oppose human cloning on ethical grounds, you must also be a bigot who hates the hundreds of thousands of cloned people who are living and working in the United States today. This kind of sloppy (and, ironically, bigoted) thinking not only clouds an already complicated issue, but it also unfairly demonizes people who are not guilty of didunophobia, especially those who...

Seattle Times

Pretending to be a clone isn't praise or inclusion. It's didunophobia.

By Vince Clinton

It took America nearly a hundred years to deal with the problem of blackface, so why is it that just decades later, we've invented a new form of the same demeaning behavior that some people unironically call "cloneface"?

Attend any college fraternity party or high school dance, and you're likely to find someone who has painted themselves blue and Quickdyed their hair in order to look like a clone.

Advocates of "cloneface" say that it helps to "normalize" cloning in communities that still harbor prejudice against people of alternative births, but the time is long past for us to call "cloneface" what it is.

It's didunophobia. It's prejudice. It's bigotry. And decent people everywhere have a responsibility to shame "cloneface" wherever they see it.

READ MORE

@Juraj Dadić: About fucking time somebody said this.

@JEG: What are you TALKING about?!?!?! Not everything is bigotry, you know.

@Os1963: "Not everything is bigotry, you know." Said someone with a picture of fucking Nelson Jenkins in their bio... SMDH

18

Jessica

Panic gripping her chest like a vise, she scrambled to her feet and raised the rifle. An agent in black tactical gear was standing over someone lying on the ground. The agent's pistol was aimed at the person's head.

Without even thinking, Jessica pulled the trigger, lighting up the dark woods in orange and sending the agent backwards.

"They took her!" shouted a voice behind her.

Jessica whirled, keeping the rifle at the ready and her finger on the trigger. A dark shape stepped from between two trees.

"Stop!" said Jessica.

"It's me," said Havana, hurrying past Jessica toward the body of the agent. She bent over and picked up his pistol. "They took her. We have to—"

Gunfire. Somewhere in the trees to Jessica's left. Bullets whistled past, some of them striking the trees and splintering the wood.

Jessica dove to the ground again, rolling until she was behind the trunk of a big oak. Her movement disturbed a group of mice, which scattered in all directions, one of them scurrying over her stomach before hopping off and hurrying into the underbrush.

More gunfire. Bullets struck the tree that Jessica was using for cover. What did you do when you were fighting an unseen enemy and you had to protect someone who might be in the line of fire? Val would know what to do, but Val wasn't here.

"Havana," Jessica hissed. "Are you okay?"

"Yes," the woman replied from somewhere to Jessica's right.

The gunfire stopped, but now there were footsteps approaching. Slow. Careful.

The shooter was working his way in their direction, probably to make sure that he had killed his targets. Should Jessica return fire and at least drive him back? Or should she wait until he was close so that she had a chance of surprising him and killing him?

Deciding that her journalist's instinct to debate a problem inwardly wouldn't serve her now, Jessica shifted to the side so that she could aim the rifle past the tree and squeezed the trigger. An orange blaze erupted from the muzzle, and the butt of the gun battered her shoulder with each round. It sent pain radiating down into her chest. No doubt she was holding the gun wrong, lying on her stomach and propped up on her elbows.

"What are you doing?" hissed Havana when Jessica stopped shooting.

"Trying to keep him away from us," said Jessica.

In the darkness of the trees ahead, there was a metallic *click*. Then something thudded on the ground several feet to her right.

"Oh, fuck."

She scrambled to her feet, moved left, and pressed her body against the tree. The grenade exploded, briefly lighting up the woods. Shrapnel cracked against the tree trunk, and the blast made Jessica's hair fly around her face.

"Havana!" Jessica screamed, dropping to the ground again. As she did, more gunshots came from the darkness, and without deliberating this time, Jessica returned fire, sweeping the gun's muzzle back and forth to cover more area.

"Jessica," said Havana, her voice weak. "Stop them before..."

"Havana?" said Jessica. The other woman sounded hurt, but Jessica didn't dare run to her yet. "Are you hit?"

No answer.

19

Merida

Wallace went to the window to peek through the blinds. "Oh, shit. I should have thought of that."

"Thought of what?" said Merida. Her pulse pounded in her temples, and she felt a little dizzy. All this way, all this effort.

Celina spoke in her mind. As odd as it was, she sounded exhausted even in her thought-voice. *Cops. DHS. SWAT.*

Wallace moved away from the window, his face stricken. "Did you steal that car?"

"Yes, we—" said Merida. "Oh."

When they'd stolen the first car outside the city, they had deliberately chosen an old vehicle that wouldn't have a built-in location transponder. But when they'd taken the EMT's car, Merida hadn't even thought about the fact that it was a late-model vehicle. If the EMT had come out of the daze and reported the car missing...

Wallace looked across the couch at Merida. His expression said that he knew she understood. Was there also anger there? She wouldn't blame him.

"Stupid," Merida said. "*Stupid.*" They'd just lost everything because she and Celina hadn't stopped to think.

"Well," said Celina, cracking her knuckles like someone about to have a fist fight. "I guess it's time for me to save the day ag—"

But a loud crash cut her off. A window pane shattered, and bits of glass and plastic blinds flew across the room. An object like a soda can hit the wall opposite the window, hissing and pouring out a grayish vapor.

"Shit!" Merida grabbed Celina's hand and pulled her away from the smoke. Looking to Wallace, she said, "Where do we—"

But Wallace threw his arm around Celina and started toward a hallway that led to the back of the house. "This way!"

Merida shoved one of the pistols from the bag into her waistband, then grabbed the laptop before racing after Wallace and Celina. She doubted that the laptop would do them any more good, though. Whatever that *buzz* had been, it seemed to have fried everything.

"We can go out the back," Wallace said, his voice oddly gruff. He had always struck Merida as a little... sensitive? Nerdy? Wimpy? Was he putting on a show in a desperate situation? Male instinct, and all that? "Maybe make it to the woods."

He led them to a bedroom with a pair of French doors that opened onto a patio in the back yard. A pair of sheer curtains hung over the windows.

"It's woods behind the house for a while, and then you run into some power lines, and then more houses," said Wallace. "You two go ahead and—"

"Nope," said Merida, shaking her head. "You're coming with us. You're not doing the noble sacrifice thing." But really, what was the point in running now, anyway? If the computer was fried, they'd lost the whole battle. Everything.

Wallace opened his mouth to respond, but before he could, a

bright white light shone through the patio door and nearly blinded them all. The steady *thumpthump* sound of a helicopter propeller filled the room.

We're not getting away through the woods, said Celina. She stood next to the patio door and peeked between the curtain and the window.

"I don't know what else we can do," said Wallace. Drops of sweat poured down his face.

Celina turned from the window and looked at Merida, her brow furrowed. The girl Merida had met just yesterday—the girl who took nothing seriously and could find something sexy in any circumstance—was gone.

Well, we're in this thing, said Celina's thought-voice. *Might as well go big.*

She closed her eyes and bowed her head, almost as if she were praying. The floodlight disappeared from the window. The helicopter was moving. Over the house. Getting lower. The sound of the propellers grew so loud that Merida covered her ears. Was it about to crash into the roof? She tried to scream for Celina to do something, but the roar of the rotors drowned out everything else.

A thump on the roof of the house. Loud, but not a crash.

Thank the gods, thought Merida.

And then came the explosion.

20

Val

The Dragonfly's fuselage groaned and creaked as the cables tightened and slowed its fall to a stop. The inertia sent Val forward, banging her head into the instrument panel and driving the control yoke into her chest. She groaned, her vision blurring. A wet trail trickled down her forehead and onto her nose. Blood.

What have I done?

If she got caught now, she'd never have the chance to tell Braden what had happened when he was sedated and lying on that rock in the creek. She'd never have the chance to remind Kim that the vision Celina had made him see had just been an illusion.

Quit whining and get your ass to work, she told herself—except that it wasn't her own voice she heard. It was Asa's. Even now, that bastard was still taunting her.

But the point was made. She wasn't captured yet.

Wiping the blood from her nose and forehead, she leaned forward and looked up through the windshield. Two Wasps were above her, the Dragonfly dangling by the cables that extended from the backs of their fuselages. The third Wasp must have been holding the Dragonfly by the back end.

So the Stinger cables allowed the target's systems to be shut down remotely. Then the Wasps could lower the enemy aircraft to the ground without damaging it or killing any people on board.

"Nice," said Val.

She looked down. Trees below. Orange and red glow about half a mile ahead. They were headed toward it, probably to set her down in the Artemis parking lot. That meant she had about three minutes to get ready.

They weren't going to kill her—at least not at first—so they would lead with drones and sedatives. One or two of the Wasps would land. At least one would stay airborne. They'd probably have to reboot the Dragonfly's system to lower the loading ramp. Drones would be ready to enter the cargo bay and sedate her. Then, agents would follow with guns ready. They'd restrain her sedated body and carry her off to God knew where.

Val stood and stepped through the doorway into the cargo area. Since the Dragonfly was dead weight, the space was completely dark. She turned to her right and ran her hands along the wall until she found what she needed: a box on the wall that held a first aid kit, a flashlight, flares, short-range communicators, and a night-vision headset. Since the Wasp pilots might see the flashlight shining and understand what she was doing, she opted for the night-vision instead. She slid the device on her head, adjusted the lenses over her eyes, and held down the power button. The room lit up in luminescent green.

Now that she could see, she walked across the room to the weapons locker, opened it, and surveyed her options. Standard rifles. Pistols. A couple of shotguns. Sedative dart guns. Grenades.

Wait, thought Val. She crouched and looked at something that lay across the bottom of the locker behind the butts of the other guns. She had missed it before and could only see it now because of the night vision.

"What are you?"

She removed the rifles and shotguns to reveal a long, oddly rectangular weapon painted with a forest camouflage pattern. Instead of a muzzle, it had an emitter surrounded by copper wiring. An EMP gun. Her unit had carried similar weapons in Iran.

"You'll be useful."

Val picked up the EMP gun and a rifle, carried them over to one of the hoverbikes, and locked the guns into the bike's weapons holsters. Then she hooked a couple of grenades into her belt loops and stuffed two pistols into her waistband—one 9mm and one sedative dart gun.

The Dragonfly suddenly swayed, nearly sending Val to the floor, and began to descend. It felt like standing on an elevator. The Wasps were lowering her to the ground.

She crouched next to the hoverbike and unlatched the parking yoke that held it in place. The bike wobbled a little, but it didn't fall. Then she climbed into the rider's saddle, fixed her feet into the foot controls, and pressed the Power button.

The bike's headlights and instrument panel turned on, flooding the space with light. In response, the night-vision lenses shut off automatically, so Val took the headset off and tossed it aside. Then she put on the helmet that hung on one of the bike's handlebars. The helmet's HUD displayed a welcome message before switching to navigation graphics.

With a loud *thump*, the Dragonfly touched down, rocking Val in the saddle. Outside, she could hear the distinct sound of lift engines slowing. At least one of the Wasps was landing. Maybe two. But one stayed in the air—right over the Dragonfly, by the sound of it.

System rebooting, came an AI voice.

Lights on the ceiling of the cargo bay flickered and turned on. Behind Val in the cockpit, a faint whirring sound meant that power had been restored to the ship's computer. If she made it out of this and managed to take down the Wasps without damaging the Dragonfly, she and Jessica would be able to fly back to Evan's farm, at least.

Alright, you bastards. Here goes.

She turned off the safeties on the bike's weapons—a minigun and a pair of grenade launchers that hung under the nose. Then she pressed the bike's Start button, and the propellers came to life with a *whir*. In seconds, they turned the room into a torrent of wind so strong that Val could barely keep her eyes open, even with the helmet's face shield protecting them.

The bike lifted off the parking yoke, but instead of settling into a steady hover, it swayed to one side and then the other. It didn't like being in the confined space. Recirculation through the props. Wind reflecting off the walls and roof. Val had to throttle down as low as possible and reach out with her hands to push on the walls whenever the bike drifted too far.

Finally, the loading ramp began to open. Val watched through the widening gap between the ramp and the roof—and saw exactly what she had expected. A pair of drones were waiting, their visual sensors blazing red at her.

Behind them, a Wasp sat parked on the ground, its lights shining on the Dragonfly. Before the ramp had fully opened, Val drew the EMP gun from the holster, aimed, and fired.

The gun vibrated faintly in her hand but made no other indication that it had been activated. It clearly worked, though, because the drone on the left spat out sparks and then fell to the ground.

Blood rushing to her head in relief, Val dropped the other drone, holstered the gun, and gripped the handlebars. Outside, a pair of agents hopped out of the Wasp's cockpit, while two more came running into view from the left side of the cargo bay door. Before any of them could draw weapons, Val fired the bike's minigun, the blast loud as hell in the cargo bay—and then she accelerated out into the night air.

Agents dove to the ground as the bike whistled past them.

That's right, you fucking—

Before she could finish the thought, gunfire erupted behind her. So much for trying to take her in alive. She veered the bike to the right, hearing bullets strike the ground behind her. Then she swerved left again and headed toward the Artemis building, which was still a blazing orange inferno surrounded by burning police cars and dead bodies. These newcomers had done their jobs well. No doubt the government would blame the attack on Val, and the news would report it dutifully.

She swerved again, bringing the hoverbike around in a wide arc, and drew the EMP gun from its holster. It was meant to be a two-handed weapon, and her arm trembled as she tried to hold it steady with her left hand while she steered with her right.

The Wasp was straight ahead, and a fresh pair of drones dropped from its underside. These flew in opposite directions, probably to flank Val and shoot her with sedative darts.

Please let this work.

Still racing toward the Wasp, she raised the EMP gun and pulled the trigger.

21

Merida

The explosion shook the whole house. Wallace stumbled into Merida, who caught him in both arms and would have gone over herself if she hadn't been so close to a wall. Merida felt a little dizzy suddenly, pinpoints of light drifting in front of her eyes.

Celina let out a groan and rolled away from the French doors. She lay on her side, grasping the back of her head with both hands. Blood seeped between her fingers from where she'd broken one of the door's bottom window panes as she fell.

"Shit," said Merida, crouching next to her. "Are you okay?" She could barely hear her own voice over the ringing in her ears.

"I'll live," muttered Celina. She grasped Merida's arm and used it to pull herself to a sitting position. "I think."

Her face, already the color of someone who rarely saw the sun, had gone even more pale than usual. She offered Merida a crooked smile, and Merida thought with a sinking feeling that she looked like someone who'd had a stroke. One side of her face had gone slack.

"You sure know how to cause a lot of trouble," said Merida. She touched Celina's face. "Are you sure you're okay? Can you walk? We'd better get our asses moving."

"I can walk." She got to her hands and knees, then struggled to her feet. A trail of blood trickled down the back of her neck. "I just keep thinking that if I have to die, I wish somebody would just kill me already. The suspense is... well, *killing* me."

"That explosion is going to bring the fricking National Guard here," said Wallace. "You need to go before they catch you."

"And you're coming with us," Merida said. "I'm sorry, but there's no way you're going back to your normal life now. You're one of us."

Wallace looked at her, his eyes sad with resignation. She had taken his life from him. But there was no time to stand around feeling bad about it. They were going to be lucky if all Wallace lost was his job and his house.

"Maybe I can—"

The sound of a crash in the living room cut him off. Somebody had broken down the front door.

22

Jessica

Running footsteps, then a burst of gunfire. Again and again. The agent was coming closer in sprints. Tree to tree. Stealing bases. Whittling away at the space between them.

Jessica crouched behind the tree and raised the rifle again, her finger against the trigger. But instead of firing, she decided to save her ammo. She'd wasted bullets trying to keep the bastard from coming closer, and all she'd done was nearly get herself killed by telling him where she was.

And I might have gotten Havana killed.

She wanted to call out to Havana again but knew that she shouldn't. That would bring the agent right to her.

The longer Jessica was pinned down here, the farther away Taylor would get—if she wasn't out of Jessica's reach already. What would Val do? Val, who had stormed a secret government facility to get her son and husband out, who had stood up to bullies over and over again when the two of them were young. If Val were here now, she'd do something bold. Take some wild chance and surprise her enemy. What would that be?

"Dammit," Jessica muttered.

She needed to try and wrap this up so that she could move on and try to find Taylor. She also needed to draw the agent away from Havana. She readied herself to run and listened for the agent, who hadn't yet moved. When he did, Jessica would sprint to a different tree. Maybe his movement would cover the sound of her own. At the very least, he wouldn't be positioned to open fire on her if he spotted her moving.

Hurried footsteps. Heading to Jessica's right.

Jessica turned left and sprinted toward a close grouping of pine trees. The way their trunks were configured gave her a good hiding spot with a space between two of them that she could use for aiming the rifle.

As she took up her place behind the trees, though, the woods became strangely quiet. The distant sounds of gunfire and Dragonfly engines coming from Artemis had died out.

Had Val killed the other agents? Had they killed her?

But Jessica drove these questions from her mind. No time to think about that now. She had to listen for the movements of the agent who was stalking her, and then she had to go after Taylor before it was too late.

More footsteps in the dark. Somewhere close to where Havana had taken cover. Moving toward the spot where Jessica had just been. In range now. The moment she saw movement, she was ready to fire.

Before she could raise her rifle to take aim, though, something cold and hard pressed against the back of her skull.

"Drop the gun," said a gravelly voice.

23

Merida

"Run!" Merida shouted.

Wallace wrenched open the French doors and shooed Celina and Merida outside.

Even now, ladies first, Merida thought. Later she might be either amused or annoyed by this. If she was still alive later, that was.

The door opened onto a large patio slab. Past that, about fifteen yards of grass lay between them and the woods.

"That way!" said Wallace. He pointed to Merida's left, where the woods were the thickest. The undergrowth would slow them down.

"That's—" Merida began, but Wallace cut her off.

"Trust me!" He gave Merida a shove in that direction, nearly knocking her over.

Her heart hammering, Merida grabbed Celina's hand and ran. She easily outpaced the younger girl and had to drag her along.

No time to get tired, she thought.

I'm coming, I'm coming, Celina replied. But her voice sounded faint, almost as if Merida were hearing it from a distance. *Can't rush a girl on the first date, you know. Besides, my head hurts.*

Just don't let go of my hand, okay?

Yes, Mommy.

They reached the woods and pushed their way into the trees, leaves and branches scraping their faces.

Behind them, a gruff voice shouted, "Stop right there!" A series of three *pop*s sounded, and something struck the tree next to Merida's shoulder. Must have been a dart.

"Shit," Merida growled.

She pulled the pistol from her waistband, turned, and crouched behind one of the trees. Peeking around the trunk, she raised the gun and aimed it toward the house. Several cops had come out of the French doors, and more were coming. She put the sights on one officer's legs.

"What are you doing?" hissed Wallace. "We need to—"

Bang.

The pistol definitely kicked, but it was more manageable than she had expected. The cops all went for cover. One knocked over a big barbecue grill and lay on the ground behind it. Another took refuge behind a wheelbarrow. A third sprinted for a small tool shed. Two more ran back into the house, then turned to aim their guns from just inside the door.

Thinking that she was already in this about as deep as she could get, Merida pulled the trigger five more times. She didn't bother following Val's instructions to just *squeeze* the trigger. She wasn't going for accuracy; she hadn't even decided whether or not she actually wanted to hit any of the cops. She just wanted to make these guys hesitate long enough for them to get away.

"Okay, okay," whispered Wallace into her ear. "Now let's—"

The cops returned fire. Merida dove to one side, knocking Wallace to the ground. Vaguely, Merida registered a thought coming from Celina, but she only caught a fragment of it—*really screwed things up this*—before she scrambled back into her crouching position, ready to fire more bullets in the direction of the house.

"*Now* can we go?" said Wallace.

Merida looked around to find Celina. The girl had sat down behind a big oak tree with her knees curled to her chest. "Can you...?"

Celina looked up. Her eyes were bloodshot. She shook her head.

"Sorry," she whispered.

Merida raised the gun and fired off three more rounds. Val had said that this gun held fifteen rounds, plus one in the chamber. So she had seven left, plus the extra magazine.

"Lead," she said to Wallace.

She grabbed Celina's hand and dragged her to her feet. As they followed Wallace deeper into the woods, she fired two more shots toward the house without looking. One of the cops barked some kind of order to the others, but Merida couldn't understand it.

They were headed down a steep incline. The farther down they went, the farther apart the trees became. The ground was covered with years of accumulated dead leaves, sticks, and pine straw. Some thorny vines bit at Merida's pants legs, a few thorns piercing through and cutting into her skin. But she barely noticed. Had to keep moving.

"Not sure how much more of this I can do," said Celina. "Head is killing me. I'm... shaking. Tired."

"We make it through this, you can sleep all you want," Merida said, her chest burning. She tugged at the girl's hand, urging her down the slope. "And I'll cook you the best damn food you ever ate."

They turned so that instead of following the slope downwards, their path ran almost perpendicular to it. Several times, Merida's ankles bent to one side, threatening to buckle under her and give her a sprain.

"Just a little farther," Wallace huffed. He glanced over his shoulder at Merida. "Careful not to fall."

They reached a power line right-of-way that ran down the slope toward a wide, multi-lane highway about a hundred yards to their left. Merida thought it was probably I-75, which looped around the perimeter of Atlanta. A concrete drainage channel followed the line of huge metal transmission towers to the bottom of the hill near the interstate.

"Which way?" Merida said, wincing at a stitch in her side.

They could go left toward the highway, across the easement, and keep running through more trees, or to their right up the slope. There were a few houses up there. Probably a few cars to steal, but they couldn't get away from the cops by running uphill.

Beside her, Celina was gasping for breath, her palms pressed against her temples. "You'd better not... make me... have to bail us... out of something... bad... again..."

Merida put her arm around Celina's waist to support her. The girl's shirt was soaked with sweat.

"I'm going to start... charging you..." she said.

"Can you swim?" said Wallace. His face was flushed to a deep purple from the running.

"Yes," panted Merida. She looked to Celina, who nodded. "Why?"

"Creek down there," said Wallace. He pointed to their left, and Merida saw where the highway crossed over a flat bridge near the base of the slope.

She looked at the pistol and then back at Wallace. Would the water damage it? And even with her life on the line, the idea of jumping into a creek didn't appeal to her. "What about the interstate? Celina could force a car to stop, and we—"

But no, Celina couldn't. Not now. Maybe not even at full strength. I-75 traffic was like an *Autobahn*. And the fact that Celina was dead silent, even in her mind, told Merida the answer to her question.

Wallace shrugged. "We can swim or we can run. I think the water is the best chance we have. We might be able to hide there or..."

Or what, Merida never got to find out, because behind them, pounding footsteps and shouted voices came toward them.

24

Jessica

"Last warning before I blow your head off," said the man. "Don't try anything stu—"

Jessica dropped and drove the butt of her rifle backwards, bellowing out a *kiai* as Val had taught her years ago.

But even as she moved, she realized that this maneuver wasn't going to work. Her right foot hit the man's leg and forced her off-balance so that when she drove the gun backwards, the butt hit him on the hip instead of the gut. He let out a low grunt and staggered backwards a little.

"Fucking hell," he said.

He drove his foot into the middle of Jessica's back, knocking her into the tree. She bounced away and fell onto her side with the rifle beneath her. The handle for the bolt dug into her ribs, sending rivulets of pain throughout her chest and abdomen. Hating herself for it, she let out a scream.

"Why the hell can't people just do what they're fucking told?" said the man.

He shoved Jessica onto her stomach and put his foot on the back of her neck, pressing her face into the earth. The dank smell of humid soil and rotting leaves filled her nostrils. Small insects scurried away.

Loud footsteps approached from somewhere nearby.

"Hart?" said a voice. The footsteps stopped just a yard or so from Jessica's head.

"Yeah," said the man.

"I got the nurse," said the other voice. "Body's over—"

"Not a nurse," gasped Jessica, her chest burning. The bastard's foot had pushed almost all the air out of her. "A *doctor*."

Even now, her eyes filled with tears. Havana was dead. And it was Jessica's fault.

"Let me shut this bitch up," said the man.

Once again, the muzzle of the gun pressed against the back of her head. Jessica arched her back and tried to get out from under the foot, to roll, to make the man stumble, *anything*. But he was too heavy, too strong. He shoved her back down. Closing her eyes, she thought of Merida and Taylor, and waited to die.

A gunshot did come, but it came from farther away than it should have. The pressure of the foot on her back relaxed, and the man crumpled to the ground beside her.

"Holy sh—" said the other man, but a second gunshot cut him off. He fell to the ground, too.

Jessica rolled, her chest burning and her head swimming, and got to her feet using the pine tree for support.

"Jessica!" shouted a voice from somewhere behind her. Someone was running toward her.

"We have to..." Jessica said. She turned and started toward the spot where Havana had been hiding. "Havana. Taylor."

Val reached her and put an arm around her for support. "We

have to go *now*," she said. "They're going to send more and more agents. I can't keep fighting them off forev—"

Jessica grabbed handfuls of Val's shirt and shook her. "They've got Taylor!" she said. "They went—"

She turned, pointing, and her heart sank. Which direction? She'd lost her bearings while trying to avoid getting caught or shot.

"I just need to get back to the other tree," she said, letting go of Val and starting toward the place where the grenade had gone off. "I'll be able to tell—"

But Val grabbed her arm, gripping hard enough to hurt.

"She's gone, Jess."

Jessica wrenched her arm free and started toward the tree again. "No! It wasn't two minutes ago that they were here. They can't have gotten far. *Help* me."

She reached the other tree. Except it wasn't the right tree. Too thin. She turned, peering into the dark, and spotted a big oak several yards away.

"That's it," she said. "If I can just—"

But now Val was standing between her and the tree, blocking her way.

"I'm sorry about the girl," she said. "And I'm sorry about everybody else. But we've almost gotten caught twice now. I have to get back to my son and my husband. If we don't get out of here now, we might not ever see them again."

The steely collectedness in her voice sent a stab of anger through Jessica. How could Val be so calm right now? How could this woman who had fought the government for the right to have a child on her own terms, who had waged a damn *war* to get that child back from them, be so fucking calm after losing Taylor?

"Get out of my way, Val. You can leave if you want, but I have to try."

"You're not going to help that baby by getting caught. We need to retreat and regroup."

Jessica's hand flew before she even realized that she was about to do it. She struck Val in the mouth with a back-fist—a move that Val herself had taught a reluctant Jessica years ago.

Val stepped backwards a little, but the blow hadn't been precise enough to stagger her. It was hard to tell in the dark, but it probably hadn't even bloodied her lip.

Should have practiced the stuff that she taught me, Jessica thought.

Instead of waiting to see how Val would respond, Jessica darted to one side and sprinted toward the big oak tree. Before she could reach it, though, there was a *pop* from behind her, and a sharp sting above her shoulder blade.

She felt the effects of the sedative almost immediately. First, a haze like when she drank her margarita too fast, and then numbness.

"You bitch!" she shouted.

She tried to throw her arm over her shoulder and pull out the dart, but she couldn't reach it. Val had known what she was doing. Then her sense of balance left her, and she fell backwards. Val caught her under the arms before she hit the ground.

"I'm sorry," Val said.

25

Merida

They were running straight down the slope, following the drainage channel toward the highway. Merida fired another couple of wild shots over her shoulder, praying that a stray bullet didn't hit some unintended target—like one of those houses she thought she'd seen at the top of the slope.

"Drop-off at the end of this," huffed Wallace. "Water falls into the creek. Deep pool. We can swim for one of the culverts."

"Just make sure we stay together," panted Merida. "Don't get separated."

Burning, stinging pain threatened to seize every muscle from her calves to her upper back. Each footfall sent a jolt through her knees to her hip joints. A nagging thought in the back of her mind said that it was time to give up.

Jessica, she told herself. *If I can make it back to her, I can deal with whatever else.*

Wallace yelped and slipped, his feet sliding out from under him. He fell on his butt, and his momentum sent him sliding several yards down the slope. Merida pounded to a stop, putting a hand under his arm and yanking him back to his feet. Then they kept running.

Thirty yards or so to the drop-off. The slope was leveling out now, and the running became easier in one sense and harder in another. Merida wasn't having to fight to keep her balance anymore, but it took much more energy to keep up her speed. Even if they made it to the water, they'd be lucky not to drown because of exhaustion.

I've never run this much in my whole life, she thought.

Me, either, replied Celina, her thought-voice flat and muffled as if Merida were listening to her from under water.

Twenty yards.

We aren't going to make it, are we?

I doubt it.

Ten yards. They could do it.

"Get ready to jump," shouted Wallace. "Swim toward the culvert to the far left."

Five yards. Celina was starting to feel like a weight that Merida had to drag along. She gripped the girl's hand harder and pulled.

"We're going to make—"

But a faint *pop* like a distant gunshot rang out behind her, and a sharp sting like the bite of a horsefly struck her in the back.

Agora: The Ideas Marketplace

American News Site: The Presidents of the U.S. and Russia caution against "unrealistic expectations" on the eve of peace talks, though both express hope for an agreement.

CNN: Lebedev says that his country won't be the first to leave the negotiation table, even as Russian forces amass on the Ukrainian-Polish border.

YLarrimore: If we want peace, we have to pray for justice.

AndreaB: Anybody who listens to Lebedev talk for five minutes can tell that he's a damn snake in the grass.

MHarper1987: Those two need to get their shit together!!!

Huffington Post: Supreme Court prepares to rule in *John Doe v State of Wisconsin*: what is the meaning of *Roe v Wade* in the age of artificial uteruses and Safe Reproductive Practices?

ABC News: SCOTUS Watch: Are men about to gain the right to abort their artificially-gestating fetuses?

26

Celina

Her head hurt.

Bad.

That was the thing that allowed everything else to happen the way that it did. It was like the time that she did the Very Bad Thing.

The thing that she tried not to think about very much any more.

When she had Hurt Someone.

She'd had to use her Power to control Nathan's mind for three days. By the end of it, her head had hurt like this, and all she could do was sleep. And Nathan had escaped.

Maybe everything that was happening now was punishment for the Very Bad Thing. That was okay. If there was a God to deal out retribution for wrongdoing, Celina could live with that. It made her feel better about a lot of things, actually. She deserved to be punished. But why did everybody else have to suffer for what she had done?

The whistle of the dart.

The *thud* of it hitting Merida's body.

More whistling.

Merida's grip on her hand went tight—the way people's hands

always do when they're about to Lose Something Important. Something they were meant to Protect.

She didn't deserve someone like Merida. Someone who wanted to protect her. Merida's fingers clasped her hand tighter and tighter, and then they went slack. She let out a noise of Despair. It was the noise you made in the moment when you first understood that you were about to Lose. And then her hand was slipping out of Celina's.

A song her mother used to sing to her. When she was drunk and feeling sorry for herself. Ashamed of what she had allowed her husband to do to her daughter. The words rang in Celina's head now.

Though the sun stop burning
And the world stop turning
I'll never let you go.

Merida dropped. Celina fell to her knees next to her, and something whistled over her head, missing by inches. Close enough to make her hair rustle.

Head hurts, she thought. *We don't have time for this, girl.*

But her mind didn't feel strong enough even to make Merida hear it.

Food. Sleep. Just needed to recharge. Then she'd whip these guys. Just had to tell them to put a hold on this thing until she was in tip-top shape again. That way it would be a Fair Fight.

There's no such thing as a fair fight, her mother had once said. *Not in real fights. The only fair fights are made-up ones. Like checkers or basketball. And even those ain't always fair.*

Somebody was shouting. Wallace? It was hard to distinguish the close voices from the distant ones. Somebody grabbed her shirt. Tugged at it. It was her stepdad all over again. That fucker wasn't ever going to touch her again.

No, that wasn't right. He was dead. She'd killed him. Who was pulling her shirt? Pulling so damn hard it might rip. Then hands gripped her arms and pulled *her*.

She summoned the last bits of strength that she had and fought back. Flailed her arms. Kicked. Fucker.

But the arms had let go of her, and she was falling.

Falling.

Cold.

PART TWO

Juana Hernandez: FOX News

We have breaking news of a second terrorist attack on American soil. An artificial reproduction facility in Georgia has been destroyed by multiple missiles fired from a Dragonfly aircraft, less than twenty-four hours after gunmen rampaged through a medical research facility in North Carolina. And the Department of Homeland Security has just confirmed these two attacks are related.

The Artemis Advanced Reproduction hospital is still in flames at this hour, and some officials are already calling it the worst terrorist incident on American soil since the 9/11 attacks. Hundreds are believed dead, including dozens of medical staff and all of the fetuses that were gestating in artificial uteruses at the facility.

According to D.H.S. officials, these two attacks were carried out by a "homegrown terrorist cell devoted to destroying safe reproduction." At the center of this organization is Valerie Hara, a former U.S. Marine and a decorated veteran of Operation Liberate Iran. Hara allegedly stole a Homeland Security Dragonfly aerial assault vehicle and used it to fire missiles at Artemis...

27

Theresa

She'd been riding in the self-driving van that Cartwright sent to pick her up for more than five hours before it finally pulled into a mostly empty parking lot surrounded on two sides by pine trees planted in evenly spaced rows. At the far end of the lot sat a rather boring two-story brick building with the words JACKSON, WILKINS & WILKINS ATTORNEYS AT LAW emblazoned over its door in silvery roman font.

A thin, red-haired woman in a business suit waited on the sidewalk in front of the building's manicured lawn.

"*Destination reached*," said the vehicle's AI voice. "*Have a good day, Theresa.*"

The van parked right next to the red-haired woman, who stood patiently with her fingers laced together, a smile frozen on her face. With a mechanical *whir*, the van's sliding door opened.

"Hi, Theresa," said the woman, her voice high and soft, almost artificially sweet. She motioned for Theresa to step out. "My name is Journey Denton. How are you?"

"I'm..." Theresa said. She climbed out of the van. Bright sunlight. Warm air. The smell of grass and pine and asphalt.

Journey stood back and surveyed her patiently, her smile sympathetic and her brow furrowed with concern. Finally, she seemed to decide that the words weren't going to come for Theresa. She filled the silence herself.

"I can't even imagine what you've been through," she said. "Nobody should ever be treated the way you were treated at that horrible Singer Institute. I'm so sorry."

"Thanks," Theresa managed. "I'm still getting used to..." She looked around at the van, the parking lot, and the office building. "...everything."

Even though it was probably rude, Theresa couldn't help staring at Journey's hair and clothes. She had never seen anyone with this woman's sense of style. She wore a suit that Theresa might have called "business-like," but instead of black, it was brightly colored—red, yellow, and green.

"I understand you're truly gifted," said Journey.

"Maybe," said Theresa.

She thought about the bloodied faces of Jones-McMartin and Tolbert. What Dr. Simmons's head had done when Bowen had shot her. All the soldiers and agents she had killed. And Bowen himself.

They had all deserved what she'd done.

But she still felt a little discomfort at the way Journey was talking about it. She wasn't a victim. Not in the sense that a lot of people would have meant. She'd chosen to kill those people because it was right. Her circumstances hadn't made the choice for her.

"I wish I hadn't had to use my powers that way," she said. "But I'd do it again if... if I had to."

"Oh, I know," said Journey, the furrow of her brow deepening. "Daniel—Senator Cartwright—has been desperate to set you free.

You wouldn't believe how much he's done behind the scenes to try and help you. We are all so very, very relieved that you were able to escape on your own. We came running to find you as soon as we heard."

On her own?

No. Not really.

That woman—Valerie Hara—had fought and killed to save her son from that place. Theresa had done nothing but take advantage of the chaos. Hara had been horrified by what Theresa had done to Bowen, but Theresa had seen something in the woman. Something they shared. Maybe it was the understanding that sometimes you had to fight back.

"I want to join the fight," Theresa said. "If you want to make the world safe for people like me, then I want to help."

Journey smiled and gestured for Theresa to follow her toward the building's front door. "This used to be Cartwright's practice," she said. "It's still a law office, but it mostly serves as a cover for our organization. We've got some rooms in the back where we work."

Theresa felt a little sick to her stomach at the thought of yet another secret facility.

It's not an underground bunker, said Journey's voice in Theresa's head. *I promise. It's nothing like that place. You won't be a prisoner here.*

As they approached the building, a middle-aged man wearing horn-rimmed glasses and a gray suit stepped out the front door and stood waiting for them on the walk, his hands clasped.

"Silvan, let me introduce Theresa," said Journey.

The man strode forward and shook Theresa's hand. His palm felt smooth and a little feminine. There was a tattoo of a moth on the back of his hand, its wingtips touching the first knuckles of his index finger and his pinky. He squeezed hard enough to hurt a little, offering a pleasant smile that managed to look sickeningly sincere and phony at the same time.

"Theresa," he said. "I've been so excited to meet you."

"Oh," said Theresa. "Uh, thanks."

He stepped back to look at her. He was shorter than Theresa, had a round face and a flabby neck that spilled over the collar of his shirt, which was buttoned all the way to the top. He wasn't overweight, though. In spite of his pudgy face, the rest of him was slight.

"Officially, I'm Mike Wilkins," the man said, pointing at the letters on the side of the building. "The second 'Wilkins' in 'Jackson, Wilkins, and Wilkins.' But you call me Silvan. That's my *true* name."

"True name?" said Theresa.

"Yes," said Silvan. "It's like this: nobody gets to—"

"Let's talk about names later," said Journey.

Silvan smiled. "Right. Getting ahead of myself. Anyway, it's really good to meet you, Theresa."

"Nice to meet you," said Theresa, but her eyes were drawn to a pair of metal statues that stood in a flower garden next to the building's entrance. Two women. The first held a set of scales in one hand and a sword in the other. The second wore a crown and had a pair of feathered wings. She stood behind the first woman, her hands lifting a blindfold from the first woman's eyes. A metal plaque at their feet read, "*Iustitia non diutius caeca.*"

"You like our sculpture?" said Silvan, who turned to look at the figures. "That's Sophia liberating Justice from her blindness."

"They're beautiful," said Theresa. She reached out and ran her fingertips along the edge of the sword.

"I'll tell you more about them sometime," said Silvan. "But right now, business." He turned to Journey. "Cartwright just called. Mission. You're up."

"What's it about?" Journey said.

Silvan looked at Theresa.

"Whatever it is, say it in front of her," said Journey. "She's one of us now, and we hide nothing. That's how you build trust."

Silvan's face fell, looking a little nervous, but then he recovered. "Right. Level Two target. Extraction. False identity mandatory."

Theresa bristled a little. He was speaking coded language. Was that just the way they talked around here, or was he still trying to conceal the truth from her? Either way, after the secrecy of the Institute, she wasn't going to put up with it anymore.

She pressed into his mind, not bothering to try and keep him from noticing her presence. For his part, Silvan didn't seem to put out any effort to conceal things from her. He just went on talking to Journey in his coded language. So Theresa saw it all, and she knew that she had to go with Journey on this mission.

"He wants me to go now?" said Journey when he had finished.

"Yes," said Silvan.

"I'm going with you," said Theresa.

Silvan and Journey both turned to face her. Silvan put on a patient, understanding expression. Journey, on the other hand, looked pleased. Almost proud.

"I appreciate your eagerness to help," said Silvan, "but you need rest, and Mr. Cartwright wouldn't want—"

I'm going, thought Theresa, pushing outward with her mind as forcefully as she could.

Silvan stared, his mouth open slightly. Finally, he said, "You'll get your chance to go into the field. Plenty of it. I promise. But first you have to be trained."

"That's what I've been doing this whole time," said Theresa. "Training. They were turning us into spies and information thieves. Killers."

Silvan stuffed his hands in his pockets, his eyes shifting back and forth between Theresa and Journey.

"I just read your mind," said Theresa. "I understand what you're doing and how it needs to be done. I can help. Trust me, this is exactly what they were training me to do. Read *my* mind if you don't believe me."

As if to get a fuller view, Journey took a step backwards and appraised Theresa. "I already knew from our source inside the Singer Institute that you were special. But you're a truly remarkable person, Theresa."

"Journey?" said Silvan, his voice slightly strained. "You *can't* take her. Cartwright would be furious. And it's irresponsible to take her on a mission like this after what she's been through recently."

In answer, Journey crossed her arms, her lips curving into a smile.

28

Jessica

She dreamed. Some of it might not have been a dream. Val had helped her walk—stumble—down the Dragonfly's loading ramp. They'd gotten into a truck. Driven along a bumpy road. Their cousin Evan had been there. They'd helped her climb some stairs and then get into bed. And then she'd been on the ground in the woods again, and Val had been standing over her. She'd been aiming a pistol at Jessica's head. Baby Taylor was in her arms. No, she was in Havana's arms now. They were together in that basement under Artemis, while the building burned down around them. Dr. Hayden had been sitting next to Jessica, his shirt stained with blood from the bullet wounds. He'd gotten up and walked into the fire. The baby had gripped Jessica's finger as her father disappeared.

Taylor. God.

Val had attacked her. Shot her. Killed her? No, that wasn't right. But Val had shot her...

Damn you, Val.

• • •

When she woke up, she thought that she was back in her apartment. A vague but terrible fear clung to her, like the remnants of a half-forgotten nightmare. Something horrible had happened. What had she been dreaming?

She rolled toward the edge of the bed and stretched, letting out a low groan as she worked out the stiffness in her body. Her joints creaked like rusty hinges, and her muscles screamed at her for moving.

No, this wasn't her bed. It was softer than she was used to. Definitely not her apartment. Light blue walls with white trim. Very country. Antique wooden furniture—a chifforobe, a dresser, and nightstands, all dark-stained wood—that could probably sell for a lot of money.

She'd dreamed about Val. A bumpy truck ride to Evan's house. Not a dream, then. She was in Evan's house right now.

Taylor. Gone.

Havana dead.

Hot tears welled in her eyes. Dripped down her cheeks. A lump formed in her throat. She saw Havana's dead eyes staring up at her. Agents had come and taken Taylor. Jessica hadn't been quick or strong enough to save her.

And her fucking sister had fucking tranquilized her.

She sat up, swinging her legs over the side of the bed, which creaked with her movements. Cool, smooth floor. Wood.

Val had said something to her in her dream. *I made sure that you got back to Merida.*

But Merida was an adult. Merida could take care of herself. If Val had just helped her, they might have saved the baby. They might have caught those fuckers before they took Taylor off to whatever government facility...

She stood, wiping the tears from her eyes.

Who was she kidding? Val had been right. She wouldn't have been able to save the baby. If she had gone after Taylor, she'd probably have been killed. Even with a gun, Jessica was just a journalist. She should have known the rescue mission would fail. Her place was in front of a camera or a keyboard, not running off into the woods with a rifle. She should have gone with Merida to—

Jessica's throat clenched. Had Merida not made it back yet?

She shook her head, wracking her brain to sort through the fragmented images and dreams that still crowded her memory. Nothing about Merida. If she'd made it back, she would be here right now with Jessica, waiting for her to wake up.

She stood, padded over to the door, and turned the tarnished old brass knob. The door opened into a hallway lined with family photos and more doors. One was a bathroom, and Jessica realized just how much she needed to pee. After she had gone, she went down the hall to a staircase. As she descended, she could hear voices.

Not Merida's, though.

"...keep a couple of crop dusters. Maybe they've got some fuel?"

"Those old things? They probably run on avgas, not hydrogen..."

She stopped at the bottom of the stairs. Ahead of her was the foyer and the front door. The voices were coming from her right. Val was talking now.

"Not a lot of places to buy that much Hydrogen-5, no questions asked."

The others didn't seem to have an answer to that. But at least everybody sounded calm. No raised voices, no strained whispers. Just the clink of metal utensils on dishes and the smell of home-cooked food. They were eating dinner and having conversation. So there wasn't any terrible news. Merida and Celina hadn't made it back yet, but they hadn't been killed or captured either. Or at least, the news had reported it yet.

Don't panic, Jessica told herself. *You knew it would probably take Merida and Celina longer to get back than you and Val.*

But how long had Jessica been asleep? It could have been hours. It could have been a whole day. How long had Merida been missing? Something else made Jessica's stomach turn, too. Was it guilt? What did she have to feel guilty about? Yes, she'd been ready to leave Merida behind to run after Baby Taylor, even if it meant she probably wasn't going to see Merida again. But what was she supposed to have done? Let Taylor go, like Val had?

Her eyes drifted up to a cross that hung above the front door. Evan had talked about church the last time she'd seen him. He'd been considering becoming some kind of preacher, if she remembered correctly. So it must be interesting for him and his wife to have Jessica in their house. Even before Jessica had moved to Atlanta and basically cut ties with her family, everyone had known that she dated women. People at their grandmother's Pentecostal church had always looked at her with something like pity. Sometimes they'd say, "I'm praying for you," and Jessica couldn't help thinking they were praying that she'd see the light and settle down to marry a man.

Looking at the cross, she saw several images: the tortured, beaten, dying Christ she'd imagined when she was a girl; the bloodied bodies of Hayden and Havana; baby Taylor sedated and pierced with needles and probes. How did so many otherwise intelligent, sane people reconcile those kinds of horrors with the existence of God?

And yet, before she even realized she was going to do it, she voiced a desperate prayer in her mind.

Please, please, let them be okay.

29

Merida

Small room. White cinderblock walls. Fluorescent lights. Metal door with a small window made of reinforced glass. Small bed. Thin mattress. Metal frame that creaked as she moved. Low to the floor. Flat pillow. Crick in her neck.

Celina. Wallace. Where were they?

The last thing Merida could remember was the darkness of sleep taking her. As she'd collapsed, she thought she saw Celina falling over the drop-off into the creek, but she wasn't sure. If they had hit her with the sedative and she'd fallen into the water, had she drowned?

A sharp twist wrenched her gut. All this way, all of the fighting and death, and not only had they lost the computer, but Celina, too. And Wallace.

Merida sat up, the springs of the bed squeaking. She shook her head against the dizziness, an aftereffect of the sedative, no doubt. Then she rested her face in her palms and let herself cry.

Her body shuddered as it let out everything she'd kept bound up tight until now. In just a few days, she'd gone from a successful restauranteur to a terrorist in the eyes of the world.

When she'd first told her family that she wanted to open a restaurant, her mom had laughed at her. She'd said that only a crazy person would try to open a restaurant in Atlanta. But Merida had done it, and she had succeeded at it. People all over Georgia knew about her food. Lots of people had told her that they'd come to the city just to eat there. She'd even been featured in *Atlanta* magazine. Now it was gone. All her employees and friends would be jobless. Megan. Marquell. Talia. Paul. Sam. Would they hate her? Would they be shocked that their employer had turned out to be some kind of crazy, government-hating radical?

Meanwhile, Jessica was out saving the world with her sister. Celina was probably dead. Wallace was who-the-hell-knew-where. Probably dead, too. And Merida was going to rot in a cell at some secret government facility. Or maybe they'd just go ahead and kill her. As long as they didn't drag it out, death didn't scare her at this point.

Then again, she didn't want to die with things not right between her and Jessica. She didn't know what was wrong or why, but she could feel it—just as surely as she could feel the ache in her back and neck. And it wasn't just because of the fight they'd had over Merida's jealousy. Something else was happening between them.

Or was that just her jealousy speaking?

All this had happened because Jessica had been given a computer. Because she'd gotten involved in something that was *none of her damn business.*

But that wasn't fair. Merida had pushed Jessica into it—and had dived over the cliff with her. After everything, she *believed* in what they were doing. That was the crazy thing. And now all of it had come to nothing. They'd gotten close—*so damn close*—only to see the whole thing fail.

Ninety-nine percent.

She wiped tears from her eyes and snot from her nose with the collar of her shirt. There was dirt caked on her arms, and she could smell her own funk when she lifted her shirt.

I hope you're happy, Jess, she thought. She imagined Jessica and Val zooming through the air in that Dragonfly. Maybe Val was fighting off other planes while Jessica cradled the little baby in her arms.

As she got her tears under control, she began to hear voices and people bustling somewhere outside her cell. Mostly they were muffled and indistinct, but every once in a while she could make out some of the words.

"—ain't done shit, man. You can't—"

"—bunch of fucking pigs—"

"—shoved me up against the wall and held a knife to my throat—"

"—oh, God, I almost died, didn't I?"

"—when my lawyer gets here, you're gonna fucking—"

She wasn't in yet another secret institute devoted to experimenting on telepaths, after all. This was a police station. This was the Atlanta PD.

At once, her heart lifted. The police hadn't delivered her up to DHS yet. They'd brought her to a local precinct and put her in a holding cell while she slept. They'd be mad as hell that she had shot at some of them—*Here's hoping I didn't kill anyone*—but maybe she could still avoid being whisked off by government goons and killed. Maybe Val and Jessica would even find her and save her.

Who was she kidding?

Val was clearly one hell of an ass-kicker, but there was no way she'd risk her family again just to save her sister's girlfriend. And while Jessica had friends and contacts in the police department, there was no way they'd talk to her or help her now. She and Jessica were both wanted criminals. Reactionaries. Insurrectionists. Grade-A, home-grown terrorists.

The door lock clicked. Her heart jumping, Merida rubbed her face to wipe any tears that were left, and the door swung open.

A tall man in slacks and a button-down shirt stepped inside. A detective. He was carrying a chair in one hand and a tablet computer in the other. His arms and shoulders filled out the dress shirt, threatening to loosen some of the seams, and when he walked, the heel-falls of his square-toed boots *thumped* on the linoleum floor. Every move he made exuded power and control. Deliberateness. He had to be ex-military.

"What happened to my friends?" Merida said.

The man placed the chair a few feet from Merida with the back facing her. Then he straddled it with his legs and sat down. When he looked at her, his gaze seemed to bore into her. Dark brown eyes. Furrowed brow. Severe cheek bones. Square jaw. Bloodshot eyes. His expression wasn't *unkind* exactly, but incredibly intense. Absolutely no bullshit with this dude.

When he spoke, his voice matched the strength and seriousness of his face. "Merida Castillo. I'm Detective Rashawn Parks. Do you fully understand why you're here?"

"I want to know where my friends are," Merida said, annoyed at the quaver in her voice. She wanted to steel herself. To be tough, as she imagined Val would be. Or like Jessica in an interview with a hardened criminal. But she might as well roll over and show her belly for all the toughness she could muster.

Parks stared at her, his frown deepening. His eyes were very bloodshot.

"They fell into the water," he said. "That creek moves pretty fast. Could take a while to find the bodies. I've got men looking for them, but you're lucky to be alive."

"Bodies," Merida echoed. "You mean they're dead."

Detective Man-Spread dropped his eyes to the tablet in his hands and made some swipes on the screen. "Unless they can swim while sedated."

"*That's your fault!*" yelled Merida. Almost of its own accord, her hand rose and pointed a finger at him. "Your men shouldn't have shot those darts at us so close to the damn water!"

Now he looked up at her, a fire blazing in his bloodshot brown eyes. He pressed a button on the tablet and held it so that the screen pointed toward the ceiling. A holographic image appeared above the device, showing a portrait of a police officer in a dress uniform. The smile looked strange on his chiseled face.

"Officer Jacob Freeman," Parks said. "He died last night when his hoverbike crashed and another officer ran over him with a cruiser. While they were chasing you."

In an instant, all of the anger drained out of Merida's body. Celina had done that. She hadn't intended to kill him, of course, but...

Parks made another swipe on the tablet, and a different hologram appeared. This one showed a wrecked police car turned upside down. Shattered glass everywhere. The body of the driver, a female officer, lay strewn out the passenger window. Bloody, matted blonde hair. From this view, it might have been Jessica lying there.

"Officer Renee Dalton," Parks said. "Also dead."

Merida struggled for a quip, something to deflect the hatred that seemed to radiate from the detective. But for once, she had nothing.

Another image. A livepic of the alley behind her restaurant. The view panned slowly over the bodies of the twelve agents, who lay on the asphalt with their guns still in their hands. One dead man stared up at the camera, his eyes wide and empty. Then she saw Marcus, who lay face-down with his arm stretched out and the long-barreled pistol in his hand. Suddenly, she wished that she had taken that damn gun as a trophy.

"These men—all federal agents—are all dead in some kind of gunfight," Parks said.

He looked at her through the holograph. His expression had taken on something new in addition to his anger over his fallen comrades. Puzzlement. His eyes lost a little bit of the fire, but his brow furrowed even further.

"DHS hasn't given me access to the bodycam footage, so I don't have enough information to say for sure what happened. But it looks to me like they all shot each other. Now isn't that strange, Ms. Castillo?"

Merida didn't know about the two police officers—and she *did* feel bad about them, despite what she had said about them defending a corrupt system last night—but these men had deserved their fate. Marcus had fucking *deserved* what Celina had done to him.

"I don't know what to tell you," she said finally.

Parks turned off the tablet, set it in his lap, and crossed his arms. He studied Merida with a mixture of anger and puzzlement. Merida had stood up to Marcus and the other agents who had taken her and Jessica, but looking at Detective Badass here, she couldn't think of a single quip. No one-liners. No smart-ass comments about his clothes or the clichéd way he sat in the chair. No "good cop, bad cop" jokes. She met his gaze as long as she could, but soon she found her eyes dropping. She was too damn tired to hang with him.

"You didn't kill any of these people," he said. "Not directly, anyway. Not deliberately. But you left a trail of bodies last night. And that's not to mention that you shot at the officers who came to arrest you at Coleman Wallace's house."

"I was just trying to keep them from following us," said Merida. "I didn't want to actually hit anybody."

"Good," said the detective. "Because I'd hate to think that *anybody* was that bad a shot. But you don't get to shoot at officers of the law and then turn around and act like the innocent victim."

Now Parks leaned forward so that his crossed arms were on the back of the chair. Merida forced herself to look at his face. He didn't seem like a bad guy, and it looked like he didn't know a thing about what had been on the computer before they zapped it.

"You have no record before last night," he said. "Not even any traffic violations. And then, suddenly, you and your reporter girlfriend are on the news for domestic terrorism. You were somehow involved in the massacre at that place in North Carolina. Then Ms. Brantley and her sister went and blew up a reproduction facility—"

Merida started so hard that she nearly fell off the edge of the bed. "Wait, *what*?"

"—and I've got four federal agencies breathing down my neck about you. They'll be here in less than an hour to take you off my hands. And once they have you, there's no telling what's going to happen."

"I don't understand," she said. The room seemed to drift around her. "You said they *blew it up*?"

The detective nodded and eyed her with suspicion. "That's what I said. Dozens dead, and that's not even counting the unborn babies. Leveled the whole goddam building."

Merida's heart sank. Could it be true? Val had seemed like a woman who just wanted to protect her kid, not like a true terrorist.

Had something else happened that the government was covering up? If so, could Val and Jessica be dead?

"They..." said Merida. "They wouldn't do that."

"Tell that to the news and the feds," said Parks. "Unless you're telling me that what the news is saying is all made up."

No, there was no way that Jessica and Val had done that. Even if Val was capable of it—and Merida didn't really know her, but she didn't believe it for a second—Jessica would never have gone along with it. It was like what had happened in North Carolina. Damn government agents had destroyed Artemis and blamed it on Val and Jessica.

"They didn't do it," said Merida. "Just like they didn't kill all those people in North Carolina."

Parks's eyes narrowed. He stood, the metal chair groaning as it shifted on the tile floor, and opened the cell door.

"Hey, Joiner," he said, shouting down the hall. "Two coffees."

"Yessir," came a voice.

Leaving the cell door slightly ajar, the detective stepped toward Merida again. He turned the chair to face her, this time a little closer, and sat down with his legs crossed and his hands clasped around one knee. He was settling in for a long talk.

"Tell me, then," he said. "Tell me what in the hell is going on."

A small laugh escaped Merida. It sounded a little deranged even to her own ears.

"I don't..." she said. "You won't believe me."

A young police officer stepped inside with two coffee cups. He handed both to Parks.

"Thanks," said Parks.

"Yessir," said the officer. He cast a withering glance at Merida and then stepped into the hallway, closing the door behind him.

Parks handed Merida one of the coffees. Warm, but not hot at all. Very dark. Normally Merida couldn't stand strong coffee, but she needed something stout right now. She only wished that there was some tequila to spike it.

"How about you just tell me what I need to know," Parks said, "and let me be the judge of what I will and won't believe?"

"You asked for it," said Merida.

30

Jessica

Val's voice drifted from the kitchen and stirred Jessica out of her thoughts. "We're putting you in so much danger just being here."

Evan's dark, deep voice let out a dismissive sound. "We're not worried about them."

"You should be," said Kim.

Another woman spoke now, presumably Evan's wife. "We've had our run-ins with the government before. Tied up with them about some farming regulations, and they tried to take a good piece of our land. We came out alright in the end."

Time to get this over with, Jessica thought.

She turned the corner into the living room and headed toward the dining room door. From here, she could see Evan's red mane, a Black woman in overalls sitting next to him, and Val sitting at the table.

"This isn't like that," said Val. "This is dead serious."

Jessica felt a stab of anger at the sight of her sister's face. Val could beat the hell out of her with both arms tied behind her back, and Jessica still wanted to go and slap her across the face.

"We know this is seri—" Evan was starting to say, but he stopped and looked at Jessica as she stepped through the doorway into the dining room.

"How're you feeling, cuz?"

"Groggy," said Jessica, not looking at her sister.

"There's food if you're hungry," said Evan.

He gestured at a buffet that ran along the wall. Several serving platters and bowls with all kinds of food—vegetables, cornbread, mashed potatoes, and some kind of roast in gravy—lay in a beautiful spread. Very traditionally southern. Right this minute, it looked like a monarch's coronation feast, but Jessica couldn't help distrusting all of it. Unless something had changed, Evan had to believe that she was going to Hell because of who she was.

"I..." she said, floundering for the words and wishing that Merida were here to tell her she was being stupid. She looked around at the other people crowded around the table. Kim and Braden were there, along with two tall, husky teenage boys with rich, brown skin. Had she known that Evan and Tasia had children? If she had, she'd forgotten it.

Finally, her eyes settled on Val, who was looking down at her plate. *You had no fucking right, you self-righteous...*

But she cut this thought short, took a deep breath, and spoke.

"Merida?"

Val looked up, frowning and shaking her head. "Not yet. I'm sorry. But I'm not surprised that they're taking a while to get back. I'm sure they're safe. There'd be fake news stories about them by now if they'd been caught. The government would want to use them to discredit us even more."

"Havana?"

Val winced at the sound of that name. Was that a confirmation of guilt? Shame? Good.

"I found her body," Val said. "Made sure that she wasn't still alive."

"And you left her there?"

Val's face hardened now. "I had to carry you to the Dragonfly. If I'd gone back for her, we might not have gotten out."

Jessica blinked away the tears that welled in her eyes. She was *not* going to be weak right now. Not in front of all these witnesses.

"I'm sorry," said Val. She stood and walked around the table toward Jessica. Jessica forced herself to meet her gaze, but in her peripheral vision she could see everyone else looking up at them in anticipation. Probably wondering if the sisters were about to throw punches.

"I know," she made herself say.

Val eased toward her, arms opening, and Jessica let her sister embrace her. Yes, Val had done what she thought she had to do. The hell of it was that she was probably right about all of it. But understanding that didn't make Jessica any less angry.

Val turned and went back to her seat. Kim, Braden, and the two teenage boys all stared at their plates. Evan leaned back in his chair, arms crossed, and closed his eyes. Was he praying? Meanwhile, his wife offered a strained smile and gestured at the buffet.

"I—uh, I know you must be hungry. Please eat when you're ready. I'm Tasia, by the way."

"Good to meet you," Jessica said, her throat tight.

To her own surprise, she *was* hungry, and if she wasn't going to start a fight with her sister or run from the room crying, she had to have *something* to do right now. So she went to the buffet and served herself green beans, potatoes, cornbread, and a little of the pork roast, which came apart easily without a knife. The smell of it all made her mouth water. None of it was expert cooking in a technical sense. Not half as fancy or experimental as the food that Merida served—*used to serve,* she corrected herself—at her restaurant. Simple seasonings. Simple ingredients.

When she turned from the buffet to the table, the younger of the sons gestured at the seat next to him. "Here. Have this seat."

Jessica sat down next to him. He was a good-looking kid, almost a man. Give him a few more years, and the women—and some of the men—would be all over him. She looked down the table at Tasia, putting on a smile. "Thanks. The food smells great."

"You're welcome. But those two did most of the cooking. They're not half-bad." She pointed at the younger of the two boys. "That's Jacob."

"Hi," said Jacob.

"And that's Isaiah," said Tasia. The older boy offered a quick smile that didn't reach his eyes. Jessica felt bad that he and his brother had to be here right now.

"It's very cool that you cook," said Jessica, hoping to ease some tension. "My girlfriend, Merida—she's a great chef. And she would be really impressed by all this." She glanced at Evan and Tasia. Neither of them seemed bothered by the word "girlfriend."

"Awesome," said Isaiah. "We've never met a chef."

"Hopefully you'll meet her soon," Jessica said, a numb feeling spreading through her. "Merida owns her own restaurant in Atlanta." She stabbed a bite of the roast with her fork, but as she lifted it to her mouth, she hesitated. "Well, she did own a restaurant. I'm not sure..."

"I'm sorry," said Evan, that deep voice booming. "Maybe once the information is out, the government won't be able to..." He trailed off, thinking. He frowned, ran a hand over his beard to smooth it, and shifted in his seat. "You know..."

"Raymond?" said Tasia, looking at him.

"Yep," Evan said. He looked first at Jessica, then at Val. "We've got a lawyer friend who helped us with an eminent domain case years ago. The government tried to take a portion of our land for a new state highway. He helped us stop them. I bet he could help you. Help your girlfriend, too. Or at least help you find the right lawyer. If it becomes necessary, we can put you in contact—"

"Why would you help us?" said Jessica, cutting him off. The words were out before she could even think to stop them.

Evan looked at her, a surprised expression on his face, and the room fell quiet. A fork clinked against a plate, and for a few long seconds, there was only the sound of someone chewing slowly.

What are you doing? came a voice in her head. It was Braden, speaking telepathically. Her instinct was to look right at him, but she fought against it and looked down the table at Evan.

"You're family," Evan said at last. "I know we ain't been close in a long time, but we're still family. And even if we weren't, I believe in what you're doing."

"You believe in what we're doing," Jessica repeated, her voice sounding flat and robotic even to herself. She looked down at her plate, scooped up a piece of meat with her fork, and took a bite.

Evan gestured at Braden, who looked a little embarrassed.

"That young man has helped me see things I would have never believed before now," said Evan. "Yes, I believe in what you're doing."

"We haven't been through nearly as much as y'all have," said Tasia, "but we have more reason than most folks to hate the whole 'Safe Reproductive Practices—'" Here, she used air quotes. "—thing. We went along with it because we wanted children, but we would never have done it their way if they hadn't forced it on us."

Evan made an exasperated noise, a scowl darkening his face. "When we applied for our first child license, the State Licensor gave us the run-around. Ordered us to have *two* 'Safe Home Environment' inspections. Then she made us drive over to Atlanta for 'ideological evaluation.'" He took Tasia's hand in his. "I think it was because of..." But he shook his head. "Well, whatever the reason, they looked long and hard at us, trying to find an excuse to deny our license. So yes, we absolutely want to help you."

"I'm sorry," Jessica said, putting down her fork and turning to face Evan and Tasia. "I appreciate your help. I really do. I just..."

She looked around at the other faces at the table. Kim and Braden were still looking down at their plates. Val stared at her, wide-eyed and unbelieving. Finally, Jessica's eyes fell on a familiar picture of an old man praying over a meal of bread and water that hung on the wall.

"I got sent a livepic of a dead pig the other day. Someone killed it and strung it up, just to send me a message. Said I was next."

"What does that—" began Val.

"It's not just the government that people hate. There's a lot of hostility out here for reporters. For the news media. A lot of good 'Christian' people who like to make threats at people like me. A lot of people who wouldn't feel comfortable inviting me into their home." She hadn't meant to say all of that. It just came tumbling out. Was it the lingering effects of the sedative? Worry over Merida? Whatever the reason, the words were out there now. She could only keep going. "I just can't help wondering why you'd help us. 'Love the sinner, hate the sin,' I guess?"

Jessica—Aunt Jessica, said Braden's thought-voice. *These are good people. They really want to help us. Please don't.*

Evan and Tasia both frowned.

"I guess I'd respond by asking you a question," said Evan, clearly weighing each word carefully. "Do you think I'd ever threaten anybody who showed up at my door asking for help? I'd also ask why you're more interested in what we *believe* than you are in how we *treat* you. You grew up in some of the same churches I did. You might've stopped going, but you know that we believe in helping people who need help. And if we've done anything to make you feel unwelcome, then I'd... I'd be ashamed of that."

Jessica tried to hold Evan's gaze, but she was about to buckle. It was like playing a game of chicken.

"After everything we've been through," said Kim, his tone artificially light, "I think it's just hard to trust anything good. You keep waiting for the other shoe to drop."

Jessica took the diversion as an opportunity to look down at her plate. A mixture of emotions boiled in her—anger at her sister, gnawing pain over Taylor and Havana, shame at her distrust of Evan's kindness, fear for Merida and Celina.

Braden's voice started in her head again. *I know you're mad at Mom. I am, too. And I know you're scared for Merida and that baby. But you—*

"Stay out of my head, kid!" barked Jessica.

Braden's eyes went wide, and then they dropped.

"Okay," said Kim. "Maybe we should—"

"Braden!" snapped Val. "I have talked to you about that."

"I'm just trying to help!" Braden shouted. "That's what you always say, right? You help when you can? You do what you *have* to do?"

He stood, knocking his chair backwards. For a few seconds, the room seemed to *tingle* with electricity, and Jessica felt dizzy. A little sick to her stomach, even.

Then the boy ran from the room, his footfalls shaking the floor. The front door slammed.

Val put her hands over her face.

"I'll go and talk to him," said Kim. "I can—"

"No," said Val. She stood. "I need to talk to him. There's some things..." But she trailed off. For a second, her gaze met Jessica's, and the anger that Jessica felt seemed to melt, leaving only an emptiness.

Finally, Val turned and strode toward the front door.

Agora: The Ideas Marketplace

Vox: In spite of precautions, people in Europe and America continue to underestimate the threat of the so-called "Samford-2" virus.

IgnacioM: I am in Argentina. Our government is failing to do its job as well. (TRANSLATED FROM ITALIAN BY AGORA LEARN)

Klaus Weber: Samford-2 isn't real, you idiots. (TRANSLATED FROM GERMAN BY AGORA LEARN)

Chen Xinyi: Samford-2 killed my entire family. The CCP won't acknowledge this, however. (TRANSLATED FROM CHINESE BY AGORA LEARN)

Juraj Dadić: Stop lying about the Chinese people! (TRANSLATED FROM CROATIAN BY AGORA LEARN)

Chen Xinyi: I AM Chinese. (TRANSLATED FROM CHINESE BY AGORA LEARN)

Juraj Dadić: So? You're still telling lies about your own people. (TRANSLATED FROM CROATIAN BY AGORA LEARN)

Chen Xinyi: This is very offensive. I lost my family, and my government won't acknowledge it. (TRANSLATED FROM CHINESE BY AGORA LEARN)

Chung Ji-Su: @JurajDadić what is wrong with you? (TRANSLATED FROM KOREAN BY AGORA LEARN)

Juraj Dadić: [THIS MESSAGE HAS BEEN FLAGGED. VIEW ANYWAY?]

31

Val

She found him in a pecan tree on the north side of the house. He was nestled in the space where the trunk split into four thick limbs. He had his knees hugged to his chest, his head down. Even now, after he had endured so much in the last two days, after he had been so brave against people who wanted him dead or locked in a cell, Val could only see the child that he always had been.

Though he didn't pick up his head at her approach, his thought-voice spoke to her. *Don't come here and tell me that you weren't really going to do it. You could have done it. You almost did it.*

"I almost did it," Val said.

She stood at the base of the tree and stared up at him, willing him to pick up his head and at least look at her. But he refused. The trouble with having a telepathic son—one who was almost a teenager—in a situation like this was that his ability to see into her mind meant he knew exactly what she wanted from him all the time. No doubt that encouraged—

Stop analyzing me, he said. *You don't know everything about me.*

But he did pick up his head and look at her. The expression on his face—fury, almost hatred—took her breath away.

She felt her feet taking her backwards a few steps. "Please... talk to me like this," she said, surprised at the quaver in her voice. "I don't think I know everything about you. I don't have your gift."

Gift, he echoed. *Is this a gift? Who gave me this "gift?" You and Dad? God?*

Val stuffed her hands into her pockets and clenched her fists. Her arms and knees trembled. "You're the one who made it possible for us to get out alive when those agents came to our house. You helped in the fight at the Institute. It might not always feel like it to you, but—"

But Braden cut her off, his eyes tearing up. "If it wasn't for me, those agents wouldn't have come to the house at all! No, it *doesn't* feel like a gift to me. It feels like..."

He looked around as if casting about for the right word. Finally, he settled on an idea and glared down at her again.

"It feels like Hell!" he shouted. "It feels like..."

But he didn't finish the thought. Instead, he made a memory replay in her head. To Val, it felt like having a dream. She was back in the creek with him. Dragonflies shining their spotlights down on her. Rifle in her hand, muzzle pointing at Braden. She was praying that if they made it through this, he would forgive her. That he would understand.

"Well, I don't understand," he said.

Whatever barrier Val had built up to hold back her frustration broke. "You spent the night stuck in that underground cell. You saw how Celina and the others had to live their lives. You saw what living that way did to them—Theresa especially. It turned her into a monster. You can't understand why I would want to keep that from happening to you?"

So "protecting me" means killing me. Got it.

"Stop that!"

But the boy was covering his face with his hands and rocking backwards and forward.

"All those people, dead," he said. "You killed all those people. You almost killed me. And I... I killed..."

A static feeling tingled the flesh of her arms, neck, and scalp. Images flashed in her mind. It was like sitting in a dark house during a thunderstorm. Flashes of lightning briefly illuminated the world around her, but their brightness made the spaces between them that much darker. Val leading Braden up the stairs at the Institute, a rifle in her hands. Kim lying on the floor of their house, a bloodstain spreading on his shoulder. The inside of the cell where they'd kept Braden. Toy dinosaurs in the dirt outside their house—Braden's hands playing with them, making them move. Theresa forcing Bowen to bash his head into the ground. Two other people—an older man and older woman—doing the same on a sidewalk.

"Braden..."

Then a single image repeated over and over in her head. An agent inside the Institute. He jammed the muzzle of his own rifle under his chin. Fired. Blood, skin, bone, and brains burst out of the back of his head. He fell.

Again.

Again.

Again.

"Please stop, Braden," Val said. "You haven't done anything wr..."

But she couldn't finish. That static feeling in the air. Goosebumps on her arms, neck, and back. The world tilted around her. Rose up to meet her. Darkness.

32

Merida

Parks sat quietly as Merida talked, never taking a sip from the coffee in his hands. He didn't even look at her except for a couple of surprised glances at some of the more unbelievable parts of the story. The first time she used the word "telepathic" got a raised eyebrow out of him. But mostly, he just stared past her at one corner of the room.

"Well?" she said finally. "What do you think?"

Parks seemed to realize that he had an untouched cup of coffee in his hands. He looked at it for a second before taking a large gulp. Then he looked into Merida's face and frowned.

"You're right," he said. "I don't believe you. It sounds like every other conspiracy theory I've ever heard about how the government is out to—"

Merida let out a laugh—more snort than laugh—and shook her head.

"I'm glad you think this is funny," said Parks. "When you're sitting in prison for terrorism and a dozen other crimes, you can laugh all the way to—"

"I knew you wouldn't believe it," said Merida, leaning forward and patting Parks on the knee. He recoiled slightly at this, sloshing a little of the coffee onto his hand.

"Don't touch—"

"But here's the thing." She withdrew her hand. "It doesn't matter if you believe me or not. Any minute, some super-secret government assholes with Little Dick Syndrome are going to show up here and take me away, never to be seen or heard from again."

Parks leaned his head a little to one side as if to study her from a different angle.

"Even if you did believe me," Merida continued, "it wouldn't actually help. Either way, they wouldn't let you keep me. The only way I was ever getting out of this alive was to get the information from that computer onto the internet, and you guys fried the damn thing before we could finish the upload."

"Those were our orders from above," said Parks.

"Yep," said Merida, tossing up her hands for emphasis. "Yep. That's what everybody says. *Nothing to see here! Just doing my job!* And now, thanks to you, my friends are probably dead, and—"

"That's not on me," said Parks, stirring in his chair finally. He'd been calm through most of this, but he clearly wasn't interested in taking the blame for Wallace and Celina. "That's on you. If you're telling the truth about all this—and I think you might even *believe* the crazy shit you're saying—then you should have come in and—"

"If I *believe* it?" said Merida, tightness gripping her chest. "So I'm crazy now. Got it."

Parks shook his head. "That's your word, not mine."

"Oh, cut the shit. It's what you—"

But a knock at the door cut her off. The door opened, and a uniformed officer peeked inside, her face wary. She almost looked afraid.

"Sorry to interrupt," she said. "There's a..." She swallowed hard and glanced back down the hall. "There's someone here to see Ms. Castillo."

33

Jessica

Kim, Evan, and Evan's family all continued eating as if nothing had happened. Silverware clinked against plates. The sounds of chewing and swallowing filled the room. Evan murmured something to Tasia about how tender the roast had turned out.

After several minutes, Jessica was unable to take any more. Fighting the urge to slam her fists onto the tabletop, she pushed her seat away from the table and stood.

"I'm sorry," she said, forcing the words. She wasn't used to this feeling—helplessness, shame, confusion, and anger rolled into one. People of all kinds had gotten angry at her in interviews. Good people. Terrible people. People who were putting on a show of outrage in order to hide something from her. People who had a right to be angry. People whose lives had been upended by trauma of all kinds—death, crime, war, politics, drugs, social media witch hunts. Through all of it, Jessica had always been able to disengage from the situation emotionally and just tell the story. Why couldn't she do that now?

"You don't need to say sorry," said Evan. "You've been through a hell of a lot. More than a lot of folks deal with in their whole lives."

Tasia put down her fork with a hard *clink* and wiped her mouth with her cloth napkin. "No, I think 'sorry' is the right thing to say," she said. "When the world is against you, you don't turn on the people who risk themselves to help you. We're putting ourselves in danger here. Our family. Our home."

Evan looked at his wife. He put his hand on her shoulder. "Tasia..."

But Tasia paid no attention to this. "We don't mind doing it. Because it's right. Because you're family. Because you're *people.* Because if we were in the same situation, we'd hope somebody would help us, too. But don't you dare slap us in the face for doing it."

A knot formed in Jessica's chest. Her first instinct was to push back, but one look at the woman's eyes shut down any retort that she might have made.

"I know," she said finally. "I'm..." But she trailed off. She knew she'd lashed out at them unfairly. She was just so angry—and so scared—that she needed to be on the attack. She couldn't just sit still. Not while Merida was out there in danger, maybe dead...

Suddenly her knees felt weak, and her skin began to tingle. It felt like her foot sometimes did after the circulation had been cut off from sitting in the wrong position too long, except that the feeling touched every part of her body.

"Do you feel...?" said Evan.

A wave of dizziness almost made Jessica stagger. She gripped the back of the chairs on either side of her to steady herself.

"I feel it," said Tasia. "What is that?"

Without a word, Kim stood and hurried to the door, using first the table and then the walls and doorframe to steady himself as he went.

The feeling began to pass more slowly than it began. The electric tingle in the air disappeared little by little. It felt almost like sitting in a tub while the water drained away around you. Was this Braden? Had he...

"Oh no," said Jessica.

She, Evan, and Tasia all seemed to have the same thought simultaneously. The three of them glanced at one another, and Tasia's righteous indignation was replaced by wide-eyed alarm.

"Val?" said Evan, and pushed back from the table.

Jessica turned and ran toward the door. Her weak legs wobbled under her, but she managed not to fall or run into anything. Outside, she stopped at the top of the front porch steps, surprised at how winded she felt. Holding on to one of the columns, she scanned the yard. Finally, her eyes fell on a pecan tree.

Val's body lay on the ground at its roots, Kim kneeling next to her.

34

Merida

Parks turned in his seat and looked at the officer.

"Did you get a name, Sergeant?" he said. "Who is it?"

The woman at the door opened her mouth to speak, but then she closed it again and looked back down the hall.

"Thompson?" said Parks. He stood. "What's wrong with you?"

But the officer stepped aside, and the door swung all the way open. Two figures appeared there.

One was a man in his early-to-mid fifties. Military uniform. Bars on his lapel. Some kind of officer. Purple skin and red hair. Clone. Something odd about him, though. To Merida, who changed her hair color using Quickdye almost as often as she showered, the hair looked too pastel to be natural (in the sense that *anything* about genetically edited clones was "natural"). But then again, cloned people might Quickdye their hair like anybody else, she supposed.

The other was a younger man, probably in his mid-twenties. Not a clone. Or at least, not a "custom" clone. Plain white skin. Brown hair and eyes. Slightly feminine face. Also military. A junior officer. He carried a briefcase and wore an anxious expression. Inexperienced, maybe?

"What is this?" said Parks.

The two officers stepped through the door. Behind them, the police sergeant cast a worried glance at them as she walked back down the hall.

Merida's heart thudded. Though the older man was the most... *interesting* person in the room, she couldn't take her eyes off the other one. The younger man's dark eyes surveyed the room nervously, landing on Merida momentarily before returning to Parks and then to the older officer. There was something familiar about his face, his eyes especially. Doe-eyes. Big. Almost feminine. But there was a severity in them, too. Strength.

You're safe, said a voice in her head. *We're not here to hurt you. Just be quiet and let us take care of this, and we'll get you out of here.*

What in the batshit crazy hell...? Merida thought.

She looked around the room, feeling a little stupid. That voice had been a woman's, not a man's. Where was she? Maybe she was in some other part of the building, waiting while these two men did their job? Or had Merida lost it finally?

"I'm Colonel O'Brien," said the purple-skinned man. "As you'll see from the documents that I've just sent to you, I have jurisdiction here. We're taking this woman into custody."

Parks looked at his tablet, and from her place on the bed, Merida could see that the screen was black. The detective swiped at it again and again, as if flipping through several pages.

"So if you don't mind," said O'Brien, "we'd like to have the room."

The man's voice sounded strange. A little high-pitched for the body that it belonged to.

Parks squared up his shoulders—almost as if standing at attention for the military officer—and his voice took on a slightly gruffer tone than Merida had heard before now. "This woman was involved in the deaths of two Atlanta police officers. She was also witness to the deaths of several federal agents while they were operating in my city."

Cute, Merida thought. He was trying to be strong. Intimidating. In an odd way, it endeared him to her just a little. He was getting ready to fight to keep her here. And even though he was mad as hell at her, she'd rather be stuck with him than "disappeared" by a bunch of military thugs.

"Before she goes anywhere," said Parks, "I am going to get some answers about..."

But he trailed off, seeming to deflate. His back and shoulders slumped, his head falling forward slightly.

"I understand, sir," he said. "Excuse me..."

O'Brien and the younger man moved aside and allowed Parks to exit the room. The detective closed the door as he went.

"Well," said O'Brien, his voice taking on a lighter tone. "That's taken care of."

What happened next nearly made Merida fall off the bed. When she looked from the door to the men, she found that she wasn't looking at men at all. They'd been replaced by two other people entirely—both women. The first had a Mediterranean complexion and slicked-back red hair—the same color as O'Brien's. Definitely Quickdyed. Probably late thirties. Tall. Slight frame. Almost wispy. White button-down shirt, red slacks, and black lace-up boots. She might have been a bank teller.

Once she could take her eyes off the red-haired woman, though, the face of the other woman made her gasp. It was the psychopath from the Institute. The one who had made that poor doctor bash his head into the floor until he was dead.

"You..." Merida said, the word coming out in a whisper. Instinctively, she grabbed the frame of the bed with both hands and gripped hard—as if holding on would keep the girl from the Institute from being able to do to Merida what she had done to the doctor. "What in the hell?"

The red-headed woman sat down next to Merida on the bed.

"You're scared," she said, patting Merida's hand. "Don't be. We're not here to hurt you."

Her heart pounding, Merida squeezed her eyes shut before looking at the two women again. A government conspiracy. Telepaths. And now fucking *shapeshifters*?

The woman smiled and shook her head.

"We're not 'shapeshifters,'" she said. "My name is Journey. I'm a telepath like Theresa here." She gestured at the girl from the Institute. "I can make people think they're looking at a couple of military men when it's just a couple of telepaths here to rescue a friend."

"A friend," muttered Merida, watching Theresa sit down on the chair where Parks had been. She was wearing different clothes than she'd worn yesterday at the Institute, but she had the same gorgeous braided brown hair.

"I hope so," said Journey. "You've been trying to help Braden and Celina, haven't you? That puts us on the same side."

"How do I know this is who you really are? How do I know it isn't just another trick?"

"That was more than just a trick," said Journey. "It took a whole lot of work. Practice. A mix of Eastern and Ignatian meditation techniques. Lots of trial and error. And I still can't do voices yet. Besides, I've got no reason to hide my face from you now. And reaching into other people's minds is not something I do lightly. We take the ethical implications of our powers very seriously."

"*We?*" Merida said. "Who the hell are you people?"

"I'll answer all your questions," said Journey, raising her hands in a *hold-on, slow-down* gesture. "I promise. Right now, though, we need to—"

But Merida pointed a finger at Theresa. "And if you want to talk about 'ethics' and 'implications,' what the hell is *she* doing here?"

Journey frowned, looking slightly embarrassed. "What Theresa did at that illegal prison was self-defense. She's not here to hurt any-one, especially not you. You haven't done anything to hurt one of us."

Bowen deserved what I did to him, said Theresa's voice in Merida's mind. *He was a piece of trash.*

Merida looked at the girl. She had a beautiful face, the kind of face you wanted to protect. There was innocence there. She might be a member of a classical choir. But there was something terrible in her eyes, too. Fury. Indignation. A vengeful righteousness.

Nobody deserves what you did to him, thought Merida, gathering what courage she had left. *And nobody—not one person who ever lived—is a piece of trash.*

Now it was Journey's turn to speak in Merida's mind. *If you knew what she'd been through at that place, you'd understand. If you knew what kind of man Richard Bowen was, you'd agree that Theresa's actions were understandable.*

Journey laced her fingers together and leaned forward, putting her elbows on her knees. She sighed. "It's hard knowing what people *really* think. What they've really been through. People have so many jumbled thoughts in their heads, and even genuinely good people think a lot of things that aren't very nice. Take that police detective you were just talking to." She raised her hand and pointed toward the corner of the room, toward what must have been the front of the police station. "When we first walked in the room, his very first thought was, 'Great, a fucking clone.' He wondered how in the hell a custom clone with purple skin had gotten to be a military officer. But then he shoved that thought aside because he's a decent guy who knows that he shouldn't be a didunophobe. But he can't really help himself. And that's one of the good ones."

Merida continued to stare at Theresa, who looked like she might suddenly burst into flames and burn the building down. No doubt she was thinking about something awful that had happened to her. Like Celina. How many people turned out as bad as Theresa or as messed up as Celina because of something that another person had done to them?

Even though she had to know that Merida was only half-listening, Journey went on. "As a matter of ethics, I try not to use my ability on someone when I haven't gotten to know them more intimately. I try very hard not to hear and I never pry." She patted Merida's knee gently, like a mother comforting a daughter, though Merida might be a little older than her. "Now we have to get out of here before—"

But Merida cut her off. "Where are Celina and Wallace? Do you know what happened to them?" Every nerve in her body said not to trust these women—especially not Theresa—but she couldn't help asking.

Journey's eyebrows contracted and lifted slightly.

"They're dead," she said, her voice soft. "I'm sorry."

Her hand acting almost of its own accord, Merida grabbed Journey's forearm and shook it. "Are you sure?"

For a second, Journey looked at Merida's hand with surprise. Then she closed her eyes and inclined her head to one side as if straining to hear some sound. "Yes. I'm sorry."

A lump formed in Merida's throat. Celina. Wallace. Both of them dead. Her fault.

"It's not your fault," said Theresa. "These people shouldn't have been after you."

Merida's voice hitched as she fought back tears.

"Just doing their jobs," she managed.

Theresa snorted.

Their jobs, she echoed. *Yeah, Bowen was just doing his job, too.*

For a moment, Merida held Theresa's gaze. Theresa stared back with a hatred unlike anything Merida had ever seen. Not hatred of Merida, though. Maybe now that Dr. Bowen was dead, she had no particular person to hate. The pressure was building inside her with no relief valve.

That's what makes you dangerous, Merida thought, fully understanding that Theresa was going to hear.

Next to her, Journey had a phone in her hand and was typing something. Merida had time to see that a messaging app was open before Journey realized she was being observed and stood up. Merida thought she saw the words, "...probably somewhere in Morgan or Walton County."

"What are you..." she began, but before she could finish the question, the lights flickered and went out. The room went completely dark except for the light from Journey's phone screen.

"They're here," said Journey.

35

Val

"I'm okay," she said. Holding on to Kim, she sat up. "I'm okay, really. Where's Braden?"

Kim's face wore the same strain as a soldier in war. Val had seen it a hundred times in the eyes of a young badass who had expected war to be like a video game and found that it really was Hell in exactly the way Sherman had meant it two centuries ago. The shadows underneath, the crinkles at the corners, the red veins staining the whites pink—all of it said that this soldier had found the world to be ruthless and unforgiving. No grace. No peace. Only survival. Or not.

"He ran off toward the old barn," Kim said. He pointed down the dirt trail that led through the woods. "I saw him running, but you were on the ground, so..."

Using Kim's shoulder for balance, Val struggled to her feet. Her head still swam a little, but otherwise she was okay. Braden had knocked her out. Had he done it deliberately? Had he meant to hurt her? Or had this just been a case of him losing control?

"He's really upset about what happened at the creek the other night. He thinks that I..."

But she didn't want to say it. Mostly because she didn't want to think about what she might've done.

Jessica crossed the yard and joined them, followed by Evan and Tasia. There was genuine fear in their faces, even Jessica's. It wasn't fear for *her*, though. It was fear of Braden.

"Did he hurt you?" said Jessica.

"No," said Val.

Jessica frowned, clearly not believing it. Val stifled an urge to yell. This wasn't Braden. This was the *situation*, and she didn't need everyone starting to be afraid of him now. And if Jessica hadn't run off into the woods at Artemis, she might have been able to get back and patch things up with him before now.

"I'm fine," she said, smothering emotions that were trying to burn out of control. "He lost himself a little bit, and I just fell down. He didn't do anything deliberately."

"We all felt it," said Tasia.

Evan put a hand on Tasia's back, kissed her on the cheek, and turned to walk away. "The boys and I will head down toward the barn and see if we can catch up with him. It might do him some good to have folks closer to his age to talk—"

"Evan," said Tasia. She grabbed his hand and stopped him, glancing toward Val. "Maybe you should... give him some space for a little while."

Evan looked down, his lips pursing. "I just don't think the kid should—"

"Evan," said Tasia, her calm voice masking urgency. She turned toward Val, this time forcing herself to meet Val's eyes. "I'm sorry. Don't mean no offense."

"It's okay," Val said, trying to offer an understanding look. She *did* understand, but she still had to fight down the urge to scream at everyone. *My son is not a danger! Every fucking kid in the world gets angry sometimes!*

But a voice answered back. Asa's voice. Again. Would that bastard ever leave her alone?

Not every kid can do what Braden just did, though.

"I'll go," said Kim. "He and I have been talking about some stuff that's been bothering him lately. You stay here and rest."

"If you're going to do that, hang on just a sec," said Evan. He hurried toward the house, calling out as he went. "Let me give you something real quick before you go."

Kim frowned at Tasia.

"He's probably getting you a Courier," she said. At Kim's confused look, she shrugged. "You'll see. Here he comes."

Evan came jogging out of the house, his footfalls *thumping* the ground under his big frame and heavy work boots. When he reached Kim, he handed him two items. The first was a flashlight, and the second was a device that looked like a phone, except that it was bigger and had physical buttons along with a touchscreen.

"Short-range encrypted communicator," said Evan. "Not legal anymore, but we've had ours since before the government banned them. Called a Courier. Preppers, privacy zealots, and militia types love them. We've got one for each of us. Doesn't use cell towers or satellite, and the range will just about cover our entire property. Just press this—" He indicated a green button on the Courier. "—and talk. You'll come through to all of our devices. Totally encrypted, so you don't have to worry about anybody besides us hearing you. It's how we communicate on the property."

"That's..." said Jessica, frowning.

Evan let out a hearty laugh. "Surely you ain't about to call us *paranoid*?"

Jessica grinned. To Val, the look of a smile on her sister's face came like the relief at the end of a long fever.

"No, I guess not," Jessica said, then turned to Kim. "Want me to come along? He doesn't know me very well, but..." She shrugged. "I'm pretty good at talking to people."

"Better let it just be me for right now," said Kim. "Thanks, though. I'll be fine. Really."

He turned and hurried down the path after Braden.

36

Merida

"Time to move," said Journey. "Now."

"Who's here?" said Merida. "Who the hell are *they*?"

Merida stood and started to inch backwards toward the wall, taking small steps to keep from stumbling in the dark. She didn't trust Journey, and Theresa scared the hell out of her. If some kind of fight was about to happen, maybe she could get away in the confusion.

Just stick with us, said Journey's voice in her head. *We'll keep you safe. I promise we're not out to hurt you or stick you in some prison.*

Fuck, Merida thought. No secrets from telepaths. It was one thing to be around a telepath like Celina, who liked to mess with people. In just a matter of hours, Merida had developed a sense of trust with Celina. But Journey...

This is going to drive me insane, she thought, feeling her fists clench. How did you live in a world of telepaths?

A light flickered in the window of the door, and then it opened. Parks stood there with a flashlight.

"This way, ma'am," he said, his voice oddly stiff. Deferential.

Journey turned to Merida and cast her a sympathetic look.

Almost motherly. In the harsh light of Parks's flashlight, it made her look like an older woman.

"Come with us," she said. Then her voice spoke in Merida's head. *I'm forcing this detective to help us. I don't want to do that to you. I hope that helps you trust me.*

"Need to hurry, ma'am," said Parks. "This way."

Merida shook her head. "If it's true that you really came to help me, I appreciate it, but I don't want your help. I'm going to—"

An explosion of sound from the front of the building cut her off. Gunfire. Yelling.

"Time's up," said Journey. The motherly look disappeared, replaced by a commanding expression that suited the military persona that she'd adopted before.

Theresa moved to Merida's other side, her eyes reflecting the flashlight's glow. The two women flanked Merida so that they blocked any means of escape. With a surge of panic in her gut, Merida understood what was about to happen.

"No," she said. "Please don't—"

But before she could finish the thought, instinct took over. Not fully realizing what she was about to do, she lashed out with both her fists. Her left hand connected with Journey's throat. The woman staggered backwards, choking and gasping. Merida wasn't as lucky with her right hand—her knuckles struck Theresa in the mouth. But it bought her enough time to throw another punch and hit the girl right in the cheek. Pain surged up Merida's arm all the way into her shoulder, and for a second, she thought she might have broken her wrist. She hadn't been in a real fist fight in years.

As awkward as the punch was, Theresa cried out and stepped backwards, her hands covering her mouth. Merida kicked her in the knee and sent her to the floor.

"What the hell?" said Parks, who still stood in the doorway. He flicked his light from Journey to Theresa to Merida.

"Help me!" yelled Merida. "Get us out of here before they—"

But a blast of gunfire erupted from down the hall. The sound made Merida's ears ring, and Parks's body shook as bursts of blood erupted out of his face, chest, and arms. He staggered against the doorframe, his eyes wide for just a second, and then he crumpled like a marionette whose strings had been cut. The flashlight fell out of his hads and rolled across the floor

37

Jessica

Jessica put an arm around Val's waist. The two of them watched Kim until he had disappeared into the long shadows of the pines on either side of the path. For several awkward minutes, they stood in silence along with Evan and Tasia, who waited nearby. The sun had sunk low in the sky now, just an orange disk barely visible behind the trees. The late afternoon quiet was punctuated by the murmuring of the two teenage boys, who stood on the porch of the house.

"He wasn't trying to hurt me," Val said finally.

"Anybody can tell that he loves you," said Evan, who stepped forward and put a hand on Val's shoulder. "And you're a hell of a good mom. He knows that. Give him some time, and he'll come around."

"I hope you're right," said Val.

A sick feeling rolled through Jessica, and she let go of Val. She suddenly needed to move—to run, even—but she wasn't going to walk away from Val after what had just happened. Even if she had shot her with a sedative.

"I'm sorry," she said. "This is my fault. I upset him. I... shouldn't have acted that way."

Val's response was quick, like she had been waiting for this admission. "He was already upset. It was going to happen sooner or later."

"I bet it wouldn't have gone like this, though." Jessica hugged her chest, wishing that Merida were here. Jessica had never been a hugger or a cuddler. She wasn't usually the type to need affection when she was worried or upset. When something bothered her, she threw herself into work. A good story—or even a bad one—was generally better at helping her through tough times than a lover or a friend. But right now, her hand could use another hand to hold on to.

"We'll give them a little bit," said Evan. "If they aren't back by dark, we all head down toward the old barn and make sure everything is okay."

"I'm sorry we brought this on you," said Val. "You're good people, and you don't deserve the kind of trouble that we bring."

Jessica felt her face flush. "I'm sorry, too."

"Okay, okay," said Evan, making a *settle down* gesture with both hands. "There's been enough 'I'm sorry-ing' around here for one night." He smiled, but the expression didn't reach his eyes. "I feel like I need to down a pint of Crown and cry, or something. Don't heap any more self-loathing on yourselves until you've got a plan, at least."

Val laughed at this. Really laughed. It was probably the first time Jessica had heard that sound in almost two decades.

"Okay, cousin," Val said. "No more self-pity for tonight. But what do you mean by *plan*? You mean a plan to get the hell off your property? Because I've already been—"

"No, that's not what I mean," Evan said, shaking his head. He frowned and crossed his arms. Together, he and Tasia reminded

Jessica of a pair of softball coaches getting ready to give their team a good, stern talking-to. "You started something when you did what you did up in North Carolina." He eyed Jessica. "And you, when you took that computer."

"We know that, Evan," said Jessica.

"And then you went and *really* stirred things up at that reproduction place," Evan said. "I've been checking the news today. There's protests and riots all over the country. Other places, too. Folks are definitely taking notice of you, and not everyone believes what the government is saying about you. Not even everyone in the mainstream media."

Jessica thought of Carlo. Would he believe that she'd helped to bomb a reproduction facility and kill hundreds? Was she a terrorist in his eyes now?

"Protests have been going on for a while," she said, thinking of the one she had seen at Artemis two days ago. God, had it only been that long? "That's nothing new."

"Not like this," said Evan. "Things are different now. California is having a special session of their legislature in two days. Looks like they're worried that the Supreme Court is about to rule the wrong way in the *John Doe* case. Worried that the ruling is going to end up being a threat to SRP. They're talking about finally making good on those secession threats they've been making all these years. Other states, too."

"Yeah, but that's just posturing, right?" said Val. "Putting pressure on Washington."

"Maybe not," said Tasia. "Georgia's talking about moving forward with its secession conference as soon as this weekend. The Senate doing what it did on the Wall of Separation Act, the B.O.R.D.E.R.S. Act, and other stuff—it's really pushed things over the edge. People are furious. And a lot of those kinds of folks would be on your side if they knew the truth about you."

"States have been making empty secession threats for a long time, Evan," said Jessica.

"It's only empty until it isn't," he said. He gestured toward the west, presumably toward Atlanta. "And when your friends out there finish their part of the job, it's going to really get going."

"*If* they finish it," said Jessica, her throat suddenly feeling dry and scratchy. She'd let Merida and Celina take the real mission, take the risk that ought to have been hers. And she'd done it for nothing at all. Baby Taylor was gone.

"They'll do it," said Tasia, reaching out and squeezing Jessica's hand. "And they'll come back here. Merida will come back to you. Have some faith in your friends—and in her."

For a second, Jessica stared at Tasia, almost angry at the thought that this woman was using her relationship with Merida against her—a relationship that she and Evan surely disapproved of.

"Thanks," Jessica muttered, trying to crush her cynicism. "I hope you're right."

"Whether you like it or not," said Evan, his voice deepening, "you two are like... you're..." He paused, looked around as if seeking the right analogy or simile. Then he frowned and looked back at Val and Jessica. "It's like you're two of the horsemen in Revelation. Two riders of the apocalypse. You're ushering in the end of something."

Now it was Jessica's turn to laugh. "If you're trying to get us to calm down and quit wallowing in self-loathing, talking about the *Great Tribulation* and the *apocalypse* isn't the way to do it."

Evan chuckled a little, but his frown didn't disappear. "That word *apocalypse*—you know what it means?"

"End of the world," said Jessica. "What's that got to do with anything?"

"That's what it's come to mean because of preaching and movies," said Evan. "But that's not what the word originally meant."

For fuck's sake, thought Jessica. *Here it comes. He's about to preach to us.*

But it was Tasia who spoke next, not Evan.

"It means 'unveiling,'" she said, her voice even. "It means that something hidden is being revealed. The veil that hides the truth is being pulled back. You're the ones who are pulling it back so everybody else can see, and it's gonna change the world."

Val shifted her stance uncomfortably.

"I didn't set out to *change the world,*" she said, not bothering to hide her irritation. "I just wanted to be left alone. And when the world wouldn't leave us alone, I had to protect my son."

"We know," said Tasia. She clasped her hands over her heart. "But you live in a world that ain't content to let folks decide how their lives ought to be run."

"And...?" said Val. She raised her hands to her sides, palms up, as if to say, *What do you want from us?*

"The point is, you need a plan," said Tasia. "Society's been hanging by a thread for a long time, and you two just went and put a match to the thread. Seems to me that if you take that kind of step, you see it to the end."

"You might not be up to the fight," said Evan, "and I understand if you ain't. If you decide you just need to hide, we've got three bunkers hidden on this property with food, water, and everything else you need to survive for three months."

Jessica glanced at Val and was surprised to see resignation in her eyes.

"You preach a hell of a sermon, Evan," she said. "You too, Tasia."

"Hell of a sermon" is right, Jessica thought. They had to "finish the job?" What did that even mean? What *could* they do beyond getting the truth out?

Evan shrugged and offered a flat smile. "Just calling it like we see it, I guess."

Jones-McMartin's words from the Institute echoed in Jessica's mind. *How many people do you know who would want things to go back to the way they were before?* But that was the problem: things *couldn't* go back to the way they had been before. The culture had changed. SRP had fundamentally changed what it meant to be human, what it meant to be a family, and what it meant to be a society. Once you had made that kind of leap, there was no way back. A way out, maybe, but never back.

38

Merida

Biting her lip to stifle a scream, Merida looked around for something to use as a weapon, but there was nothing. The only objects in the room were the beds and the flashlight that Parks had dropped, which was too small to do her any good.

We're trying to help you, you idiot! screamed a voice in her head, its intensity so great that it made Merida clap her hands over her ears. Theresa's voice. The girl wiped blood from her mouth with the back of her hand.

Merida tried to match her intensity. *You gonna make me smash my head into the floor like you did that doctor?*

Just stay out of the way, said Theresa.

She shoved Merida toward the corner of the room just as a man in SWAT gear stepped into the doorway, his rifle raised. Theresa dove to one side, narrowly avoiding a short burst of fire from the gun. Then the man stopped, his body going slack.

"Did you get them all?" said someone down the hall. "What about the primary targ—"

The gunman in the doorway spun and fired down the hallway. Screams. A few *thumps* as bodies hit the floor. Then the man put the barrel of the gun under his own chin. Suddenly, his face turned to an agonized grimace. He groaned so hard that spittle flew from between his clenched teeth. The muzzle of the gun must have been burning the soft flesh under his jaw.

"Wait," gasped Journey. "Don't."

"But—" began Theresa. She clearly had an appetite for the guy's blood, wanted his brains all over the ceiling. Merida thought that it didn't matter one bit what had happened to her at the Institute. There was *nothing* that could make Merida feel sorry for someone so completely empty of basic humanity.

Do you hear me? thought Merida. *It's horrible what they did to you. But nothing justifies what you're doing right now, you selfish bitch.*

Journey got up from the bed, her knees shaking visibly. "He can help us... get out of here."

Damn, I got her good, thought Merida as she watched Journey struggle to stand. *I wish Jessica and Val could see this.*

Yeah, said Journey's voice in her head. *It was a good hit.*

"I am so sick of this shit!" shouted Merida, fresh anger surging through her. "How the hell can anybody stand not being able to keep their thoughts private?"

"You're going to get used to it," said Journey. "Privacy is overrated, anyway." Her voice sounded raspy, and probably would for a while. There was that, at least. If nothing else, Merida had proven in the last two days that she was as tough as anybody.

She stepped toward Journey, her fists clenched. The hell with caution. "Maybe you'll think twice before you try to take over my mind again, huh?"

Journey frowned. Then smiled sadly.

Well, shit, Merida thought. *That was a stupid thing to say.*

39

Jessica

Val, Evan, and Tasia sat down on the front porch steps to talk plans and contingencies while Jessica stood by and listened. After a while, Jessica said that she wanted a shower. Tasia took her inside, gave Jessica some of her own clothes to wear, and showed her where to find towels and washrags.

Like the rest of the house, the bathroom was impossibly old-fashioned. Standing next to the pedestal sink and the vintage claw-foot tub, Jessica imagined that she had traveled back in time. How different things were now from when this house was built. Had the world become better or worse in the intervening time? But that way of looking at it was too simple. No doubt it was better in some ways—but it was definitely worse in others.

She turned on the shower, setting the temperature hot enough that a plume of steam rose out of the tub and filled the room, and stepped under the water. She felt a little guilty for doing this after Evan's sermon about Val and Jessica's responsibility to follow through on the "apocalypse" they had started, but she wasn't going to have anything meaningful to contribute to a conversation or a plan right now. There wasn't a good chance that she'd have much to contribute to *anything* anymore. "Horsemen of the apocalypse," Evan had said. That might be true of Val, but it wasn't true of Jessica.

The problem was that she had insisted on trying to save the baby. Should have focused on the computer. Shouldn't have sent her girlfriend and a nymphomaniac telepath to do the job. Shouldn't have let guilt and sympathy for the baby drive her decisions. If she and Val had gone with Merida and Celina to get the computer, she wouldn't be staring down the possibility that Merida and Celina had gotten caught or killed—or that the computer had been taken.

No use in thinking along those lines, though. In her profession, she'd seen a lot of people lose themselves in thoughts about what they should have done and what might have been. *There's no such thing as what might have been*, she had once said to a woman who had been doing sexual favors for a corrupt state representative. That woman had been tortured by the thought of what might have happened if she hadn't given in to the bastard's advances in the first place. But now Jessica's own words mocked her. There was no way she'd have been able to live with herself if she hadn't at least tried to save the baby. What were they doing if not fighting for the innocent, the weak, and the voiceless?

Pushing aside these thoughts, she washed her hair with shampoo that smelled like green apples and scrubbed her body clean with a masculine-smelling soap in the soap tray. When she had finished, she turned off the water and stood for several minutes to let the water drip from her body.

"You've started something," Evan had said. It reminded her of something she'd heard from her political science professor in college. What was his name? Dr. Cheek, that was it. He'd devoted a class session to civil disobedience, discussing the tradition of people saying ‘no’ to their rulers from the Greek tragedy *Antigone* all the way to Martin Luther King. What all these great lawbreakers had in common was that they willingly accepted the consequences of their actions, Cheek had said.

Her heart hammering against her ribs, she thought that she was beginning to see what her part in this apocalypse would be.

40

Merida

It kind of felt like when Merida put too much gin in her martini. The flush in her skin. The dullness in her mind. The feeling of not quite having control.

No, that wasn't it.

Maybe like the first dive into a pool on a hot day. One second, you're dry and warm. Then you're slapped in the face by the cold, by the water rushing and swirling around you. Sounds become deeper. Duller. Muffled. Your eyes have to adjust to the slightly distorted way of seeing things underwater. Colors become softer but deeper.

No, that wasn't right, either.

A dream, maybe? It was like one of those dreams where you find yourself somewhere without knowing how you got there. You move toward the edge of a roof, your mind warning you that this is dangerous, but you can't stop yourself from edging closer. Closer. Closer. Or you find yourself in public wearing nothing but your underwear, and you can't run away and put on clothes even though the panic is clawing up through your chest and into your throat.

That was closer, but not exactly right, either.

Maybe it felt like nothing. You were empty. A vessel.

no

She looked at Journey.

i'm here

"I'm ready to go with you," she said. But it wasn't her saying it, was it? It was her voice. Her lips, tongue, and teeth formed the sounds. But someone else was speaking.

i'm here

Journey seemed sad, like someone who was performing an unfortunate duty. Maybe Merida should tell her that it was okay—

no this shit is definitely not okay

She was moving now. They were moving. Following the man with the gun down the hall toward the front of the building, the light mounted to the bottom of his rifle illuminating their way. Merida was careful to step over Parks's body—

wake the hell up girl do you see what

—which lay in a pool of blood. He had seemed like a decent guy. Just a guy doing his job.

he's fucking dead girl what the hell are you

Theresa fell in line behind Merida. Now they were hurrying to the front of the station. Fast movements. She felt like she might fall down at any moment, but somehow she kept moving. Moving underwater. In a dream. Intoxicated. All of these at once.

Hallway. Doors. Bulletin boards with flyers and memos pinned to them.

More bodies at the end of the hall. More guns. More puddles of blood. Bullet shells lying in the puddles. Scattered across the tiles.

You won't understand this right now, thought Merida. *But trust me. I'm just helping you.*

that's not my fucking voice

no that is definitely not me

Just trust me. I'm on your side.

She moved—it almost felt like gliding—into the front of the station. Long, wide hallway. Doors. Water fountains. Bathrooms. Front desk. Waiting area. Chairs. Tables. Magazines. Holograph projectors with images of Atlanta police officers hovering over them.

Main entrance. Front doors.

The man with the rifle led them to a side door and opened it, checking to see if the area was clear before waving them through.

Another hallway. Narrower. Cinder block walls. Red stripes. Fire alarms. Extinguishers.

girl please you've got to

You're safe, she thought—no, somebody else did. *You don't need to feel anxiety.*

They reached the end of the hallway, and the man raised his left fist. A "halt" sign. He opened the door slowly. Orange-yellow sunlight. Almost dusk. Voices outside shouting. Distorted. A loudspeaker.

"Drop your weapon!"

Theresa moved ahead of her.

you can run girl what the hell

Theresa at the door. Behind the man with the gun. Journey beside her.

Merida, get a hold of yourself.

It felt like she had come out of the water. The clarity of sight and sound. The weight of the water no longer pressing down on her. She was free.

Holy shit, Merida thought. Why had they let go of her?

Not sure that her legs were going to respond to her commands, she took one step backwards. Then two. Outside, a short burst of gunfire went off. Someone yelled something.

Now's the time.

She turned to run back down the hall.

Stop, Merida. You're still coming with us.

First it was her legs. Suddenly they felt heavy, as if she'd just overdone it on a jog.

"Oh hell, no, you don't," she groaned, straining to keep control of her own body. Heat and tingling pain moved through her limbs as she fought to move. But it did no good. The desire to resist dissipating like smoke, she turned back toward the exit. Toward Theresa and Journey. Why was she fighting, anyway? She was supposed to be going with them, not back to the prison where the men who had killed Celina and Wallace wanted to keep her.

Footsteps. Down the hall. The man with the gun was gone. Outside, probably. Journey watched her approach. Patient expression, like a teacher. Theresa frowning. Then the two of them stepped outside. Merida followed. Into the sunlight.

girl fucking run

Outside, two police cars. A couple of hoverbikes floating above the cars. The riders holding rifles. A few drones. A police van. Prisoner transport. Blue lights flashing. Cops with pistols pointed. Cops putting handcuffs on Theresa and Journey.

Merida put her hands behind her own back before the young cop with the ponytail even told her to. The cop turned her by the shoulder and cuffed her wrists. Cold metal against her skin.

this is not right

scream

tell them what's happ—

It's going to be just fine. Merida's voice. But not Merida's thoughts. *This is how we get to safety. Just trust me to keep you safe and out of their hands.*

but we're in their hands right now

A cop led her, Theresa, and Journey in handcuffs toward the prisoner transport van. Big. Black. Double doors open in the back. Dark interior. Climb up. Doors shut.

Then Merida's mind came back, and the van was moving.

41

Jessica

Her hair wrapped in a towel, she left the bathroom and padded down the stairs to the foyer. After the shower, the air in the house felt chilly. Jessica didn't mind at all. The last two days had felt hot and oppressive, and a little chill in the air came as a relief.

At the bottom of the stairs, she looked through the frosted glass of the front door. She could see Evan's large frame moving back and forth in the yard and Val's smaller form sitting on the porch steps. Val was talking, but Jessica couldn't understand the words. She ought to go out and join them, but she stood frozen in the foyer—as if the cool of the air conditioner, the smooth wood floor under her feet, and the quiet of the house were holding her in an embrace. It felt like home, and she wanted to hang on to that feeling as long as possible. She might not know it again for a long time—especially if she followed through on what she had decided to do.

"You okay?" said a voice behind her.

Jessica turned. Isaiah and Jacob were coming down the stairs, flashlights and Couriers attached to their belts. Isaiah wore a friendly expression, while Jacob eyed her a little warily.

"I'm fine," said Jessica. "Just trying to decide if I want to go out and get sweaty again."

The boys reached the bottom of the stairs. Isaiah's eyes were a little too wide, like someone who was trying to look more interested than he actually was. Jacob, a little shorter than his brother, hovered behind him.

"Make yourself comfortable," Isaiah said. He gestured toward the living room, which was furnished with a comfortable-looking plush couch that had a very inviting chaise lounge at one end.

Jessica put on a grateful smile. "Yeah, I think I might do that. Some peace and quiet will do me a lot of good."

"Oh, we'll get out of your way," Isaiah reassured her. Jacob seemed to relax at the idea of leaving Jessica alone.

"I'm sorry," said Jessica. "I didn't mean that you had to be quiet or leave or something." She shook her head and rubbed her face. She was really on a roll at being a pain in the ass for her cousin and his family.

"It's not a problem," said Isaiah, glancing toward the front door. "We're going out anyway."

"Oh?" said Jessica.

Now Isaiah looked embarrassed and stuffed his hands in his pockets. "Yeah, we're, uh..."

"We're going out to help look for Braden," finished Jacob.

"But we don't want our parents to know until we're gone, okay?" blurted out Isaiah. "I mean—please."

Jessica had to stifle a small chuckle. *Good Christian teenagers rebelling against Mom and Dad...* She made a zipper gesture over her lips. "Not a word."

Isaiah sighed as if he'd been holding his breath.

"Aren't they going to come look for you?" added Jessica.

"We've got our Couriers," said Jacob. "They'll just call us and fuss." He put on a stern face. "Mom and Dad should have gone looking. It's getting late, and Braden doesn't know this place. Neither does Dr. Hara. We've got a lot of land out there to get lost in."

Jessica's thoughts turned back to Baby Taylor—how she had nearly shut Jessica, Beck, and Havana down when she had started crying. "I think your Mom just wants to be cautious. Braden's a different kind of kid."

Jacob crossed his arms. "Maybe, but he's still a kid. We can't just leave him to wander around out there after dark. Mom should know better."

Jessica let out the chuckle that she had suppressed. *Even the "good" kids think they know better than their parents.* "That's fair. I won't rat you out, but if they ask, I'll tell them where you went. Like I didn't know you weren't supposed to be going."

"Thanks," said Isaiah.

The two boys glanced at one another, and then they turned and walked past the stairs toward the house's back entrance.

42

Merida

The back of the police van was lined with chairs built into the walls on each side. Merida stared at Theresa, who sat on the other side with her hands folded on her lap. Journey was sitting up front with the officer driving the van.

"Nothing that has ever happened to you can justify what you do to people," said Merida. "You know that, right?"

For a moment, Theresa stared back at her, her eyes defiant and her lips pursed. Then her gaze fell to the floor. All the violence and anger, all the control she held over other people's minds, and she couldn't even win a staring contest. The shock of it deflated Merida.

"I don't need to justify anything to you," the girl said after a while.

I know you don't understand this, came Journey's thought-voice, *but Theresa only did what she had to do.*

"I can't get away from your eavesdropping and snooping even when I'm locked in the back of a van, huh?" Merida shouted toward the cab.

I hope I can change your mind eventually, said Journey. *This isn't a kidnapping. We just got you out of a bad situation. There was no way you were ever going to be free again once DHR and DHS got their hands on you. We came to save you from them—and from yourself.*

Merida snorted. *From myself?*

I know you and your girlfriend think that you're helping people like me, but you're not. You're actually stopping us from being able to make a better world for ourselves. A better world for everybody.

We're trying to get the truth out there about what the world is doing to you! thought Merida, heat rising in her face. *And it wasn't you who stopped me, anyway. The Atlanta police did that when they zapped my friend's house.*

I hope so.

You hope so? What the hell is wrong with you?

I appreciate the risks that you and Ms. Brantley and the others have taken to help people like me, but if you'd succeeded, you'd have done more harm than good.

Merida banged the back of her head against the headrest of her seat several times and groaned aloud through her gritted teeth. This was too damn much.

Just shut the hell up and leave me alone, she thought. *Stay the fuck out of my head, or next time I see you, I'll give you another throat-punch.*

Across from her, Theresa shook her head, almost smirking.

Merida closed her eyes and leaned her head against the wall of the truck. Her teeth clicked and chattered sometimes as the van hit bumps in the road, but the point was to ignore Theresa. She might be able to read her mind, but that didn't mean that Merida had to pay attention to her. Still, Merida couldn't help wondering what Theresa would look for if she were reading her mind. Would she try to find out where Val and the others were?

What the plan was after their respective missions had been accomplished?

She went on like this for a long time—enough time for them to get out of the city. And she could tell by the way it was driving that the van had left Atlanta. No more weaving in and out of traffic, no more complete stops at intersections; the driver now stayed at a steady speed in a single lane. They were probably on a two-lane road now.

For the most part, Merida kept her eyes shut the whole time. On the few occasions when she did open them, she found that Theresa was staring toward the front of the van, her arms and legs crossed in an almost lady-like pose. She was a beautiful girl—beautiful in a conventional way like Jessica. She could easily be a model for one of those holographic ads that greeted you at store entrances or in clothing aisles.

Watch it, or I'll tell Jessica you're thinking about other girls.

Merida barely held back a startled jump at the sound of the voice in her head. To cover any movement, she shifted in her seat and crossed one leg over the other. The voice had been faint, like someone speaking at a distance. And it wasn't Theresa's or Journey's.

Actually, I'm getting a little jealous myself.

Celina.

Put on your seatbelt.

Feeling stupid, Merida turned her head slowly to look around the van and make sure that no one else was back here besides Theresa. Nothing. The rows of seats. Walls. Doors. No place for anyone to hide.

I'm not in there with you, you sexy idiot, said Celina's voice. *Now put on your damn seatbelt.*

Suddenly Theresa's eyes narrowed. She looked around, too—

first at the back door of the van, then at the front, and then at Merida, whose heart skipped a beat.

Now!

Fear clenching her throat, Merida watched Theresa's eyes widen with realization as Merida pulled her seatbelt around her body and buckled it.

"What is going on?" said Theresa. She uncrossed her legs and moved forward in her seat as if getting ready to spring at an intruder.

DONE! Merida yelled in her mind, willing the thought to be as loud as possible.

Theresa was closing her eyes, probably to focus her mind on a telepathic search of the area around them. Was Celina in a car nearby?

Somewhere behind them, there was a loud crashing noise—the sudden, horrible sound of metal smashing into metal, then an ear-piercing *skreeeeee* as it skidded across asphalt.

Are you okay? Merida thought. *Whatever you're going to do, you'd better do—*

Before she could finish the thought, Theresa let out an angry yell like someone struggling to lift a heavy weight. At the same time, a loud *bang* and *screech* came from the front driver's side of the van. The tires squealed as the front end lurched to the right and the van began a sideways slide. Then the seatbelt jerked against Merida and pushed all the air out of her as the van began to roll. Before she blacked out, Merida saw Theresa's body tumbling like a doll.

43

Val

"What are you going to do now?" said Evan, pacing back and forth in the front yard.

Val stood and climbed the porch steps, then sat down in one of the four wooden rocking chairs. She leaned her head back, closed her eyes, and rocked.

During the war, she'd never been uncertain about what she had to do. Sometimes she'd wondered if what she had to do was *right*, but she'd never had trouble with knowing what was required of her. There was always a mission. And the mission was always clear because she had good commanders. Now, though, there weren't any commanders. There was just Val and Kim.

The screen door opened, its spring creaking, and Tasia came out. "Jessica's out of the shower if you want one. Make sure to give me your dirty clothes so I can wash them with Jessica's."

"Thanks," said Val. She looked at Evan, who stood in the grass at the base of the steps. Hands in his pockets. Head down. "I don't know what we're going to do. Not yet."

Evan nodded, still looking at the ground.

Tasia leaned against the front porch rail and crossed her arms. "Got any options in mind?"

Val stifled her irritation. She appreciated the help that Evan and Tasia were giving them, but she needed just one damn day to recover. One day to not think about what the plan was. One day to worry about how to fix what had happened between her and Braden before she decided what to do next.

But you've spent twelve years pretending that this day wouldn't come, she thought. *Time's up. No more pretending.*

"We still haven't figured out the fuel question," said Val. "That's got to come first. The Dragonfly's going to need a lot of Hy-5 to get us out of the country. And if you two start buying up a bunch of hydrogen fuel, it'll bring the whole DHS here within the hour."

Evan put one foot on the second porch step and propped himself with his elbows on his thigh. He glanced up at Tasia, frowned, and then looked at Val.

"What if you stole some?"

Val raised her eyebrows. "You think that will bring less attention than buying some?"

Evan seemed to barely register that she had spoken to him. He was staring out into the dusky woods, his brow furrowed with deep thought. "Actually, we wouldn't be stealing it, exactly. How fast could you fill it up? The Dragonfly?"

"Probably about fifteen or twenty minutes," she said. "Why?"

But Evan didn't answer. He turned suddenly, looking west with his head cocked curiously to one side. "Do you hear...?"

Val stood, her heart pounding. Just from experience, she expected to hear the sound of drone propellers racing toward the house.

Evan turned back to Val and Tasia. "Sorry. I thought I heard something. Must have been a gas-burner on Highway 83."

But Val was already running toward the trail where Braden and Kim had gone. "I think it's time I found my family."

"We'll all go," Tasia shouted after her. "Let me get the boys, and we'll head that way, okay?"

But Val was already halfway to the woods. Maybe Evan had just heard a distant car, but she wasn't going to wait to find out. She had just gotten her family back.

"Wait up!" shouted a voice—Evan this time. "I'm coming with you!"

Val slowed her pace a bit to let him catch up with her, but she didn't stop. When he reached her side, she saw that he carried a Courier in his left hand and an old double-barreled shotgun in the right.

"I brought supplies," he said. "Just in case."

44

Merida

The ceiling lights in the back of the van. Barely working. Flickering. The sound of bent metal creaking.

Merida was lying on her back. Still in the seat. The seatbelt had done its job. Her head hurt like hell, and she couldn't feel her legs or arms. Or could she? She wiggled her toes. Her fingers. Tried to pick up one leg. Sharp jolts of pain in her hip and ankle. Same with the other side. Definitely two legs there. Arms, too. Thank all the gods and fates for that.

A banging noise from the back of the van. A voice in her head. Celina.

...come on, you crazy woman, answer me...

I'm here. I think I'm dead.

Dead. What about Theresa?

A sharp pain went off in her neck as she turned her head to the right, toward the front of the van. Theresa lay unmoving across the seats. Arms and legs splayed, but straight. Didn't look like any of them had snapped in half. Too bad. There was still a chance that her neck was broken, though...

"Come on!" shouted a muffled voice outside the van. Merida

turned to look in that direction, and with a loud screech, the back door swung open and banged into the ground. The white light of a car's headlamps silhouetted a pair of figures.

Celina and Wallace.

"Oh, God," she burst out, and tears filled her eyes. "Is it really you?"

They climbed into the back of the van. Both looked like hell. Stringy hair plastered to their heads. Dirt covering their clothes and skin. Small scratches all over their faces and arms.

"I thought you were dead," Merida said. "It's you? Really you?"

"Unfortunately, yes," said Celina, and let out an exaggerated sigh. "But if I'd known you were going to put us through all this, I would have just died and saved myself the trouble."

"But Journey..." said Merida. "She can... How do I know it's really you?"

Celina crouched next to Merida, looking right into her eyes. "Hey. It's me, girl. Cross my heart."

"Are you okay?" Wallace asked.

"Yeah. Banged up, but yeah," Merida said, rubbing her face and feeling like someone who has woken up from a nightmare and found a bunch of other people sitting around her. "Better than that little shit, anyway." She pointed toward Theresa's body.

Celina closed her eyes as if straining to hear a distant sound. Then she looked down at Merida again. "She's alive. Let's get moving before she and the other one wake up. I'd rather not have to duke it out with the pair of them."

"Journey is strong," said Merida, as Wallace removed her seatbelt. "She can make you think she's someone else..."

"Tell us about it while we drive," said Celina. She offered Merida a hand to help her up. "We gotta move."

The two of them helped Merida hobble out of the back of the van. She hadn't broken anything, as far as she could tell, but she felt like she'd been beaten with a tire iron. Outside, she gasped. They were in the middle of nowhere. Two-lane highway. Tall, straight pines on either side. An old billboard, overgrown with kudzu. The sun was behind the trees, close to setting, and the sky was a deep, heavy shade of blue.

The van had rolled off the road, leaving a wide gash in the grass maybe thirty yards long. A small car was parked next to the road.

"That's our ride," Celina said. "Let's hurry before anybody—"

Don't do this, said a voice in Merida's head.

"Oh, shit," said Celina. She must have heard it, too.

"We have to go," Merida said. "Now."

They ran. At first, Merida thought that she might not be able to. Her legs didn't want to pick up her feet high enough. They kept dragging her toes against the ground. But she pushed herself. They had to get to the car and as far from Journey as possible.

You're going to destroy any chance we have! said Journey.

Feeling—praying—that her strength and coordination were coming back, Merida picked up the pace. Wallace was yelling something about the car, but she barely registered this. All she could think about was Journey. About the way she had made those soldiers and police officers shoot one another. The way she was able to control what other people saw. Celina was strong, but there was no way she was as strong as that.

Thanks for the confidence, said Celina.

Merida glanced over her shoulder toward the van. Journey was crawling through the shattered windshield.

I can't let you go, she said in Merida's head. *You're going to ruin everything.*

"Go!" Merida shouted at Celina and Wallace. "For God's sake, go!"

A sick feeling ran through her body, starting in her stomach and spreading through her chest and into her head. Dizziness. Nausea. Still another twenty feet to the car.

"Don't give in," said Celina. "Almost there. And she's weak from the wreck. You can beat her."

I'm not your enemy, said Journey. *I'm just fighting for my kind. And the world would be... so much better with... my kind...*

They reached the car, and Wallace jumped into the driver's seat. Celina shoved Merida into the back seat and slid in beside her.

"*Go!*" she screamed as she slammed the car door.

But Wallace hesitated. Sitting straight-backed in his seat with his hands at two and ten o'clock on the steering wheel, he looked like someone waiting for a traffic cop to approach his window.

"Oh, God," said Merida. "Journey's got him."

Celina held her palms over her temples, her eyes squeezed shut and her teeth bared in a grimace. Slowly, a sound like a growl rose in her throat.

After a few seconds, Wallace let out a surprised *huh*. He shook his head, put the car into Drive, and then accelerated, rocking Merida's head backwards as they sped down the highway.

45

Kim

Night had nearly fallen when Kim finally found Braden in the pecan grove that stretched out for several acres to the east of the barn.

"Hey," said Kim. He turned on the flashlight and waved the beam back and forth to get Braden's attention.

At first, the boy stopped and stared at him, his stance wide and low—like someone who was about to run. Kim picked up his pace to a jog, ready for a sprint if Braden made a break for it. But rather than run away, Braden staggered to one side and collapsed with his back against a pecan tree.

"Braden!" Kim yelled, hurrying forward. When he reached Braden, he crouched next to him and put a hand on his shoulder. "You okay?"

"Pulled something," Braden said, grimacing and holding his hands over his side.

"Maybe next time, don't run away. Now isn't a good time for that."

Braden sighed. Nodded.

Kim stood, slid the Courier out of his pocket, and pressed the button. "Anybody hear me?"

"This is Evan," came a voice from the device's speaker. He sounded a little out of breath. "Go ahead, Kimiya."

"I'm with Braden. He's okay. We're in the back lot. Pecan grove."

"Good deal," said Evan. "We'll be there pretty soon. Valerie and I are walking down."

Kim looked at Braden, who swiped away a tear and stared miserably at the ground.

"No need. We'll meet you at the house," said Kim into the Courier.

Pause. Then Val's voice.

"I'm glad you're okay," she said. "I'm glad you found him. Tell him... I'm sorry. Tell him I love him."

"I will," said Kim. "We'll be home in a little while."

Another pause, and then Evan answered. "Understood, Kimiya. Be safe. We'll see you at the house."

Kim put the Courier back in his pocket and dropped to one knee next to his son.

You want me to forgive her, came Braden's thought-voice.

"Yes, that's exactly what I want you to do," said Kim. "Desperation does things to people."

I know. But we're still in a desperate situation, aren't we? When will we ever not be in a desperate situation again?

"Our situation right now isn't like you and your mom at the creek that night," Kim replied. "We're safe and with—"

The sound of footsteps made Kim whirl and try to scramble to his feet in the same motion, but he tripped over his own feet and fell onto his side.

"Sorry," said a young voice. One of Evan's sons. "Didn't mean to scare you."

Jacob stepped out of the shadow of a pecan tree and walked

toward them. He held out his hand to help Kim to his feet. Kim took it, and the young man pulled him upwards with surprising strength.

"I heard Dad on the Courier," he said. "I get that you want some alone time. I'll just wait over there—" He aimed his flashlight at the barn. "—and then we can walk back together, if that's okay."

Kim nodded. "Of course."

"I'm fine," said Braden. He stood. "Let's go back now."

You sure? thought Kim.

Braden started toward the path without answering him.

46

Merida

As the car sped away from the wreck, Merida leaned forward to look into the rearview mirror. A pair of headlights was pulling over next to the overturned police van. A good Samaritan offering help.

They'll regret that, she thought.

"Can you warn them?" asked Merida.

"Warn who?" said Celina, turning to look through the back window. She sighed. "Too late for that now. Too far away."

The car stopped, and the driver got out and ran toward the van. But before Merida could see what happened next, they rounded a curve so that trees blocked her view.

"I hate it for whoever that is," Merida said, facing forward again. "Journey and Theresa will probably kill them."

"Who the hell is Journey?" said Wallace. He met Merida's eyes in the rearview mirror. "What does she want with you?"

"She wants to 'build a better world.'" Merida shook her head. "Or some such shit."

"Yeah, my mother used to say that I was gonna help change the world," said Wallace. "Got no use for that sort of talk, myself.

People who think it's their job to change the world always end up destroying things, and not just the bad things."

"Maybe," said Merida, thinking of Val and Jessica. *Had* they blown up that Artemis facility? "Maybe not all of them. Anyway, this Journey chick is strong."

Her stomach tightening like a fist, Merida turned to Celina. Grabbed her thigh. Squeezed her shoulder. Cupped her face in her hands. Would touching her make it easier to know the truth? To see through one of Journey's tricks?

"Hey," said Celina. "At least buy me dinner first. Yes, it's me. I promise."

"Sorry," said Merida. She hugged Celina tight. The girl smelled like dirt and pond water. "It's just... I thought you were dead, and then Journey and Theresa made me wonder if I'd lost my mind. They can disguise themselves. Trick you into seeing them as someone else. I really saw this old military guy when I looked at her."

"That's pretty badass," said Celina, her eyebrows lifting. "I could think of some great uses for *that* trick."

Merida laughed, feeling a little giddy herself. She'd narrowly escaped capture, and maybe death. And now she had Celina back—and Wallace. Her friends.

"What about you two?" she said. "What happened to you?"

Wallace and Celina exchanged glances in the rearview mirror.

"You can tell it," Wallace said.

"Well," said Celina, her smile fading. "It's not what you went through, but it wasn't fun, either."

"Shit," said Wallace, all mirth drained from his voice. "Incoming. Behind us. Look."

Merida turned, her neck complaining, and looked back. Headlights. Coming up fast.

"Is that...?" she said.

"I can feel her," Wallace said. "She's..."

Celina turned so that she knelt in the seat of the car, facing backwards. "Just drive. Focus on the road."

Merida.

Goosebumps broke out all over Merida's arms, neck, and back. *Just leave me alone,* she thought.

Now Celina spoke in her mind. *Don't respond to her. Just focus on what you see.*

"Here," Wallace said. He tossed a pistol over his shoulder. It landed on the seat next to Merida. He did the same with a magazine. "Hopefully it fires. It got soaked when I fell into the creek."

Merida picked up the gun. It was the pistol she'd given him when they were being chased by the cops. Now she didn't even question the confidence and security that it gave her to feel the cold metal in her hands.

"Need some help here, doll," said Celina, who had her head bowed with her hands flat against her temples. "You can start shooting any time now."

...you don't... that gun, I'll make you... on them. Journey's voice was broken and faint, like a holocall with someone over a bad connection.

Wallace put down Merida's window, letting in a blast of humid night air.

"Give 'em hell," he said.

Her heart pounding, Merida turned her body to face backwards and leaned out the window. The wind whipped her hair into her eyes. With one hand, she held it out of her face, and with the other she pointed the pistol in the direction of the pursuing car.

Damn you! screamed a voice. Not Journey's. Theresa.

Please, prayed Merida, not sure whom she expected to hear or listen, let alone answer.

Click. Bang.

The gun recoiled and flashed. It worked, at least. But it might as well not have, for all the good it did. She'd clearly missed. The other vehicle inched steadily closer, maybe four or five car lengths behind them now.

The movies make this look so easy, thought Merida.

She tried to aim more carefully, but the car kept bouncing. She fired again. Two more times. Three. No hits, as far as she could see. The car kept coming. Didn't even swerve.

Can't do this much longer, said Celina's thought-voice. *Not against two of them.*

Bang. Bang. Nothing. Probably not much ammo left.

Come on, she thought.

"I can feel her in my head!" screamed Wallace. "Do something about this now, or we're gonna—"

Bang.

Journey's car swerved, first to the right and then to the left.

Yes, Merida thought. *Come on, you insane...*

The car was sliding sideways, tires squealing.

Come on. Wreck. Flip.

It didn't flip, but it skidded sideways to a stop in the grass next to the road. A hand grabbed Merida's arm and pulled her upper body back inside.

"You did it!" said Celina. "You hit her! I felt it!"

"Thank God!" said Wallace.

Merida fell back against her seat and gasped. Her ears popped with the changing air pressure inside the car as Wallace shut the window.

"Any luck, and that crazy woman is dead," said Celina. "Wish we could've got Theresa, too, but I'm pretty sure she's okay."

Merida's stomach twisted at the word *dead*. She hadn't wanted to kill Journey, even after what she'd done to Parks and who knew how many other officers. But she looked down at the gun in her lap, tightened her fingers around its grip, and made a mental note that she should thank Val when she saw her again. *If* she saw her again.

"Got to find another car," said Wallace. "Y'all help me keep a lookout for one. Soon as we do that, we can get the information out there."

Merida's heart skipped a beat. "What are you talking about? They fried the computer."

Wallace glanced at her in the rearview mirror, grinning like a maniac. "Oh, ye of little faith. You think a little EMP burst can stop a badass IT guy like me?"

47

Theresa

Everything was noise—Journey yelling, tires screeching, car motor whining, the AI's bizarrely calm voice saying something about traction control and automated steering. Then the car skidded to a stop next to the woods—just feet shy of a big tree that would have done a lot of damage if they'd hit it at full speed.

"Oh, God, it hurts," Journey said, groaning through clenched teeth.

Theresa—whose right hand lay in her lap, her wrist swelling and radiating pain—gave Journey her left hand to squeeze.

"I can help," she said. "But you'll have to trust me."

"*Calling for emergency services,*" said the car's AI voice.

"Cancel that!" shouted Journey, her voice cracking. "No help. Don't call for help."

"*Are you sure?*" said the voice.

"Yes!"

"*Canceling.*"

Theresa's body felt bathed in pain. Her right arm was probably fractured. Almost every part of her was bruised. She had several cuts on her face, arms, and legs. Probably a concussion. If she could do anything she wanted right now, it would be to get in the back of the car and go to sleep. Maybe never wake up again.

But.

Her parents. The accident. She had been here before. A young girl in a wrecked car. Her parents too close to death. Her ability still developing. Nothing she could do.

But this time was different. She hadn't been able to save her parents, but she could save Journey. *Would* save her.

"I can help," she said again.

"What... can you do?" Journey said. Moving slowly, as if her arm had become extremely heavy, she reached up to put pressure on the bullet wound. As soon as she touched it, she cried out.

"Bite down on the steering wheel," said Theresa. "I'm going to help, but it's going to hurt, I think. Pretty bad."

Journey looked at her. Tears streamed down the woman's face, and her lower lip trembled. "I don't understand."

It was an odd thing for a telepath as strong as Journey to say. She should be able to read Theresa's mind and see immediately what she could do. What she had done for Bowen's eye. What she had done for her father when he had cut his arm open with a screwdriver. What she had done a hundred times with more minor injuries. But the pain of the bullet wound must have sapped all of Journey's strength of mind.

"Do it," said Theresa.

She reached into Journey's mind and forced her to obey. It didn't take any effort. Without resisting at all, the other woman turned to the steering wheel, opened her mouth, and bit into the vinyl.

"Just try to be still," Theresa said.

Setting aside her own pain as much as possible, she closed her eyes and reached deep into Journey's mind. Hallways echoing with fragmented thoughts. Chambers full of memories both recent and distant. A blood-red hue of pain. A high-pitched steam-whistle sound of agony. A frantic voice screaming for something to end the pain. Another voice wondering whether Journey was going to die. Going on and on about things that Journey had left to finish. The ambition to replace Cartwright as the head of the organization. Faith in their mission. The hope that, one day, telepaths would be lords over a worldwide peace. A name. Set aside. Forgotten. Whitney. People to save. A world to build.

Finally, Theresa found what she was looking for—a deep place in the mind. A dark foundation. Barely used, but powerful. She reached into it. Pushed and turned. It awoke and began to do its work.

Journey's body jolted and strained. Her teeth clenched down on the steering wheel. Her voice grew louder, first as a groan and then a scream.

Be still, Theresa thought as she worked at that dark place in Journey's mind. Almost as if it were her own body, she sensed the wound in Journey's shoulder begin to heal. First, torn and ragged muscle squeezed against the bullet, working it slowly toward the entrance wound. With the bullet came all of the smashed and mutilated dead cells that had been in its path. Then, living cells pushed together and reconnected with one another as severed veins, arteries, and capillaries sealed back together. And all the while, Journey screamed and bit down on the steering wheel.

Theresa reached out and touched Journey's leg, which vibrated like the plucked string of a guitar. Her thigh muscle was painfully, impossibly tight.

"It's almost over," said Theresa.

Journey let go of the steering wheel, threw her body back against the seat, and screamed. But then she stopped, her body going limp.

"Oh, my God," she whispered, her chest heaving for breath.

Theresa leaned back in her seat, realizing only now that she had broken out into a cold sweat. The pain of her own injuries returned, along with a dizzy, nauseated feeling.

Journey reached up and touched her shoulder. Her fingers dug inside the bloody hole in her shirt and brought out a small object. The bullet. It looked like it had been crushed by the impact. Theresa had expected it to be smooth and pointed, but it looked more like a mushroom.

"How did you do this?" Journey said, still whispering.

"It's just..." said Theresa. To her, the ability to heal had just been a part of who she was. It went hand-in-hand with her telepathy. Only at the Institute had she discovered that her healing ability might be unique. As far as she knew, Celina and Francis weren't able to do it. "I've always been able to do that."

The two women looked at one another. Journey's eyes reflected the green and blue lights from the car's instrument console. Stringy with sweat, her hair clung to her face, and tears were drying on her cheeks.

"You're..." said Journey. "You are amazing."

Theresa leaned her head back against the headrest and thought that if she were so amazing, then her parents ought to be alive today. She took a deep breath, wincing at the pain in her chest.

"Why don't you heal your own injuries?" said Journey.

Theresa shook her head. "I can't. Doesn't work that way."

Journey's eyes dropped. She looked at the bullet, turning it over in her fingers. "I'm sorry."

"Your name isn't Journey," said Theresa. "It's Whitney."

Journey let out a small gasp, almost inaudible. She turned in her seat, slowly at first, as if she expected pain.

"My name *is* Journey," she said. "'Whitney' is the name my DNA donors gave me."

"Your... what?" She looked into Journey's eyes.

"My genetic parents."

Theresa thought of her mother, then. Her mother, who had taught her to bake banana bread when she was seven, who had sung to her every night when she was a little girl. "Summertime." "Count Your Blessings." "You Are My Sunshine."

"I know you loved your parents," said Journey. "I'm sorry you lost them. But only *you* can decide who you are. What your identity is. My DNA donors decided that I was Whitney before I even came into this world. But *I* decided that I was Journey." Her eyes were wide, almost stern. She was a teacher who needed her student to get this lesson. But Theresa's mind reeled at the thought of rejecting her parents.

I'm not saying you should reject them, said Journey. *You're happy with the name your DNA don—*

"My parents," said Theresa, a surprising jolt of anger surging through her.

Your parents, corrected Journey, her expression softening. *You're happy with your name. That's all that matters. I wasn't, because it wasn't who I am. My DNA donors don't get to decide who I am.*

Theresa looked out the windshield and into the night. Her own reflection, which glowed blue and green with the car's dash lights, stared back at her. She had always defined herself by her parents. By heritage. By the kindness of her father and the love of her mother. By their strength. By the name that they'd given her. They gave her something that she wouldn't have otherwise. Context.

Meaning. The fact that her identity wasn't just something that she fashioned herself, but that she inherited. It gave her a connection to the people who had come before her and a firm foundation on which to build something neither entirely new nor outworn.

I rejected my DNA donors because they were afraid of me, said Journey. *Because they regretted me. And when I escaped them, I promised myself that I would be my own person from then on.*

Theresa tried to hold on to the image of her parents in her mind, to see their kind faces as reminders that there was some good in this world, but another image arose unbidden—her parents on their knees, looking at her in terror, just before they bashed their heads into the ground. Again. And again.

She reeled at the thought, shaking her head to drive the image away. If they were alive now to see what she had become, they would be even more afraid of her than Journey's parents had been of their daughter.

Journey shifted in her seat, placing her hands on the steering wheel. "Now. Is Theresa, the daughter of Jason and Renee Strickland, going to help us make a better world? Because we have work to do."

48

Val

Standing on the porch with Tasia and Jessica, Val waited for Jacob to lead Kim and Braden back to the house. The evening had turned to night, and the stars had come out in their full brightness. Even the floodlights on the outside of the house couldn't outshine them. Somewhere in the distance, a coyote howled. If it weren't for her pulse pounding in her temples and the sick feeling of dread in her gut, all of this would have felt like home.

"Everything's going to be okay," said Tasia.

Val met Tasia's gaze for a second, offered a polite nod, and looked out into the night again. She couldn't be that kind of optimist. Not that she was a pessimist, either. To Val, the optimist and the pessimist made the same mistake—both thought they knew something that they couldn't know. Better to be something else—"realist" wasn't it, either, but Val didn't know what the right word was. The healthy, sane thing was to know that you can't see the path more than a few steps ahead. Good or bad, the future was a fog.

After about ten more minutes, a flashlight flickered at the place where the path left the woods. Val's heart skipped a beat at the sight of it. She had to fight off the urge to turn and walk inside.

What was wrong with her? She was a combat veteran, for God's sake. But she'd never had to face a real, meaningful conflict between her and Braden. She'd never had to endure him thinking that she was wrong. Not just *wrong,* but that she had wanted to kill him. Compared to this, the Iranian Revolutionary Guard had been easy.

"There they are," said Jessica, relief in her voice.

The three of them emerged from the woods and crossed the patch of grass that surrounded the house. Val couldn't see their faces, which only increased her anxiety. And Braden walked with a limp.

I'm okay, came Braden's thought-voice. *I just pulled something when I was running earlier.* There was something odd about his voice, though. It sounded faint. Muffled, maybe.

I'm sorry, thought Val.

Nothing major. Dad says it'll be better tomorrow.

That's not what I meant.

I know. Me, too.

Val met them at the bottom of the stairs and hugged Braden. The boy stood and let her hold him, but he returned the embrace with a stiffness that wasn't just the result of a pulled muscle.

I'm fine. Really. Sorry that I...

He let go of her and looked around as if casting about for the right words.

I'm okay, she thought. *No harm done.*

The others—Kim, Jacob, Tasia, and Evan—all climbed the stairs and went inside, clearly to give Braden and Val some privacy. Kim looked over his shoulder as he went, offering his most reassuring *good luck* smile.

"Well," said Val.

Braden turned his back to Val and took a few steps toward the woods. "I did some thinking while I was out there," he said. He put his palms against his temples and gripped chunks of hair. For a second, Val thought that he was about to pull some of it out. Then he dropped his hands to his sides. "I can't stop thinking about that baby. I want to save her."

At these words, Val let out a breath that she hadn't known that she'd been holding. She had expected more angst and anger from him. But this was Braden, truly—the compassionate kid who just wants to help others like him. This, she knew how to handle.

"I know," she said. She stood next to him and put an arm around his shoulders, but he pulled away and turned to face her.

"Don't say that." He wasn't angry, but there was something in his voice and face that made her step backwards. "Don't treat me like a kid."

"What are you..." said Val, renewed anger rising in her. She tamped it down with a deep breath. "I just—I know you want to help the baby. Why are you mad about that?"

Braden shook his head and rubbed his neck with one hand. "You were going to say, 'I know, but you don't understand how hard it will be.'" He crossed his arms and stared right into Val's eyes. In the shadows of the evening, he looked more like a man than she had ever seen before. "You were going to talk about the risks. Don't tell me that it's too dangerous."

"I wasn't," said Val. "It would be dangerous, but we're stuck with danger whether we want it or not. That's not the problem. The problem is—"

"That we don't know where they took her," he said. "But maybe we could find her. Maybe they took her back to that place where they took me."

"No," said Val, "that's not likely at all. That place is on the news now. Probably crawling with investigators—and with the government agents trying to keep the investigators from discovering anything. The people who have Taylor will take her to some place that isn't compromised. There are bound to be other facilities like that."

Braden's eyes welled with tears. One spilled over onto his cheek, and he wiped it away. He blinked, scrubbed his eyes, and drew himself up. "So why don't we try to find her? You're... if anybody can find a place like that, it would be you."

Val's heart sank. He might still be angry at her for pointing a gun at his head, but he also put too much faith in her. She remembered what that was like—thinking that her role models were the strongest, most capable people on Earth. She'd thought of her grandfather in that way.

"Right now, we're coming up with a plan to get some fuel for the Dragonfly," she said. "We'll need that to get someplace safe, and we'd need it to try and save the girl, too. In the meantime, I'll think about how we might do that. Will you take that answer for now?"

Braden's gaze seemed to harden. He was reading her mind, trying to see if she was just pacifying him.

I'm not saying that I'll be able to come up with something, she thought. *I'm just saying we'll try. I promise we'll try.*

Braden nodded. His body seemed to relax, and the almost-man that he had become seemed to wilt like a dying flower.

"We ought to get some sleep now," Val said. "Come on."

Braden hesitated.

"What?" said Val, wincing at the impatience in her own voice.

"I'm..." said Braden. "Something happened tonight. I'm worried..."

He stared at the ground.

"What's wrong?" said Val, tightness building in her chest. She had to suppress the urge to shake whatever it was out of him.

"Sorry," he said finally. "I'm worried that... I—I think I might be losing my power."

Joe Tessio: *Atlanta Journal-Constitution*

Governor Brooks has set this Saturday as the opening date for a special session of the Georgia legislature to discuss possible secession from the United States.

On day one, members of the general public will be invited to voice their opinions and concerns directly to legislators in a joint meeting of the State House and Senate. Speaking slots will be assigned on a first-come, first-served basis, and citizens are already setting up lines of tents on the sidewalks outside the Georgia Citadel building to ensure they're among the first in line to make their voices heard.

Although the issue of secession was originally planned for debate in the fall when the legislature returns for regular session, Governor Brooks today declared that the State of Georgia must act now, before the Wall of Separation Act is signed into law.

"The President may think she can intimidate and bully our churches into silence with this grotesque and unconstitutional law, but the people of Georgia won't give up our God-given right to free speech so easily," said Brooks. "That's why I asked the legislature to give the microphones over to the public on the very first day of their special session. The people must be allowed to speak, and their voices should be the first and loudest ones we hear."

Brooks said that she hopes the special session will lead to a state referendum to decide whether Georgia will move forward with secession.

"The time has come for Georgia to take stock of its relationship to the rest of the States," she said, speaking alongside Secretary of State Vance, House Majority Leader Clark, and Senate Majority Leader Xiao. "The time has come for us to ask ourselves whether or not the Federal government helps or hurts Georgians. The time has come for us to decide whether or not Washington has become the tyranny that the American Founders fought to escape."

Brooks went on to cite broad public support in Georgia for secession, as well as concerns about SRP, increasing levels of controversy and violence surrounding SRP, and other recent developments in national politics.

In response, Atlanta Mayor Jackson Wilkes has called for protests at the Georgia Capitol, saying that secession will "plunge Georgia back into the days of..."

READ THE FULL STORY
VIEW COMMENTS

Josephine Clinton: About damn time.

Vinn63: the south has risen again!!!!!!!

Courtney Baxter: This isn't the Confederacy. Stop perpetuating that lie. We're not going to suddenly become the Old South again. Nobody wants to bring back slavery. This is about OPPOSING the NEW slavery of government control over women's BODIES. The Federal government has trampled on the Constitution for long enough.

MAJ1963: I guess you've never heard of the 30th amendment?!?!?!?!

49

Merida

"All the information is in my online data locker," said Wallace, grinning as he spoke. "All I need is internet access, and I can activate it."

He's pretty proud of himself, said Celina. *It's funny how sexy a smart brain can be.* She patted Merida's thigh with her hand. *Don't be jealous, though. I'd take you over him any day.*

At another moment, Merida might have slapped Celina's hand away, but right now she couldn't even begin to feel annoyance about much of anything. She felt light-headed, almost drunk with relief. Was it possible? She was almost afraid to let herself believe it. But the giddiness in Wallace's voice was infectious, and as much as her mind rebelled against the idea of entertaining hope, warmth radiated from her heart to the rest of her body.

Wallace tapped a button on the car's entertainment console, and the dash on the passenger side opened to reveal a holographic projector and a touchscreen.

"We just need to find a new car first," he said.

"This car can't connect to the web?" asked Merida.

"Oh, it can. But the moment I log in to my account and dump

that information, somebody will track the login to this car's computer. We'll need another car ready to go, so we can ride off into the... well, into the night, I guess."

Unable to restrain herself, Merida leaned forward and put her arms around Wallace.

"May every god that ever existed bless you," she said, kissing him on the cheek. "Tell your boss that you need a raise, okay?"

Wallace shook his head. "I don't think I'm going to have a—there!"

He slammed on the brakes, rocking Merida forward. She let out a dull *huh* as her chest slammed into the back of the driver's seat. Then she rocked sideways into Celina's lap as Wallace jerked the wheel right, tires squealing, and then stopped.

"What the hell?" said Merida.

They were sitting in a driveway, their headlights shining on a small wood-frame house. In the driveway, a middle-aged man in coveralls stood staring at them, his eyes wide. He was frozen in place, posed as if he'd been about to open the driver's side door of his very old, very rusted Honda Civic.

"Sorry," said Wallace. "Do your thing, Celina."

"I'm on it," the girl replied. She opened her door and got out.

"Give me some warning next time, Dale Earnhardt," said Merida. She winced at a sharp pain in her back. "I've already got whiplash."

"Sorry," said Wallace. "Who's Dale Earn—whatshisface?"

"Never mind."

Merida leaned forward between the driver and passenger seats to look through the windshield. This house was the only one in sight. Overgrown yard. Pieces of rusted scrap metal strewn here and there. An old truck on cinder blocks nearly overtaken by ivy. The car that they were apparently about to steal looked like a late 2040s model. The paint was peeling, and the back window was missing, covered with duct tape and plastic sheeting. Merida hoped that the thing ran.

Celina approached the man in coveralls. A big guy with arms and shoulders that looked like they could stranglehold a bear. He rose up to his full height and gestured angrily toward the car that had just swerved into his driveway.

"The fuck y'all doin'?" he shouted. "Damn near plowed right into my..."

But he trailed off, his shoulders slumping. His mouth, which had been stretched into a sneer, relaxed and hung open slightly. He muttered something that Merida couldn't make out, handed Celina a set of keys, and then turned to walk into the house.

"Okay," said Wallace. He opened his door and got out of the car.

Merida got out, too. "What now?"

"Now, I do *my* thing," Wallace beamed.

He strode around to the passenger side of the car and got in. When she'd met him at company parties with Jessica, Wallace had always struck Merida as one of those aimless men who never seemed to have any goal in life beyond performing the daily tasks of a job and gratefully accepting what little fun there was to be had. But now, he moved like a man with a purpose. Looking at him, you wouldn't know that his whole life had been upended.

Celina's voice spoke in Merida's head. *Piece of cake.*

The girl leaned against the front quarter panel of the car and crossed her arms. She put on a self-satisfied smirk.

"You're feeling better, I take it?" said Merida.

Oh, I'm ready to go now.

Merida leaned against the car next to Celina, the questions that had been waiting in the back of her mind finally spilling out. "What happened to you two? How did you get away from the police?"

Still smirking, Celina glanced over her shoulder at Wallace, who was working on the car's computer.

There's a lot to him, she said in Merida's mind. *You think he's just a nerd. But he's really got some stuff. I think I might keep him as a pet.*

What's that supposed to mean?

I got tranqed right after you did. But Coleman's dart got caught in his shirt under his armpit. Never broke the skin. After we both fell in the water, that beautiful, nerdy, cloned man pulled me into one of the drains that went under the bridge. When I woke up, we were in the woods somewhere. Absolutely filthy. Stunk like a sewer. But I was looking up at him, and I thought he was an angel. First chance I get, I'm going to reward him.

You know, thought Merida, *you might just try saying "thank—"*

The car rocked a little as Wallace climbed out and shut the door.

"That's it," he said, his face pale. "The whole world knows. Now let's go before somebody tracks this car down."

50

Val

Val and Braden stood on opposite sides of the porch steps, each leaning against a handrail. Braden hugged his own chest and hung his head, almost as if in shame.

"When I was out there," he said, the words coming slowly, "when Dad found me, I could read him. I could send my thoughts to him, and I could hear his. Like normal. But then he started to fade, like somebody walking away while talking. Then, when Jacob showed up, I couldn't read him at all. I lost Dad completely for a while, and then he came back a little bit. When we were walking home, I tried to have a private conversation with him, and I couldn't."

Val crossed the stairs and leaned next to Braden, putting an arm around his shoulders.

"You're just tired," she said. "We've all been through so much in the last two days..."

But Braden was shaking his head hard. "No. That's not it. It's not like that at all. Even right now, I'm having trouble reading you. It's like you're far away."

"Either way, you need some sleep," said Val. "Maybe it'll help. And if it doesn't, we'll be able to think through it better in the morning. Why don't you go inside and get in bed? We've got some rough times coming, I think. I'm going to need you rested and in good shape."

The boy nodded and pulled away from her. Still hanging his head, he went up the stairs and opened the screen door. Stepping inside, he—

Braden. Cowering in the corner of a featureless room. Cinderblock walls. Bare cement floor. Braden was rocking back and forth, his knees drawn to his chest in a fetal position, his hands on his head. Men gathered around him.

"I can't stop them," Braden whispered. "I can't stop—"

She found herself staring at Braden—the real Braden—who was still holding the screen door open for her.

"Mom?" he said. "You okay? What's wrong?"

"You didn't—?" she said.

He frowned and cocked his head to one side. "Didn't... what?"

"I just... had this weird thought. Never mind," she said. "I'm fine."

She stepped past him into the foyer. There were voices coming from the dining room. The warm light of lamps. The ticking of a grandfather clock's pendulum. Things around her seemed both hyper-real and unreal at the same time. Like it had after the first time Braden accidentally projected one of his dreams into her mind.

"You get some sleep," she said, turning to face Braden. "I've got to talk some plans over with the others, and then I need some rest, too."

She hugged him, pressing her lips to the top of his head.

"I'm sorry," she whispered. *I promise I would never hurt you.*

If he heard this thought, he didn't answer. When she let go of him, he turned and trudged up the staircase to the bedroom. Her mind reeling, Val watched him until he disappeared down the hallway. What was happening to him? His ability to read other people seemed to have weakened, but he had projected a thought into her mind so strong that for a few seconds she had forgotten where she was—and he didn't even seem to know that he had done it.

"Val."

Kim stepped into the foyer from the living room, his face wearing an expression Val couldn't read. Eyes wide. Lips pressed together in thin lines. Using his good arm, he put a hand on her back and led her through the living room toward the dining room where Tasia, Evan, and Jacob were gathered around a hologram projector on the dinner table.

"You need to see this," said Kim.

Agora: The Ideas Marketplace

StanleyFord: I'm looking through the documents and videos just published by @JesscaBrantleyANS, and I'm not sure what to think. It all looks authentic to me.

Dr. Marquize Hughes: My field of expertise is deepfake footage analysis, and my initial impression of this video is that it's real. I'll say more later when I've had time to examine the footage more carefully for deepfake artifacts.

JaMarcus Stone: Fake news!!!

David Vess: telepaths? give me a fucking break

M. Klinger: I knew it! I can read people's minds!!! And I thought that I was the only one!!!

Blake Fogg: Y'all forget the fucking telepaths. Do you realize what this means for the Samford Virus?!?!?! The government deliberately infected billions of people and caused millions of fucking babies to die of birth defects!

Janice Joiner: This has to be fake. I don't like the current administration, but I don't believe that ANY government would do this.

Dante Solomons: quit trippin. you really think the u.s. government wouldn't do something like this??????? they put japnese and german americans in internment camps durig ww2!!!

Janice Joiner: @DanteSolomons: You're talking about something that happened OVER A HUNDRED YEARS AGO!

Dante Solomons: @JaniceJoiner: yes! and the simple fact they did it then mns they could do somethin worse now!!!!

Blake Fogg: It's not just the American gov! The documents show that other governments went along with this stuff!

Dr. Marquize Hughes: Let's not rush to judgment. It will take time to sort out the truth from the fiction.

PART THREE

50

Val

"It's stupid!" said Val. "A waste! You won't even make it into the building, let alone get anywhere near the legislature or the Governor!"

Jessica stood across the dining room table from her sister. "Val—"

"No!" said Val, pointing a finger at Jessica. "It's just like what you pulled at Artemis. You're running into a burning building just when it's about to collapse!"

Kim put a hand on Val's back. She took a deep breath, but from the scowl on her face, Jessica could see that a little bit of air wasn't going to calm her.

"I was wrong at Artemis, okay?" Jessica said, struggling to keep her voice from quavering. "I admit it. Is that what you want to hear? But this is different. Just think for a second."

"I don't have to fucking think about it!" spat Val.

"Val," said Evan, who sat at one end of the table. "There ain't any need to—"

But Val slammed both her palms down flat against the tabletop. "*You're* the one who needs to stop and think. The legislature is meeting to talk about secession, maybe even civil war, and you're a wanted terrorist! You think they're just going to hand the microphone over to you so you can talk about telepaths and secret government assassination squads? If you don't get killed, you'll at least get arrested—and somebody's going to force you to tell them where we are and where we're going. Hell, they'll probably drum up a fucking telepath to get the information out of you."

"Then don't tell me what your plans are," said Jessica.

Val threw up her hands. "You already know too much!"

"Come on, Val," Kim said. "Maybe dial it down a notch or two."

Val glared across the table at Jessica, whose heart pounded so hard that she felt it down to the pit of her stomach. This was unlike anything Jessica had seen out of her sister before. Gone was the superhuman control that gave Val the ability to think through even the most stressful situations.

"Fine," said Val finally. She sat down. "Let's talk this through."

She wasn't yelling any more, but her tone was too carefully measured to really sound calm. Her body became still—but still with a tension and fixedness that might break her if this conversation continued to go sideways.

"I didn't expect you to love the idea," said Jessica, "but I didn't think you'd act like this."

"I'm not acting like anything," said Val, her tone dangerously even. She looked down the table at Evan, whose face was weary and shoulders slumped. The effect was to make the mountain of a man look weathered and defeated. "Sorry, Evan."

Evan nodded. He closed his eyes and rested his face on his folded hands.

Val turned back to Jessica. She crossed her arms and leaned forward. "Now. You say you've thought this thing through. You've got a plan and a rationale. Convince me. Show me why I'm wrong."

For God's sake, Val, thought Jessica.

"Val," she said, "you started this whole thing to rescue your husband and keep your son out of government hands. You did that. Now, it's time for you and your family to find a safe place and wait this thing out. I know you and Evan were up half the night making plans. And that's exactly what you and your family should do. But that's not what *I* set out to do."

Val's eyes seemed almost to bore into Jessica's. Any minute, she was going to blow up again—but Jessica pressed on.

"My job is to make sure the world finds out the truth. And I let Merida and Celina take on that job for me. They risked their lives to get it done, just so I could lead us on a wild goose chase. That's on me, and I'm sorry. I'm sorry that you had to tranq me to keep me from dragging you even further into danger. I can't change any of that. I can only choose where to go from here. And I've still got work to do. Don't you see it, Val? I've got a mission. And that mission's not over yet. It's not enough to get the information out there—I need people to *believe* it. That's the whole reason I got mixed up in all this shit to begin with! I've got to give this thing credibility. I've got to..."

Fuck.

Jessica couldn't bear to look at Val anymore, at that impossible fury. That unconquerable will. She put her face in her hands, surprised by the hot tears that suddenly spilled from her eyes. If she were being honest with herself, she had to admit that she was lying about one thing: she wasn't at all sorry that they tried to save Taylor. But even so, it ought to mean something that she had said the words.

"Dammit, Val," she said. "For all I know, Merida might not even make it back. She's still out there, still fighting, and I'm not just going sit on my ass while she's risking everything! I'm the one who set this thing in motion. Not Merida, not Celina, not even you. Now

I have to finish it. My face is already all over this thing. Don't you realize what it'll look like if I just dump a bunch of files on the internet and disappear? I've got to stand behind it. I've got to lead the fight, make people believe it."

She wiped the tears from her face and looked up at the others. Val's expression had softened a little now. She was still defiant, but something that Jessica had said had disarmed her. The men, too. Kim had leaned forward, almost in anticipation.

"I believe that this is the last step in the mission I took," she said finally. "I believe that when somebody defies the government the way I have—"

"The way *we* have," said Val.

"—they have a responsibility to accept the consequences," Jessica finished.

"But that's true for us, too," said Kim. "We broke the law in having Braden. We did that a long time ago. And if we turned ourselves in, then Braden would have nobody."

"No," said Jessica. "It's different for you and Val."

"No, it isn't," said Val. "It's the same—"

Jessica banged her fists on the table. "Do *not* try to take this from me! Your first responsibility is keeping your family safe. Mine isn't. I don't have Braden to protect. What I have is the truth. That's *my* responsibility."

Val leaned back in her chair, her eyes still fixed on Jessica. Before she could voice another protest, Jessica pressed on with her plan.

"The Saturday session is reserved for the public. If I can get into that session, I can get them to listen to me—"

"No," said Val, shaking her head with careful patience, "Even if you could get into the building without getting tagged by security—and you won't—there's no way they'd let you speak. You'd be lucky if they only tranq you and lock you up. I don't want to see your brains all over the Citadel floor."

"Jessica," said Evan, "if what I said yesterday in my little sermon is making you want to do this, I'm so sorry. I didn't mean that you should go on a suicide mission or sacrifice yourself."

"Are you sure, Evan?" said Jessica. "What the hell did you think we would take from a 'finish the mission' speech? What else is there to do but to stand up and fight?"

Evan opened his mouth to speak, and then closed it again.

Jessica shook her head. Did none of them get it? She was a *reporter,* for God's sake. She was supposed to be good at talking to people, explaining things—but Val, Kim, and Evan seemed hell-bent on not hearing her.

"I'm not trying to make myself a martyr," said Jessica. "I'm not doing this out of self-pity or something. This information we put out there just might tear the country apart. I'm not just going to lob that grenade at the American people and walk away."

"The country was already tearing itself apart," said Val. "That's what was always going to happen."

"I'm choosing to put more faith in people than that," Jessica said. "Maybe this is the issue that could unite everybody. Maybe..."

But she stopped. Did she really have that kind of faith in people? Maybe. Maybe not. It had been *people* who had leaked Genovirus-1, *people* who had decided to give the government control over women's bodies. But those had been people in positions of power. Maybe ordinary people—the ones who hadn't been corrupted by ideology, anyway—could be trusted to do the right thing.

"I'm *choosing* to put my faith in people," said Jessica. "I'm choosing to believe that people who know the truth will do the right thing. I'm choosing to believe that seeing somebody stand by the truth will inspire people to do the same."

"That's all very nice," said Val, "but it will take time for the effects of the leak to play out. I expect some rough times first. And as noble as your plan might be, it doesn't matter because *you won't be able to get in the damn building!*"

Actually, I can help with that.

A voice in Jessica's mind. A familiar voice. And judging by their expressions, everyone else had heard it, too.

"Did you...?" asked Evan.

Kim nodded. "Was that...?"

Didn't think we'd make it back?

The front door creaked open. Footsteps in the foyer. Making their way through the living room. Three people stepped into view. Jessica gasped. Merida, Celina, and...

"Coleman Wallace?" Jessica said, gaping at the newcomers.

"Yeah, it's a... well, it's quite a story," said Wallace, his blue skin flushing a deep lavender.

"Hey, babe," said Merida. She gazed across the room at Jessica.

Jessica pushed her chair back from the table slowly and stood, heart pounding. "I..."

Celina put on an affronted tone, crossing her arms. "I fight off a bunch of bad guys, nearly drown, fight off more bad guys, and then get everyone all the way back out here to the boonies safe and sound, and you're more interested in the techie nerd and your sexy girlfriend than you are in me? I'm hurt."

Celina and Wallace were both filthy, like they'd wallowed in mud. Merida looked... gorgeous. Her hair was just the right kind of messy, and her makeup had mostly been washed or smeared off. Jessica had always preferred her natural look.

"Sounds like you've got to get yourself into some high-security place," Celina said. "I'm good at that kind of thing. Do you want to see my résumé?"

She let out an exaggerated sigh and looked at Merida.

"Actually, I'm not sure that you all appreciate me enough to deserve my help."

52

Val

Jessica led her by the hand to the back yard where a pair of swings hung from an old oak tree with huge, twisted limbs that nearly touched the ground. They hugged wordlessly for a long time, and she could feel Jessica's heartbeat. Heavy, but slow. She smelled strange, like men's soap, and she was wearing clothes that Merida didn't recognize. Must have come from Evan's wife. Finally, after a long silence, Jessica kissed her quickly, let go of her, and sat down on one of the swings.

"I missed you," she said, wiping a tear from her face. "I was afraid you weren't going to make it, and then when we saw that you'd dumped the information..."

"I'm sorry we took so long," said Merida. She sat on the ground and leaned against the tree trunk. Then she reached and slid her hand under the cuff of Jessica's jeans so that her fingertips could brush the skin of Jessica's calf. A little stubble grew there. "It's... it's a long story. A lot happened."

Jessica, who wasn't wearing any shoes, rubbed Merida's thigh with her foot. "How did you know to come to the house?"

"Celina," Merida said. "When we didn't find you at the barn, we walked the path toward the house, and Celina just 'listened' for you, if that makes sense."

"So I guess you know what I'm planning," said Jessica. She took her foot from Merida's leg, stood, and walked a few steps from the swing and the tree.

Merida stretched her legs out in front of her and let her head rest against the tree. "I know. I support you—as long as you understand that I'm going with you."

Jessica knelt down in front of Merida and then turned to lie back with her head on Merida's chest. Taking Merida's hands, she pulled them around her stomach. "I know you want to."

She poked Jessica in the stomach with her index finger. "I *am* going with you. Let's just skip the argument and get to the part where you acquiesce, okay?"

Jessica chuckled a little at this. "Nothing I can say to change your mind, huh?"

Merida kissed her ear, taking the lobe between her lips and sucking lightly. Warmth spreading through her like a good shot of whiskey, she squeezed Jessica tight. Her fears of the last two days had come to nothing. They were going to be alright.

"Not a damn thing," she said, pressing the side of her face against Jessica's.

"We've got preparations to do, then," said Jessica. "We can't just waltz into a secession convention and say 'hi.'"

She stood and offered a hand to help Merida to her feet. Then she kissed her—slowly, lips parting, tongue lightly touching Merida's, a real kiss this time. Merida drank her in, thinking that the world was new, that whatever happened now, she and Jessica would be side-by-side. Together, they were going to change the world. Or the plan would end in disaster. Merida could be fine, either way.

When they pulled apart from one another, Merida took Jessica's hand, and they walked toward the house.

"You know," Merida said, "I have some ideas about how to get ourselves inside."

"You're turning into quite the spy, huh?"

Merida smiled. "Actually, it's right up my stylistic alley."

53

Val

Evan, Jacob, and Isaiah took Val to the shed behind the main house. It was a small, wooden outbuilding with double doors and two small windows. Looked like it was built to house a riding lawnmower. What was odd about it was that it had an air-conditioning unit on one side.

"This is where I keep my tools," Evan said as he unlocked the shed. He opened one of the double doors. Inside, Val saw exactly what she expected to see: a zero-turn riding mower, weed trimmers, leaf blowers, rakes, and other equipment.

"You want me to cut the grass, Evan?" said Val.

"Not quite." Evan stepped into the shed and turned on a light. "This way."

Evan led them to a set of shelves holding small tools and boxes. Evan and Isaiah took places on either end of the shelves.

"You going to help there, son?" said Evan. He was looking at Jacob.

"Oh," said Jacob. "Sorry."

He joined his brother at the far end of the shelves, and the three of them heaved to one side. The shelves slid along the wall, groaning and creaking, until Val could see a door into what looked like the back wall.

More secret doors, thought Val. "You offering us a place to hide?"

"Not here, no," said Evan. "Tools, I said. Remember? Though I do have the bunkers if you change your mind about staying a while."

He and the two boys dusted off their hands, and Evan opened the door. It was a sealed exterior door, but instead of opening to the outside, it revealed a dark staircase. Evan turned on a light and stepped through. Val, Jacob, and Isaiah followed.

As soon as Evan opened the door at the bottom of the stairs, Val smelled it: metal and oil. Even before he turned on the light, she understood. He had brought her to a room directly under the shed, and it was a damn arsenal.

Weapons racks lined every wall, each space filled with a rifle, shotgun, or pistol of some kind. Most looked vintage, but all were in excellent condition. There were also maybe a dozen bows and crossbows with arrows and bolts on wooden stands in the middle of the room. Several crates, probably full of ammunition, were stacked near the far wall.

The air in this room was surprisingly cool and dry, and Val realized that this was what the air conditioner was for. The climate control kept the weapons from rusting.

"Here we go," said Evan. "My mother's side of the family—Pawpaw Rick Heaney's people—spent years building this collection. All the way down to me."

"Wow," said Val. "Planning to fight a war?"

"I know how it looks. But like I said before, if anybody should understand, it's you."

Val walked to one of the racks, reaching out to touch an old

Springfield 12-gauge shotgun. Pump action. Wooden stock so polished that she could almost see her reflection. Beautiful. Probably a hundred years old or more, but it could have been built yesterday. Someone—probably several people—had taken very good care of it.

"I understand," said Val.

She walked the room slowly, touching each gun as she passed. Bolt-action .30-06. A few .30 .30 Winchesters. AR-15s. Chinese and Russian SKSs. Several kinds of shotguns in 12, 20, and .410 gauge. Several .22s. Some 1911 .45 pistols. Even a .50 cal sniper rifle. Many were fitted with silencers—not the regular ones, but advanced modern silencers that could suppress the sound of a gun by seventy percent and more.

"Why are you showing me this?" Val said, turning to look at her cousin, who picked up a very fine recurve bow and ran his finger along the edge of one of its limbs.

"After seeing all this, you won't believe me when I say that I've always considered myself a pacifist," he said. "Or at least close to one. I think people have a right to defend themselves. I would absolutely defend my family if someone threatened them. And I was proud of you when I heard you'd joined the Marines. But I hated the Iranian war. We never should've gone there. And even when the government was after our land, even when Tasia and I had to choose between our morals and having children—I ain't never had aspirations of armed rebellion."

He put the bow down and looked at Val.

"But my great-grandfather started this collection a century ago, and my grandmother continued building it up, and then my dad and mom. I'm the one who added the bows. I never bought any of the guns, of course. Almost all of them were illegal by the time I was a man grown. I promised Dad that I'd take care of these in case the world ever went to hell. In case it was ever needed."

Val turned slowly and looked at the collection. There were probably a hundred thousand dollars or more in this arsenal. Enough weapons to equip a small militia. Ten years ago, Val would have seen this collection and judged its owner to be a dangerous paranoid. Now she didn't. But did she need any of these guns? There were already weapons on the Dragonfly—more than she and her small crew needed already. And the goal was to get someplace where she'd never need weapons again. Still, some of these might be helpful if she found a way to do what Braden wanted and save the—

Val tried to cough but choked on blood. It filled her lungs. Drowning her. She looked down to find herself lying on the ground, blood flowing freely from a dozen bullet wounds. Men in military uniforms dragging an unconscious Braden away. Then she saw Kim on the ground next to her, a bloody hole between his wide eyes.

What the hell was wrong with her? She shivered and shook her head.

"I could use a couple of the shotguns," she said, still fighting to drive the images out of her mind. "And probably some of the ones with the silencers."

"We've shot several of those," Evan said. "They're really quiet."

"Pacifist, huh?" said Val.

"We do hunt," said Isaiah.

Evan nodded. "And in my experience, a gun is less dangerous when you understand it. So I made sure that Tasia and my sons understand them."

Val picked up the old Springfield, pumped it to check that the chamber was clear, and then aimed it at the wall. It was long and heavy—a relic of a time that had ended decades ago.

"We've got ammo for just about everything in the room," said Evan. "Full metal jacket. Hollow point. Even got rubber bullets."

"Rubber bullets, huh?" said Val. "Those might be useful tonight. I don't want to kill anybody there, but we might need to scare somebody off if things go south."

"Nothing is going to go south," said Evan. "I don't want to hurt anybody at that farm. They're good people. It's bad enough that we're taking fuel from them—even if I am leaving money for it."

"Look," said Val. She put the Springfield back in its spot. "If you're not comfortable with this..."

"Val," he said, then took a long, slow breath. "I could be wrong—*hope* I'm wrong—but I have a feeling that we're all going to have to do a lot of things we ain't comfortable with from here on out."

54

Kim

They spent most of the day preparing. Val, Kim, Braden, and Evan would be flying the Dragonfly to the Fuller farm sometime after midnight to take fuel from their airfield. At the same time, Jessica, Merida, Celina, and Wallace would leave in the old car that Merida and company had used to get here. They'd dump that car and steal another one as soon as they could, then head to Atlanta.

Kim tried not to think much about what would happen once everyone was underway, but questions nagged at him. Would he, Val, and Braden make it to the border? And what would they do once they got there? Would they ever see the others again? Val had just gotten her sister back, and both Kim and Val had become pretty fond of the others, as well.

Kim had thought himself in circles about this, but as long as Jessica insisted on going through with her intention to try to get a hearing at the convention, he couldn't come up with a plan other than the one that they were getting ready to carry out. He'd flee the country with his family, leaving Jessica and her crew to infiltrate the convention. And hopefully, Evan, Tasia, and their sons would get back to their normal lives without a visit from the authorities.

Tasia and Isaiah had left for town to get new clothes for the group, as well as cosmetic supplies for Jessica, Celina, and Merida, who were going to Quickdye their skin and hair so that they could appear to be clones. Merida even planned to shave her head, reasoning that the more conspicuous they made themselves, the less likely they were to look sneaky and suspicious.

"If we go in wearing sunglasses and hoodies," Merida had said, "they'll be on us in a minute. But if we go in looking like the Rainbow Clone Squad, they won't pay attention to us. And probably a little didunophobia will work in our favor."

To Kim—and Evan and Jessica, too—this idea had seemed nonsensical, but Val threw her support behind it. She said that she had seen enough guerrillas and suicide bombers who walked in the open completely unnoticed until the moment of the first strike. Kim suspected that Val was supporting the idea partly as a way of apologizing to Jessica for coming out so hard against her plan, or maybe to help patch things up after what happened at Artemis. Whatever the reason, though, Val's support sealed the deal.

That part of the plan settled, Tasia and Isaiah had made a list of things to get from the store—Quickdye, durable body paint, wipes made for removing body paint, colored contacts, clothes, a pair of burner phones, and a computer that Wallace would need to help carry out Jessica's plan at the convention—and left.

While they were gone, Kim helped Jacob and Val move guns and ammunition from the bunker under the shed to the Dragonfly. They took two semi-automatic shotguns, four of the .45s, and two hunting rifles. Evan also insisted that they take three of the bows, a crossbow, and two dozen arrows and bolts. As they loaded the weapons onto a golf cart and took them down to the old barn, Val kept telling Kim not to help because of his bad arm, but he wasn't about to sit around and watch the others do all the work. He had one good arm, after all.

"You're not the only hard-headed member of this family," he said.

Evan also packed old military Meals-Ready-to-Eat, fresh fruit, bags of pecans, bottled water, and other food items into crates. When Kim saw the crates stacked in the back of Evan's gas-burner truck, he protested that it was too much.

Evan laughed and leaned on the truck's bedside. "You wouldn't believe the amount of survivalist supplies that I've collected over the years. I've still got a basement full of MREs. Trust me—we've got more than enough. A lot of what I have came from my parents—they prepped and never had need for it—and so far, I haven't needed it either, thank God."

He picked up one of the green MRE bags and inspected it, almost as if seeing it for the first time.

"Truth be told," he said, "I think I've been prepping all my life because, one day, *you* were going to need it. It's interesting to think how... how connected all of our..." But he trailed off and shook his head. "Sorry. Never mind."

"What is it?" said Braden.

Evan waved a dismissive hand. "Nothing. Just a silly idea."

Kim thought that he knew what Evan had been about to say, though. The word that occurred to him was "fate," though Evan probably wouldn't have put it that way. He might have talked about "God's plan." "Providence," maybe. Or "mysterious ways." But it all amounted to the same thing, didn't it? Whatever it was that determined human destiny had brought all of them together at this moment—two distant cousins who had never been very close, the son of Japanese immigrants who'd spent his early life hoping for honor and recognition as a doctor, Jessica and Merida, Celina, and now this Wallace guy. All of them following different paths that they did not know had always been meant to converge. Kim had never been religious, but he wanted to believe that Evan was right. Hoped that all of this wasn't just an accident.

Jessica went with light pink skin while leaving her hair its natural color, and Celina chose lavender skin with red hair. Merida chose a dark shade of green.

When it was time to shave Merida's hair before coloring her skin, everyone gathered on the front porch to watch. Merida sat in a dining chair, and Tasia did the cutting. Merida cried a little as her hair fell onto the porch planks.

"You're still dead sexy," said Celina.

"What, like a sexy cue ball?" said Merida.

Tasia smiled. "It'll come back and be just like new."

Later, they ate a meal of boudin with mixed vegetables—a simple affair compared to the meal they'd had the night before, but to Kim, it was delicious. Afterward, Braden threw a football with Isaiah while Merida, Celina, and Wallace went upstairs to try to get some sleep.

Kim followed Val and Jessica down the path to the Dragonfly so that Val could check the software settings and inspect some of the hardware. Jacob tagged along, wanting to see a Dragonfly up close.

"You could come with us," Val told Jessica as they walked the trail. "We've got plenty of food and water. You could wait it out with us and see what happens first. Maybe things will go the right way on their own. Or maybe there'll be a better time for you to jump in and take a stand down the road."

Kim didn't know if Jessica could tell, but Kim knew his wife's artificially light tone was there to conceal something. Maybe lingering anger. Exasperation. Puzzlement. It was the tone that Val used when she had already tried arguing, found that it hadn't worked, and was trying a different approach.

"That's the thing about taking a stand," said Jessica. "Waiting to do it is the same as not doing it at all. Either you're taking a stand or you aren't."

They walked in silence for a minute or two before Val finally spoke again.

"I get it," she said, kicking a small rock and sending it rolling down the path. "I think. This is some kind of role reversal, isn't it?"

"How's that?"

"You don't see it?"

"She went off and fought in a war," said Kim. "And you didn't want her to go."

"And now I'm tucking tail and running while Jessica goes into battle, in a sense," Val said.

Jessica stopped walking and gazed off into the trees, as if trying to read the future in the underbrush. Or maybe the past. "I've always been in a battle. It's just... now I understand where the real fight is."

"You fought in the war?" said Jacob to Val. "What was it like?"

"Bloody and dusty," said Val. "Not much to tell other than that."

"I've thought about the military," Jacob said. "The Navy would be my thing."

"The Navy's great," said Val. "If you're a wimp, that is."

Jacob laughed an odd laugh at this—deep and throaty at first, and then the sound slipped into a high, boyish tone.

"So, the Marines, then?" he said.

"Marines."

Kim took Val's hand in his own. "By the way, you're not tucking tail and running. You promised Braden that we were going to try to find Baby Taylor and rescue her."

"I know, but not until—"

Val stopped, her hands going to her head.

"Val?" Kim put his other hand on her arm. "What is it?

For a second, Val didn't answer. She shook her head as if trying to wake up fully, blinked, and then looked at the rest of them.

"I'm... fine," she said. "Just tired, I guess."

Kim and Jessica exchanged a glance.

"Maybe we should head back and let you get some rest," said Kim. "It's been a day."

"It's been a *few* days," said Jessica.

"No," said Val. She straightened her back and started forward again. "No, I'm fine."

Agora: The Ideas Marketplace

AmericanNews Site: World Health Organization: "Samford-2" Virus near pandemic level. Almost every nation in the world reporting cases. CDC confirms cases in NYC, Jacksonville, and Brandon, Oregon.

DeshawnWhitmerCNN: In response to the announcement from WHO, the President has taken to Agora to ask secessionist states, especially Oregon, not to hold their upcoming secession conventions. "This isn't about politics anymore," the President said. "This is about the health and safety of the citizens in each of your states."

JennyThomas: In a holocast speech, Governor Brooks of Georgia has reaffirmed that her state's secession convention will begin on Saturday, despite pleas for caution by the CDC and the President. "They're not going to deter us from following our self-determined path with fear-mongering about a virus that, frankly, the evidence suggests was created by the federal government," Brooks said.

55

Celina

Secrets.

Celina had never known what they were like. They didn't exist in her world.

Everything was Laid Open to her like pages torn out of a book and scattered on the floor. All she had to do was to pick up a page. Read. Turn it over. Read.

But something was Different in this place.

Her power was Different. It was... weak?

No, that wasn't right. Not weak. Cloudy.

It wasn't that her Sight had been blinded, or her Hearing deafened. It was as if someone had put a piece of cloth over her face and cupped their hands over her ears. Glimmers of light filtered between the fibers of the cloth. Faint hints of sound made it through—but they were muffled and indistinct.

Braden thinks he's losing his power, but that's not it.

someone is interfering.

he's close—

no, not a he?

she? hard to tell.

—she or he is interfering with my ability to see and hear. Braden's too.

where?

Someone was keeping a Secret. Someone close by. Among them. Someone who never let a single glimmer of light through the cloth. Completely dark.

The process of elimination left only one person. But how to Do Something About It without letting on that she knew that there *was* a Secret...

so stop thinking about it and Do Something.

Breitbart

"Brantley Dossier" A Hoax?

By Damonda Rickard

Several notable digital forensic experts, including two Nobel Prize-winning computer scientists and seven university professors, have taken to Agora and Twitter to vehemently deny that the documents and videos released by Jessica Brantley provide any evidence whatsoever that telepaths or telepathy are real.

H.H.S. Secretary Michael Jones-McMartin goes even further, calling the Brandley Dossier a "pack of lies and terrorist propaganda" and an "insult to the memory" of his wife, Senator Nancy Jones-McMartin, who was murdered two days ago in a terrorist attack allegedly orchestrated by Brantley's sister...

CNN

DHS Ties North Carolina Terrorist Attack Directly to Brantley Dossier

By Alexia George

DHS officials confirmed this evening that they believe Jessica Brantley was present and involved in the terrorist attack at the

David Singer Institute in North Carolina, and they are in the process of filing multiple charges of murder and terrorism against her.

One agent told CNN under the condition of anonymity that the DHS's working theory is that the attack was orchestrated specifically for the purpose of giving Brantley a cover story for how she obtained the allegedly classified files in the dossier, all of which are being denounced as fraudulent by the agency.

When she released the dossier last night, Brantley did not specify how she came to be in possession of any of the files, but speculation has run rampant on the internet that she took them from the Singer Institute during...

Fox News

Ten Suicides in the Wake of the Artemis Tragedy

By Akira Hunley

In addition to the horrifying death toll in the attack on Artemis Advanced Reproduction, ten parents of unborn children gestating at the facility have committed suicide.

Three of them livestreamed their deaths on social media, collectively garnering more than two million views worldwide before Agora, Twitter, and other sites deleted them.

Several organizations have stepped in to provide grief counseling to parents and families of the victims, including mental health staff from Emory University, the Catholic Archdiocese of Atlanta, and...

American News Site

Statement on Jessica Brantley

By Carlo Moyers, News Director & Chief Editor

ANS strongly condemns the actions of Jessica Brantley. Furthermore, we had no advance knowledge of her intended actions or the contents of the so-called "Brantley Dossier." At this time, ANS is fully cooperating with authorities to help them apprehend Ms. Brantley and investigate her connection to and involvement with domestic terrorist organizations.

Ms. Brantley not only broke the law and betrayed her country, but her actions have also threatened the stability of our society and represent a terrible betrayal of the principles that she claimed to stand for as a journalist and a reporter of the...

The New York Times

Safe Reproduction: Living with an Uncomfortable Truth

By Robin Stanley

...Nobody except for a few religious nuts, political reactionaries, and members of the so-called "Alternative Feminism" movement want Safe Reproductive Practices to end. So we have to ask ourselves whether or not we can live with an uncomfortable truth: good ends can come from unpleasant means.

If the "Brantley Dossier" isn't a hoax, then the actions taken decades ago by Reginald Samford and others within the federal government were despicable. Anyone involved should be prosecuted to the fullest extent of the law, assuming any of them are even alive at this point. No matter what your preferred party or political ideology, no reason-able person could ever deny that fact.

But I defy anyone to deny another basic fact: artificial reproduction technologies and the various Safe Reproduction laws around the world have finally and definitively put women on equal footing with men. If these laws came about because of false pretenses—and that's a big "if"—does that mean that the laws themselves are unjust?

Freedom is precious and fragile, and the actions of two deranged women threaten to destroy it for women all around...

Libertarian Free World

Brantley Is Right

By Jenna Maxwell

It is absolutely disgusting to see how many journalists, politicians, celebrities, and others are beclowning themselves and clamoring to defend "Safe Reproductive Practices" after the revelations that have come out of the Brantley Dossier.

Jessica Brantley and her sister have sacrificed everything to give us the truth about the government's efforts to control women's bodies...

ABC News

The Hunter Report

ROLL VO OFF TOP

Show famous telepathic characters from movies, TV shows, and comic books

((ANTHONY HUNTER))

Imagine you thought that these people were real. Not movie heroes. But people who could *really* look into your head and see what you're thinking. People who can *really* read your thoughts and know all the secrets that you keep there. People who could possibly make you do things that you don't want to do. Imagine men who could rape women without physically forcing them to or giving them drugs.

ON CAM 1/FULL

Now let me ask you, America: if people with this kind of *illness* were, in fact, real (and even after looking at the Brantley Dossier, I have serious doubts), then don't you think the government would be right to try to control them? Even stop them from being born? Not only for our good, but for their good, too?

Agora: The Ideas Marketplace

Stephen Killian: Who the hell actually believes that crap that Jessica Brantley released?! Telepaths? Come on, man...

Vickydoll: JESSICA BRANTLEY=HERO

Paul Grigorovich: So much "footage" and "documents" are just fakerys. How do we know who to believe? The Government? Jesica Brantley? That TERRORIST Valerey Harah?

SarahB: I would LOVE to screw a telepath . . .

June Devon: As far as I'm concerned, they can go ahead and euthanize ANYBODY who can read people's minds, thanks.

Talisa Evans: Jessica Brantley was always anti-clone and anti-SRP. Now shes trying to destroy the hole thing. look at what she did at that hospital and artemis

BF109: Don't believe those videos of Jessica Brantley "destroying" that Artemis place. Y'all know that shit was faked.

Cassie Mathers: SRP was just yet another way for the gmnt to control women's bodies. That's what men always do.

VinnieVincent: That "dossier" ain't proof. Everything in it could easily be faked. Probably IS faked.

56

Val

She was dreaming of home when Celina woke her up. Tending the roses. Repairing the split-rail fence. Walking the property with Braden and Kim.

Hey. A hand shook her shoulder gently. *Val.*

She opened her eyes. Pale light from the window. A face hovering in the dark. Eyes narrow and alert. Celina.

Come on, lady. Wake up.

"What's wrong?" said Val, sitting up.

Her military instincts, slowed only a little by retirement, worked to wake up her mind. She had trained a hundred times to wake up from a dead sleep and spring into action. She had done it a hundred more times during the war. Her body was moving before she even began to assess the situation. She sat up, swinging her legs off the bed. Cold floor under her bare feet. Someone was here. DHS had found them. Braden was gone.

"Don't freak out and go all G.I. Jane on me," whispered Celina. "Not an emergency."

In the bed beside her, Kim stirred. "What..."

"Come with me," said Celina. "There's something you need to see."

Val looked at the old-fashioned alarm clock on the nightstand. Only 11:04. Still an hour to sleep. If nothing was wrong, why was Celina waking her up?

"What's going on?" said Val.

"Just trust me," said Celina.

I trust you as far as I can throw you, thought Val.

Ouch, said Celina. *That's not nice.*

Sorry.

No, you're not.

"What is it?" said Kim, who was also getting up. Down at the foot of the bed, Braden stirred on his pallet.

Celina put a finger to her lips.

Let's not wake him up. Get some shoes on and come with me.

Val and Kim had slept fully clothed, so they put on their shoes and followed Celina out into the hallway, stepping carefully to avoid making noise and waking up everyone else. Celina led them to the next bedroom down, which was where Isaiah and Jacob slept.

What are we doing? thought Val.

Celina held up her index finger in a *hold on* gesture and then eased the boys' bedroom door open. Val peered into the room, Kim looking over her shoulder. By the glow of the boys' nightlight, Val could see cast-off clothes lying here and there on the floor, a set of bookshelves, and a pair of beds.

On one bed, she could see the shape of a boy under the covers. The other bed was empty.

Where's the other one?

It's Jacob. He's not here. Come on.

Val and Kim followed. They crept down the stairs, and Celina eased the front door open. The sound of crickets drifted inside.

Will you please tell me what in the hell we're doing?

"Val? Kim?" said a voice behind them. "What's up?"

The three of them turned. Evan stood beside the stairs in pajama pants, slippers, and a T-shirt. He had the double-barrel shotgun in his hands.

"Ask her," said Val, pointing at Celina. "Sorry we woke you up."

Celina's voice spoke in Val's head. *I don't think it's a good idea for him to see what we're about to see. Especially not with that gun in his hand.*

What the hell do you want me to do?

"Celina wants to show me something," said Val. "She hasn't told me what it is yet."

Celina shook her head, annoyed and resigned at the same time. "Come on. I'll show you. But we should be really quiet."

Celina led them in a circle around the house, her head turning this way and that as if she were listening for something. Val and the others followed her lead, straining to hear sounds other than crickets chirping and the light breeze that rustled the trees. The girl took them near the equipment shed where Evan kept the stockpile of weapons, then along the edge of the woods away from the house.

"Celina," said Evan. "What are we doing?"

Either the girl didn't answer, or she answered Evan in his mind.

After a few more minutes of walking and listening, she turned suddenly and led them in a straight line across the yard toward a spot at the edge of the woods where a trail led to one of the cattle fields. When they were about twenty yards from the trail, Val realized where the girl was taking them—an old shed just beyond the edge of the woods, too run-down and overgrown to be used.

"What do you think is in there?" she said.

Wait, came Celina's voice. *Watch and listen.*

As they neared the woods and the shed, Val began to see a pale blue light through the cracks between the boards of the shed's walls. It flickered and moved a little as they approached.

"What is that?" murmured Kim.

"Video screen," whispered Val. "Or a hologram."

"Somebody's there," said Evan.

Val heard the distinctive sound of the shotgun's hammers clicking.

Drawing closer to the shed, Val also began to hear a voice. Hoarse. Deep. Probably male. At first, it was indistinct, but when they were about twenty yards away, Val began to make out some of what it was saying.

"My fucking eye started bleeding tonight! My *eye!*"

Oh, God, thought Val.

Definitely not God, said Celina's thought-voice.

Now a different voice spoke. This one sounded tinny and slightly distorted with static. Coming through a speaker.

"I know you're frustrated," it said. Male. Calm.

The person in the shed snorted. "*Frustrated?* I'm fucking exhausted! There's ten people here now, including two telepaths. Two! It was hard enough to keep the kid under control, and now this Celina chick is going to give me an aneurysm! If they weren't both asleep right now, I'd be fucking dead."

Evan started forward, but Kim and Val grabbed his arms to stop him.

"Wait," whispered Val. "Listen."

Evan let them hold him back, but his body was trembling. His breath came in long, deep blows through his nostrils.

I told you he didn't need to come with us, said Celina's thought-voice.

"I know you're tired," said the voice over the speaker. "But you're almost done. The intel you've provided has been invaluable, but we still need—"

"Wait," hissed the person in the shed. "Dammit. I've got to go."

There was a click, and the blue light inside the shed disappeared.

Footsteps on the floor of the shed. A static tingling in the air. The door creaked open, and a familiar face peered out into the woods, searching between the trees. It was Jacob.

Oh, shit, thought Val.

57

Merida

wake—

She was running. No, falling. No, she was a little girl, and she was running along an alleyway in Atlanta. Something was chasing her. A glance over her shoulder. A boy. No, a man. A man with Jacob's face.

"I'm not here to hurt anybody," he called after her.

—wakeup—

But fear drove her on.

"Merida!" screamed a familiar voice. Above. Echoing down the walls of the buildings on each side of the alley.

She looked up. Jessica. She was leaning over the edge of a building. Looking down at Merida. Screaming. "Merida! What's happening?!"

Merida tried to call to her, but her mouth wouldn't make a sound.

She glanced back. Not Jacob. A man she didn't know. Young. Dark-haired. Wearing Jacob's clothes.

Another scream. She looked up. Jessica was falling. Falling. She would hit the ground in seconds. But she never seemed to stop falling—

—wakeupyousexywoman—

Now Merida was falling. But instead of falling down, she was falling sideways. The buildings all disappeared, the world turned into a blur, and suddenly she was standing in an open, grassy area. Dense trees yards away. People. She couldn't tell who they were. Indistinct voices yelling.

Falling sideways again. Now she was surrounded by white. Nothing but white as far as she could see. Ground, sky, everything. But then Celina was standing there, her brown eyes big and bright. She was—afraid? But Celina didn't get afraid.

—staywithme—

—gottohelpmeouthere—

—i'mallbymyselfinthis—

Now she was being pulled away again. Back in the alley. Jacob was there, cowering on the ground. He peeked at Merida from behind his forearms, which were in front of his face as if to ward off an attacker.

"Please help me," he said. "She's hurting me."

—don'tlistentothatinnocent—

—getbraden—

—help—

58

Celina

I'm going to be

really

damn
lucky
not
to

59

Jessica

The falling wouldn't end. Brick walls raced past her. It was like watching the asphalt when you're in a car. But the ground never came closer. Merida never came closer. And then Merida was gone. God. She was going to fall for—

—wakebradenup—

—ever. The wind in her face. Her scream. Burning in her throat.

But now she was somewhere else. A stadium. Crowded with people. A quiet murmur as she walked toward the stage in the middle of an arena. Two groups on either side of her. Senators and representatives. The Governor, Lieutenant Governor, and Cabinet on the dais. She was almost there. They were waiting for her.

—getbradenplea—

Now she was at Artemis, in the room with Antonio, Mel, and Dr. Hayden. Flames filled the room. A column of it reached up like a hand to grip the baby's glass and plastic uterus. It blackened Hayden and Mel's skin.

"You did this," said Mel. She pointed a flaming finger at Jessica. Touched her on the chest. And the heat spread inside Jessica like anger or love. "You killed my son. You burned him."

—wakeup—

She was in bed with Merida. Making love. No, not Merida. Celina. No, Hayden. She was crying out, grasping handfuls of sheet as pleasure—no, agony—ripped through her.

She opened her mouth, and fire came out.

Her bed.

Artemis.

The alley.

Artemis.

The stadium.

Antonio's gestating room.

She was breathing flame, engulfing Artemis in it. Burning the people at the stadium. Burning the world.

—help—

60

Celina

bleed out
of
my eyes and
ears and
everything else
before
this
is

61

Val

She had only ever tried an illegal drug once in her life. This had been in Iraq, just before the Allied invasion of Iran. Her unit had been based in al-Hillah, and two nights before the invasion began, Val, Asa, and several members of her unit had tried something called *Ahlam Jamila,* a rare drug extracted from a local desert plant. Just a few drops of the yellow liquid under her tongue had made the world strange: the pale blue desert sky had turned orange; the faces of friends around her had become like reflections on the surface of the water, now looking normal, now distorted, now entirely different from the faces that she had known.

Just now, Val felt like she had taken several drops of *Ahlam Jamila*. The night air, which had been humid and oppressive, seemed charged with electricity. The hair on her arms stood on end and then relaxed—and did this repeatedly. Strangest of all, though, was Jacob's face, which seemed to melt, turn into a completely different face, and then suddenly become normal again.

"What's happening, Celina? What are you doing?"

The girl's body was frozen in a strange stance, her feet staggered and shoulder-width apart as if to brace against an aggressor. She held her hands out as if she were ready to spring on someone and bear-hug them.

notmecan'ttalk

Val turned to Kim and Evan, who appeared frozen themselves.

"We need to get back to the house," she said.

Before she could move, though, a wave of something that felt like heat, sound, and pressure hit her and sent her reeling. What was odd, though, was that the force had seemed to come from *inside* her. Or at least to move through her and not just against her. She stumbled, barely regaining her balance before she fell down.

"Val," groaned Kim.

He staggered forward, grasping at Val's shoulder for balance, and Evan fell backwards onto his ass, dropping the shotgun.

"What the hell is happ—"

Iran. Khorramsh. Night. She and six other Hellhounds were carrying out a strike on a Revolutionary Guard ground force. Beep for target lock. Asa fired missiles. They trailed white and yellow as they raced toward their—

"Val!" yelled Kim. He had her by the shoulder.

"I'm okay," she said, shaking away the vision of Iran.

Kim's face was close to hers, stricken with fear. "I don't understand it, but I think Jacob's a telepath, and Celina's fighting him."

notforlongifidon'tgetsomehelp

Val looked at Celina and the boy. Judging by sight alone, nothing was happening except that the two of them were staring at one another, each holding a strange, aggressive pose, and each wincing occasionally.

But in Val's mind and gut, it felt like standing in the middle of a storm. Invisible violence filled the air around them like the winds of a tornado or the shockwave of multiple bombs exploding at once. It hit her in wave after wave. Distorting her sight and hearing. Clouding and jumbling her thoughts. Filling her head with thoughts that weren't her own.

"How do we stop them?" shouted a deep voice. Evan. He had gotten to his feet, but the psychic violence was taking its toll. His eyes had turned bloodshot, his face flush.

needsomedamnhelphere

Celina was flagging. You could see it looking at her. Her knees and hands trembled visibly. Tendons stood out in her neck.

But then, Jacob didn't look great, either. Dark trails, almost like running mascara, dripped down his cheeks. Blood? He'd said something about bleeding from his eyes.

Clenching her fists, Val started forward. If she could just get a few blows in, she could take the kid out. But almost as soon as she'd started walking, a white-hot light exploded in her head.

no

That wasn't Celina's voice.

Val fell to her hands and knees. For a few seconds, she thought that she had gone blin—

Artemis. She was climbing out of the wreckage of a Dragonfly. Crashed. Completely demolished.

Voices around her in the darkness. Murmurs. Accusations. Blackened, smoking corpses walking. People who wanted her dead.

She could feel their hatred burning into her like the flash of a nuclear explosion.

"It wasn't me," she said. "I didn't do it."

"You destroy everything in the name of your precious 'freedom,'" said a familiar voice. She turned, and Taylor Hayden stood there. "You don't get to say—"

Kim was beside her.

"What do we do?" he groaned through clenched teeth.

Her vision returning, Val inched forward on all fours. But the farther she moved, the more intense the pressure in her head.

isaidno

Val fell onto her face now, her mouth and nose pressing into the grass. She tried to get up, but every movement sent pain tearing through her flesh. Thumps and groans on each side of her told her that Kim and Evan had also hit the ground. A sound like a whistle grew in her head, first low—

didn'twantohurtyou

—but growing quickly to a fever pitch. There was nothing that she, Kim, or Evan would be able to do now. Celina was on her own.

wantedtohaveyoualljoinus

nowjustyourson

ineedhelpfrom

The last word was cut off, but Val knew who Celina needed.

Braden! she thought, her own inner voice drowned out by the whistling sound building inside her head.

62

Celina

Over

63

Jessica

She woke with a start. Merida was next to her, jerking in her sleep. Probably having a bad dream. Had she been dreaming, too? It hadn't *felt* like a dream. It had felt more like—

—ohgoodyou'refinallyawake—

—when Francis had probed her mind.

Oh, she thought. *Oh, fuck...*

—yesthat'srightnowgetyourassmovingplease—

Jessica turned to Merida and shook her.

"Wake up," she said.

Merida groaned. Sat up.

"Oh, shit," she said, her eyes widening with realization. "You, too? I was sleeping right through it."

Jessica threw the covers off and half-jumped, half-fell out of bed. Something was happening. She didn't know what, but Celina was in trouble. She needed help that only someone like her could give.

"Have to wake up Braden!"

Jessica hurried out the door and into the hallway. When she wrenched the door open, she found Tasia and Isaiah standing there.

"Why were you shouting?" said Tasia. "Where is every—"

"No time," said Jessica, shoving past them. "Talk to Merida."

She ran down the hall to Val's bedroom, her bare heels hammering on the old wooden floor. Before she could get there, though, a jolt of something like electricity filled the air around her—

didn'twanttohurtanyofyou

—and sent her into the wall.

That... wasn't Celina, she thought.

A sound like wind roared in her ears. Behind her, Tasia, Isaiah, and Merida were all shouting, but she couldn't hear the words over the noise.

Jessica lunged at the door, dizzy, off-balance, crashing into it. She clawed at the doorknob, twisting it, and the door swung open under her weight. She fell to the floor again with a wave of dizziness so intense she almost threw up. The whole room seemed to be spinning downward and to the left.

"Braden!" she screamed. She shut her eyes tight and army-crawled on her forearms toward the bed. "Braden, wake up!"

She felt the bedskirt against her fingertips, then clutched it tight in her fist and pulled herself toward the bed. Reaching blindly with her other arm, she slapped at the top of bed again and again until she connected with the boy's legs.

"Ow!" he said. "What—"

The storm in Jessica's head suddenly calmed but didn't disappear entirely. She opened her eyes to see Braden staring down at her from the top of the bed, a strained look of fright on his face.

"Go help your mom!" Jessica screamed.

Braden seemed to understand at once. He jumped out of bed and ran from the room.

Jessica staggered into the hallway after him, but she couldn't keep up. For a few seconds, she wasn't even sure she could hold herself upright. She put out her hand and supported herself on the wall, looking down the hallway toward the stairs where Braden had disappeared. Then Merida and Wallace appeared.

"You okay, baby?" said Merida.

Jessica nodded. "Feel a little sick, but I'm okay."

Jessica forced herself to walk without support. She took Merida's hand and started for the stairs. They had to go join the fight if they could.

"We need to get down there and see if—"

Before she could finish, a burst of light—not natural light, not sunlight or lamplight—blinded her. It felt as if she'd been shut in a darkened room for a long time and then hit in the face with a camera flash. Instinctively, she covered her eyes with her hands.

Wallace let out a yell. Merida screamed. And Jessica felt herself falling.

64

Celina

though the sun stop burning
and the world stop turning—
i'll never let you

65

Val

She had plenty of faults. She could be too critical of other people. Some people thought that she was self-righteous, probably. But one thing nobody could accuse Val of was being a coward. Only now, cowering was exactly what she was doing.

Through the noise—a high-pitched scream of terror mixed with the roar of a tornado—she barely registered that she was on the ground, her knees drawn to her chest and her hands over her head. None of this did any good, because the bombardment was in her mind, not in the world around her.

Somewhere close by, Kim and Evan were alternately groaning and yelling, but Val couldn't tell which direction they were in. She groped with one hand, hoping to find Kim's body. If she could only touch him, they might both find a little more strength. Maybe—

Tehran. Yesterday Asa had told her that he wanted to work things out with his wife. It still felt like a wound right in her gut. A knife wound that...

No, she was at her grandmother's house. Fighting with Jessica, who was angry that Val had decided to join the Marines.

"How could you want to go off and kill people?" Jessica said. "But that's what you are, isn't it? A killer."

staywithmeplease

Celina's voice. Grass under her. The tips of the blades brushing against her face. The smell of green, of growth and earth and nighttime dew.

Something was different now. The scream and the roaring were still there, but weaker. The feeling that some force was passing through her—it was there, but *slower*. Something was pushing back.

"*Mom! Dad!*"

Braden.

She opened her eyes and took her hands from her face. Braden stood over her, staring toward Celina and Jacob. Feeling almost drunk, she got to her hands and knees and struggled to her feet. Beside her, Kim did the same. She wanted to tell Braden to be careful, to not risk himself for their sake, but what would she say? How did she advise him on using a power that she'd never had and couldn't explain?

"Get... behind me," he said, speaking through clenched teeth.

"Braden," said Kim, struggling to reach out and touch his son.

NOW!

The voice was in Val's mind, but so loud that it *hurt*. Val wasn't sure how that made sense. But she and Kim backed slowly away, leaving Braden to move alongside Celina, his steps small and stiff.

Together, the two of them formed a triangle with Jacob, whose face had become just a blur to Val's eyes. Was his power distorting his appearance somehow? Did an increase in strength or intensity have that kind of effect on a telepath? If so, she wished even more that her son could have been born normal.

"What can we do?" said Kim. "How can we help them?"

Before she could answer, though, Val gasped. A pair of figures had appeared on the grass in front of her. A man and a woman. Fucking. There was no other word for it. The woman was on her hands and knees, and the man was fucking her from behind. Hard. It was grotesque—a teenage boy's idea of what "hot" sex must be. The man reached forward, grasping a handful of the woman's hair, and wrenched her head back savagely. And Val's stomach turned at the sight of her own face looking up at her, a grimace of intense pain and pleasure on her face.

Then she looked at the face of the man. Of course it was Asa.

that'snotmeisweari'mnotdoingthat

Val looked at her husband, who was clearly seeing the same thing. How was this happening? The image was not in her mind. It was just feet away from her. She could see the sweat beading on Not-Val's back, face, and arms. She could see Not-Asa's ab muscles flex and tighten with each of his thrusts. Val thought that if she stepped closer, she'd be able to punch the bastard right in the face.

"It's not real," said Kim, his voice strained.

The Not-Val let out a ridiculous porn-star scream as not-Asa yanked her head back even farther, pounding her ass with his hips.

it'snotmedoingthatladydon'tblame

As suddenly as the coupling pair had appeared, another pair of figures appeared in front of Braden, and Val's stomach turned at the sight. She was looking at another version of herself now—as she had been the night that she and Braden fled their home.

This Not-Val was standing next to a copy of Braden. The boy

was lying on a rock, his eyes closed, and not-Val was aiming the muzzle of a rifle at his head.

"I'm going to kill him!" the second Not-Val screamed. She was looking right at Val, almost defying her to try and save Not-Braden.

momisthatwhatitwaslike

valdon'tletitgettoyou

While the naked Not-Val moaned and ground her ass against Not-Asa's hips, the other Not-Val fired the rifle. Muzzle blast flared, and Not-Braden's body shuddered. Real Braden screamed and covered his eyes.

It's not real, Braden, Val thought. *Please—just focus on helping Celina.*

"That's not Jacob!" shouted Evan.

Val and Kim tore their eyes from the illusions to look back at him. He stood just behind them, staring at the spot where Jacob had been standing. And when Val looked for herself, she saw what he meant. Whoever it was that stood in the doorway of the old shed, it definitely wasn't Jacob. A grown man, early twenties, slight build. Blonde hair. Fair skin. He was wearing Jacob's clothes.

gladyoufinallyfigureditout

momidon'tknowifwecandothis

You and Celina can do it, thought Val. *You are stronger than him.*

Even as she encouraged Braden, Val felt her limbs come free from the force that had held her in place. It took effort, but she moved one foot. Then the other. It felt like trying to run in a pool. Her legs, body, and arms felt sluggish. Heavy. But pushing herself, she made her way forward—first past the coupling pair, and then past Braden. Just a little farther and she'd reach the man-who-wasn't-Jacob.

Keep the pressure on him, she thought, hoping that both Braden and Celina could hear her. *Just give me the chance to reach him.*

As she moved closer, she could see that the man's whole body was trembling, almost vibrating like someone being shocked by electricity. If he was aware of Val's approach, he didn't indicate it at all. He stood with his feet fixed, his arms by his side. Muscles stood out in his neck and arms.

whateveryou'regoingtodogetitdonenow

don'tknowhowmuchlongerwecandothismom

Finally, Val reached the impostor, clenched her fist, and threw the punch. She focused on hitting with perfect form, swiveling on her feet, twisting her hips, and bringing her arm straight out.

But as she swung, the impostor's eyes widened. He became aware of Val, and his appearance changed. His face seemed to melt, and for a half-second, Val thought that it was going to become Braden's face. But she didn't give him time to finish the transformation. Her knuckles struck his mouth, sending him backwards, and his face took on its natural appearance.

that'sitladywe'vegothimnow

"That shit won't work with me!" Val said. "I know my son, and I know who you—"

A fresh wave of nausea moved through her.

momgetback

Blood dripping from his mouth, the impostor screamed at Val like a wounded animal. Power radiated from him like heat from hot coals, and Val stumbled backwards. Not-Jacob stood over her, his eyes red and swollen, his mouth twisted in rage.

getbackgetbackmomhe's

A new image appeared in Val's mind. A boy. Jacob. Sleeping.

Maybe dead. His naked body was lying on what looked like a bench seat in a pickup truck.

Oh, my God, thought Val. *Is he dead? Is that... real? Is it true?*

Before anyone could answer, something exploded behind her.

66

Merida

When the white light blinded her, Merida was standing close to the top of the stairs. She recoiled, and when she did, she felt her foot step into empty space. She groped, hoping to find purchase on a handrail, a doorknob, or maybe Wallace, but there was nothing to grab.

And then she was falling. Tumbling.

The back of head hit the edge of a stair tread, and then her legs pitched over her head and made her roll end-over-end. She tried to twist her body to get her arms underneath her and stop the fall. When she hit the floor, she felt her left forearm give way. Snap.

She screamed, and for several minutes, there was nothing but the sound of her screaming and the roaring noise that seemed to be coming from outside somewhere and from inside her own head at the same time. She rolled onto her back, clutching at her broken arm with her good hand. Halfway between her elbow and wrist, the two bones of her forearm were completely severed and moved freely. She could feel the rough and ragged ends grinding against one another, sending rays of white-hot agony up her forearm and into her shoulder.

Through the pain and the noise, she thought that she could make out voices. Fragments of sentences from multiple sources. Sometimes Celina. Sometimes Braden. Sometimes a voice that she didn't recognize. Even Jessica's voice a few times.

"Merida!"

A thumping noise. Somebody coming down the stairs.

"Merida! Are you—oh, God!"

Jessica.

"Your arm..."

More footsteps coming down the stairs.

"Is she hurt?"

Wallace.

"My arm," Merida ground out. "Broken."

"Okay," said Jessica. "Okay. Let's..."

Merida tried to open her eyes, but the pain coming up her arm forced them shut.

Breathe, she thought. *Breathe through it.*

"Let's get her to the couch," said Jessica. "Baby, can we help you up?"

Merida nodded, but she wasn't sure that she'd be able to move. The pain was bad, but it wasn't the only thing. Something that Merida could only describe as waves of *pressure* were passing through her. Coming from somewhere else. Outside. Something bad was happening outside.

Hands under her arms. Behind her back. Lifting her to a sitting position and then to her feet. The jostling sent fresh jolts of pain like electricity up to her shoulder and down to her fingertips. They helped her to the couch and sat her down. Hot tears pouring down her face, she cradled her broken arm in her good one.

"Looks like it didn't break the skin," said Wallace. "That's good."

"Got to get some kind of splint," said Jessica. "I don't know what..."

"Bet this Evan guy has some kind of first aid kit around," said Wallace. "Probably one in every room."

"I'll sit with her," Jessica said. "Why don't you look around? Or just find Ev—"

But the sound of a gun cut her off.

67

Val

The slugs from Evan's double-barrel shotgun tore through the young man's torso and sent him stumbling backwards through the shed door. As he fell, the image of Jacob dead on the ground disappeared, and both Celina and Braden collapsed to their knees.

"Where is he?" Evan screamed. He ran toward the spot where the impostor had fallen.

Val rushed to Braden and knelt down beside him.

"You did good," she said, pulling his body close to hers. "You did so good."

"Did you see it?" he whispered. "Did you see what he made me see?"

She kissed his head and breathed in the smell of his hair. "It wasn't real."

Kim was next to them now. He pulled Braden to him with his good arm. "You were a badass, kid. You saved all of us."

"*Where is he?*" screamed Evan again.

Val stood and limped toward the shed. Evan had lifted the impostor's body by the shirt and was shaking him. He wasn't dead yet, but it was a matter of minutes, maybe seconds. The 12-gauge slugs had ripped a pair of huge holes in his chest. His head lurched, and he made a gurgling sound in his throat. He was trying to speak. But his body shuddered, and finally he became still. Evan let the corpse fall with a *thud* onto the shed's rotting wood floor.

"Where is my son?" Evan whispered.

Val put a hand on her cousin's elbow, which trembled with rage. "We'll find him," she said, hoping the image that the impostor had conjured up had been a lie.

"Evan!"

Running footsteps. Tasia and Isaiah were beside Evan now. Val moved to one side to give them space. Tasia, who was carrying a flashlight, stared down at the impostor. The light made the corpse's dead eyes glimmer.

"That's not..." Tasia said.

"No, it wasn't him," said Val. "He's a telepath. He made us all think we were looking at Jacob."

Tasia cupped her mouth with both hands as if she were about to be sick. "What did he do to my son?"

"He's sedated," said Celina. She stood in the doorway now, her breath coming in gasps. Tasia turned, shining the light on her.

"How do you know that?" said Tasia, her voice dangerous.

"I read his mind," said Celina, nodding toward the impostor. "He's in... a truck. An old truck, I think. It's all grown up with vines."

Before anyone could say anything else, Isaiah pushed past Celina, nearly knocking her over, and ran into the night.

"The old F-150," said Evan. He hurried after Isaiah.

Tasia's knees gave way. She collapsed to the floor and let the flashlight roll out of her open hand. "You're sure?"

"Don't worry," said Celina. "He's alive. This guy—his name was 'Shimmer,' I think—he kept Jacob alive but sedated. I think he needed Jacob's mind as a... resource. He had to keep reading him to make sure that he had all the information he needed to fool us."

"Oh, my God," said Tasia. She turned and spat on the impostor's body. "You son of a bitch."

"This Shimmer guy was... talented," said Celina. "I need to work on some self-development, or something."

Careful, Celina, thought Val. *Show a little sensitivity for once, maybe?*

Sorry.

Tasia glanced up at Celina, frowning. "What do you mean, *talented*?"

"He didn't just trick us all into seeing Jacob, but hearing him and smelling him and all of it, too," said Celina. "And he was blocking mine and Braden's powers. I thought I was going crazy at first. Or that I was losing my abilities."

"Braden did, too," said Val, nodding. She looked back through the shed door at her son and husband, who were still kneeling where she had left them.

"And those illusions that you saw," said Celina. "You servicing that sexy Marine's knob, you shooting Braden in the..."

Val and Tasia both glared at her.

"Sorry," said Celina. "The things that he made us see—they were all out in the real world. I can make you see things in your mind, but you know that it's just your imagination. It's like dreaming. But this guy... he made you see them like they were really there." The girl's mouth spread into a rueful smile. "He had some seriously dangerous talents. I kind of hate him for it."

Tasia stared at Celina, her eyes wide—whether in disbelief at what the girl was saying or at her envy of this "Shimmer" character, Val couldn't tell. Probably both.

"It was too much for him, though," said Celina, her tone chastened a little. Maybe by something she'd heard in Tasia's mind. "He couldn't handle fooling all of us at once. I think it really messed him up when my crew showed up—"

A series of beeps from somewhere in the dark cut her off.

"What was that?" said Tasia.

As if in answer, a blue light shone from the floor near where Shimmer had fallen. The holograph projector had activated. A translucent figure appeared above its oval lens. A man in a suit. Middle-aged. Vaguely familiar to Val, but she wasn't sure where she'd seen him before.

"Valerie Hara," he said. "You and your family are..." His gaze fell to the body on the floor, and his expression turned from urgent to sad. "I know you won't think so, but Shimmer was a good person. I wish you could have known him under different circumstances."

"Who are you?" said Tasia.

The man looked up, the urgency returning to his face. "Valerie Hara, you and your family need to get moving."

"Evan! Tasia!" shouted a voice from outside the shed. Val turned. Wallace came running up to the doorway, panting. "We need help, please. Merida's arm is broken."

At this, Celina shoved past him and ran off into the darkness.

Tasia glanced down at the holographic projector, and then at Val. There was conflict in her eyes.

"Take Kim," said Val. "I'll be right behind—as soon as I hear what this guy has to say."

Frowning, Tasia nodded. "Get some damn answers for me."

"I will."

As the others headed toward the house, Val picked up the holograph projector and looked into the man's face.

"I hope that Ms. Castillo's situation doesn't slow you down," he said. "You need to be moving."

"Tell me who you are."

"Who am I?" The man crossed his arms. "Probably your last hope."

"The hell is that supposed to mean?"

"It means you need to run," the man said. "It means that they're coming for you."

68

Jessica

Merida sat hunched on the couch, tears dripping from her face onto her broken forearm. Jessica sat next to her with one arm around her waist and her face pressed into her shoulder.

"I'm so sorry, baby," she said. "We'll get this fixed."

"You're going to leave me," whispered Merida.

Jessica sat up straight and looked at her. "What are you talking about? I *love* you. I won't ever leave..."

But Merida was shaking her head. "That's not what I mean."

Before she could explain, though, the front door burst open, and people began to file inside. Tasia ran down the hallway past the stairs, Wallace ran toward the kitchen, and Braden, Kim, and Celina hurried into the living room. Kim knelt in front of Merida, while the others gathered behind the couch. Celina leaned over and kissed Merida on the cheek.

"Okay, Merida," said Kim. "Have you ever broken a bone before?"

Merida shook her head.

Jessica started to move, but Kim put a hand on her leg to stop her.

"Stay with her," he said.

Tasia came back with a splint and a first aid kit.

"You're really prepared," said Kim, taking the splint from her and setting it on the couch next to Merida.

"We try to be," said Tasia. She opened the kit and took out gauze and medical tape. "Celina, see that liquor cabinet over in the corner?"

"Yes," said Celina, her voice robotic.

"Get me a bottle of whiskey, please," she said.

"Oh, God, yes," groaned Merida. "Whiskey."

Celina went to the cabinet, grabbed a brown bottle, and brought it back.

"A little alcohol always brightens your day, doesn't it?" said Jessica. She took the bottle from Celina and unscrewed the cap.

"Damn right," said Merida. Grimacing, she slid her good arm out from under her broken one and took the bottle out of Jessica's hands. Tipping it back, she took a huge gulp.

"Slow down," said Tasia.

"Good stuff," Merida said. She took one more gulp and then handed the bottle to Jessica.

Their eyes met, and Jessica began to understand what Merida had meant a minute ago. With her arm broken, there was no way Merida could go to the convention. Jessica would either have to forget about her plans, or she would have to leave her lover behind. Merida obviously thought she knew which choice Jessica would make—even though Jessica didn't know yet herself. Or did she?

Celina's voice spoke in her mind. *She wants you to go.*

I don't believe that, thought Jessica.

Jessica? Can you hear me?

Jessica started a little. That had been Merida's voice, not Celina's.

I have some impressive talents, too, said Celina.

Jessica looked up at Celina. The girl grinned and winked, but her face looked stiff, like someone nursing a bad migraine. *Talk to her.*

Turning back to Merida, Jessica thought, *I can hear you.*

You need to go to that convention, said Merida's thought-voice. *I know how important it is to you.*

You're more important to me, thought Jessica.

"Okay, Merida," said Kim. "I'm going to need to set the bone. It's not going to feel great."

"You've only got one good arm," said Braden.

"I can help him," said Tasia. "Done this before." She took a short piece of thick dowel rod out of the first aid kit and held it up to Merida's face. "Bite down. This is going to hurt pretty bad."

Merida took the dowel rod between her teeth and closed her eyes.

I know you love me, her voice said in Jessica's head. *But right now, going to that convention is more important to you. Being with you is what makes me happy, but I can't be happy with you knowing that I held you back from doing what—*

But the thought was cut short as Tasia lifted Merida's broken forearm into an upright position. Merida let out a groan, and her teeth bit down on the dowel.

"It'll hurt pretty bad at first," said Kim. "But you're going to feel relief as soon as I get the bones into place. Just hold on."

Jessica took Merida's good hand. *I'm not going to leave you.*

Merida squeezed Jessica's hand hard enough to hurt, but Jessica held on.

I promise.

She can't hear you anymore, said Celina in her head. *Sorry.*

Using his injured arm, Kim gripped the lower half of Merida's broken forearm. He did a brave job of hiding it, but Jessica could see the muscles of his face tighten at the pain from his own injury. With his other arm, he reached to take the upper half.

"Here we go," he said. "Get ready, Merida. I'll be as quick as I can, but I have to do this right or your arm won't heal properly. Braden and Celina, hold her shoulders."

Before Kim could begin the work, though, the front door opened, and Val appeared. She had rifles slung over both of her shoulders, plus a pair of pistols and several replacement magazines stuffed into her waistband and pockets.

"Whatever you're doing," she said, "do it fast. Company's coming."

69

Theresa

She leaned forward to look through the doorway into the Dragonfly's cockpit, hoping to catch a glimpse of the world through the windshield. All she could see, though, was the glow of the plane's heads-up display and darkness beyond it.

Theresa had always wanted to fly, but because she was an "undocumented birth," her parents had never been able to take her on an airline. When Journey had told her that they'd be flying to the farm where the Haras had gone into hiding, she'd felt her heart flutter and lift a little—both with excitement and fear. What if she got sick? What if they got into the air and she found that she was paralyzed by fear?

The reality turned out not to be what she had imagined, hoped for, or feared. The back of the Dragonfly, which was made for carrying cargo and troops, had no windows—just metal walls lined with seats, weapons racks, and a pair of hoverbikes locked into parking yokes in the middle of the floor. Theresa sat strapped into a chair near the back loading ramp next to Journey and stared at the floor, the ceiling, the hoverbikes, or the cockpit so that she would not have to look into the faces of the two dozen black-clad agents who sat around the compartment.

Don't be nervous, said Journey. *You're here because you are the most gifted telepath we have ever seen. You're here because you can help people in a way that none of the rest of us can. We're going to save the telepaths at that farm, and they're going to thank us when they understand what we're doing. When they understand that we're not like the people who've been hunting them.*

And the others? Are we going to kill the parents? The people who own the farm?

Journey patted Theresa's leg. *We're not here to hurt anybody. What happens to Valerie Hara and the others is entirely up to them. We can't force our help or mercy on anyone.*

The Dragonfly banked to the right, making Theresa's stomach lurch. She leaned forward again to look toward the cockpit. This time she could see something besides darkness beyond the HUD graphics. There were other Dragonflies ahead. Maybe a dozen of them.

The cockpit's instrument console issued a *beep,* and a staticky voice spoke. Male. Both suspicious and authoritative. Loud enough to distort the speaker. "UATC-11. This is Commander Patel, U.S. Special Forces. This airspace is currently restricted to unauthorized aircraft. Please exit the area immediately. Transferring no-fly zone coordinates to you now."

Two of the Dragonflies ahead broke off from their group and flew away in wide arcs. Theresa thought that they must be circling around to get behind them.

Journey spoke in Theresa's mind. *Don't panic. This is part of the plan.*

"Copy, Commander," said the Dragonfly's pilot. "We have

been instructed to rendezvous with your group and assist you with your mission. Authorization code 117-616-P3."

"*Assist* us?" said Patel.

There was a pause. The Dragonfly continued to draw closer to the group.

"Stand by," said Patel.

They don't know about us? thought Theresa. She looked at Journey.

Commander Patel is one of the top men in the most secret special forces in the world, said Journey's thought-voice. *The work that he and people like him do is known only to half a dozen officials in the entire U.S. government.* Her mouth spread slightly into a thin, knowing smile. *But even people like him, with all of their resources, have no idea that our organization exists. DHS, DHR, FBI, CIA—none of them know about us.*

Finally, Patel's voice came over the speaker. His tone was different this time. Surprised, maybe. Almost chastened. "Authorization code accepted, UATC-11. Good to... have you along."

"Roger, Commander," said the Dragonfly's pilot. "Always happy to help."

70

Val

Forty minutes. At most. That's how long they had until the attack came, according to the man in the holograph.

Forty minutes—actually, less than that now—and then the whole property would be surrounded by DHS craft and swarming with armed agents. There would be no attempt to capture any of them—not even the telepaths. Every agent was instructed to kill anyone on Evan's property on sight.

Was the message a trap? The only person who could give her any insight was Celina. So, while Kim set Merida's arm, Val leaned the rifles against the wall by the front door and told Celina to follow her outside.

I know what you want to know, said Celina's thought-voice as Val rounded on her in the yard.

"Well?" said Val.

All I can tell you is that the man in the message sent the impostor. He—

"Like this," said Val.

Celina frowned in confusion for a second, but soon realized what Val meant. "The impostor's job was to spy on us, find out our plans, and encourage division between you and Braden. That's about all I could get out of him."

Val's stomach turned. Division between her and Braden. That made sense. All the anger she'd felt over the last day. All the unwanted thoughts and images of Braden being hurt. Whoever the impostor had been, he'd been trying to force her to change her mind about trying to save the baby. She'd made a promise to Braden, and they—whoever "they" were—wanted her to break that promise. Was it to keep her from getting to Baby Taylor, or was the goal just to drive a wedge between Val and Braden?

"Some of what I said might not be exactly right," said Celina. "Trying to make sense of his mind was like being stuffed in a washing machine with a bunch of torn-out book pages and trying to read them."

"Dammit," said Val, clenching her fists. She had escaped the first attack at their house, fought off three Dragonflies, rescued both Kim and Braden, and fought off more Dragonflies and the Wasps at Artemis—only to fail here?

The man in the holograph definitely wasn't on their side, but they couldn't ignore his warning. So, did they stay and try to put up a fight? If they did, could they possibly survive what was coming? There was no way it would be just a couple of Dragonflies.

Did they run? If they decided to run for it, did they just pile up in a car and drive, knowing that the authorities would be on the lookout for any vehicle that left Evan's property? Did they steal cars from here on out? Did they take the Dragonfly and try to steal fuel?

"I'm a little tired after the fight with Fake Jacob," said Celina, "but I'm recovering, and my range is pretty far. I could influence anybody who came close enough to me. Make them do things."

Val, who had been pacing the grass and clenching her fists while she ran through all the possible scenarios, stopped and looked at the girl. "What do you mean?"

Celina rolled her eyes. "I'm saying that I can *help*. If it comes down to a fight between us and those Dragonfly things, I can help. Braden could, too."

"You could help."

Val considered this. Telepaths against Dragonflies. And there were more than just the Dragonflies themselves to contend with. Each Dragonfly had long-range weapons, and most importantly, they had drones. Celina and Braden wouldn't be any good against drones.

Val could take out drones with a gun, and she was betting that Evan and Tasia could do it, too. But in the dark, the drones had the advantage. They'd all be shot with sedative darts—or bullets—before any of them could target a drone with a rifle or a shotgun.

And then there were the troops. A troop carrier or two would probably drop troops away from the house to sneak up on them. Even if they survived the drones and Celina and Braden took out the Dragonflies, they'd be overwhelmed by troops. Braden and Celina were powerful, sure, but they'd only be able to keep up the fight so long.

Val stared at Celina. Troop carriers. UAD-9s. *Wait.*

"I think..." she said. "Maybe..."

A plan was forming in her mind. An insane plan. But a plan.

That's right, said Celina's thought-voice. *"Maybe" is good enough for me. That's all I've ever needed.*

71

Jessica

The minutes it took to set Merida's arm seemed like hours. Merida screamed and bit the dowel so hard that Jessica thought she would break it (or her teeth). Meanwhile, Kim grimaced at his own pain while he struggled to put Merida's broken bones back together.

Finally, Merida's screams and groans turned into gasps of relief, and she fell still, her clothes drenched with sweat. The dowel rod dropped from her mouth and fell into her lap. There were deep teeth marks in it.

"All done," Kim said in a strained but soothing voice. "The worst is over now."

Braden, who had been helping to hold Merida still, let go of her. "Remember what you told me, Dad? When we were sitting in the hayloft, waiting for everyone to come back?"

"That I wasn't up to setting a broken bone with a bad arm?" said Kim.

The boy's face lit up with pride in his father. One day, Jessica hoped, he would have someone to brag to about this. *Let me tell you about what* my *dad did...*

Tasia went to work wrapping and taping the arm, and Kim sat

back on his heels to rest. His breath came in slow heaves. He was clearly breathing through pain of his own.

"I'm sorry," Merida half-whispered, half-sobbed. "I'm sorry."

"You did great," said Kim.

"But your arm..."

"Actually, it's doing much better today than it was yesterday." Kim looked at the shoulder where he had been shot. "I'm a bit amazed, to be honest. Maybe we've got luck or the universe on our side, after all."

"Yeah," said Tasia with a wry smile. "'Luck.' Or 'the universe.'" She looked up at Merida. "Okay, baby. I'm about to put on this splint. Let's just do it slow and easy, okay?"

"Thank you," said Merida. "Thank you both."

"My pleasure," said Kim.

"I'm just sorry it happened," said Tasia.

Watching the woman work, Jessica felt a sting of shame over her behavior at dinner the day they arrived. She'd always thought of herself as anything but judgmental, but she had judged Tasia and Evan before she'd even spoken a word to them.

Merida's spirits seemed to have lifted. She smiled at the superhero print on the sling that Tasia was helping her into.

"I guess *we're* the superheroes now," she said. "Except I'm slightly tipsy, and my arm is broken. So I can't be a superhero anymore."

"Baby, you've already done your superhero work," said Jessica. "You might have saved us and the rest of the world singlehandedly. I just sat here, waiting for you to come back."

"Well," said Wallace. "It wasn't exactly 'singlehandedly.'"

"Sorry," said Jessica.

"And I didn't do it for the world," said Merida, all trace of mirth draining from her face. "I only did it for you."

Val and Celina came back inside. "I'm sorry to rush things, but we've only got a few minutes. It's time to hunker down."

Kim got to his feet. "We're not running? Taking the Dragonfly?"

Val shook her head. "No time for that. They'd run us down easily. Tasia, Evan mentioned some bunkers. I think we should break into two groups and head for those."

"We'll need to hurry, then," said Tasia. "They're a little ways from the house. And I need to find my men."

She crossed the room to an end table, opened it, and brought out two of the Couriers.

"Take this," she said, handing one of them to Val. "And listen close. Head down the path to the front field. When you get to a sign that says, 'Home is Where the Heart Is,' turn right into the woods. You'll see a rusted-out Chevy El Camino with no wheels. It's got a wooden floor in the bed. Looks like a piece of plywood. That's the hatch. Lift the end of it, and the hatch will open, and you'll find a ladder. The hatch locks from the inside. It's fully ventilated and well stocked, so you can stay in there a while."

"Got it," said Val. "Take Celina with you. She knows what the plan is."

"Celina is coming with me, Val," said Jessica. "You're not going to use this to keep me from going to—"

"Yes, you're going to the convention," said Val. "You, Celina, and Wallace are all going. It's the right thing to do, and I want you to do it, okay? But we have to survive this first."

Jessica gaped at her.

"If you leave now, you'll get caught. But as soon as this is over, you should get out of here. In the meantime, hunker down with Tasia and Evan while Celina does her thing."

Trust me, said Celina's thought-voice. *I'm going to be magnificent, and you're going to want to be there to see it.*

If Val heard this, she ignored it. "I'll be communicating with you throughout, and when it's safe, I'll give you the go-ahead. You'll want to drive north at first, for maybe an hour, then ditch the car and look for another to take back south toward Atlanta."

"Why north?" said Wallace.

"DHS is going to find that car, and when they do, we want them to think you're headed away from Atlanta," said Val. "Just make sure you switch to a vehicle that won't be trackable."

"Val," said Jessica. "I'm..." She hesitated, biting her lower lip. What was she trying to say? She was glad for everything that had happened in the last few days because it had brought them back together? That she was sorry for the way she'd acted after Artemis? "I'm glad..." But she didn't know how to say it. All of these years making her living through words, and she couldn't find any now.

"Dammit, Jess," said Val. She crossed the room, threw an arm around her sister, and pulled her close. "Me too, okay? Me too. Now let's move."

72

Theresa

The pilot's voice came over a speaker in the ceiling of the cargo compartment. "Ten minutes out, ma'am."

Journey didn't respond aloud. Listening in on her mind, Theresa could tell that she was speaking to the pilot telepathically. The other UAD Dragonflies—the ones that carried only a pilot and a gunner—were going to create a perimeter around the property, send out drones, and close in toward the house slowly. Meanwhile, the troop carriers would land at a barn where Hara had parked her stolen Dragonfly, disable the craft, and spread out for a ground search.

"So what are we going to do?" said Theresa. "How are we supposed to get the telepaths out safely if these guys are there to kill everyone?"

We'll start at the house. It should be a lot faster for us to reach out and find them telepathically than a bunch of commandoes can with night vision goggles. If you sense anyone, try to persuade them to come with us. Just be careful about what you let on.

I might not be able to help it, thought Theresa. *They're telepaths, too, you know.*

Stick with the truth. We're here to rescue them. We're liberators.

We protect telepaths and their freedom. We'll protect the non-telepaths, too—as long as they don't get in our way. Don't try to lie. You just need to be careful how you present *the truth to them.*

Theresa considered this. When you spoke to people, you could use your tone and body language to shape how the other person heard what you had to say. She'd practiced this skill during the time that she was at the Institute, and that had paid off when Bowen underestimated her abilities. Could you do the same thing with thoughts?

I promise, said Journey's voice, *you're ready for this. Remember, there's nothing to hide from them. The only thing that matters is how you* think *about the truth when you're dealing with the two telepaths. We're the good guys here, and they'll see it when we rescue them.*

How can we get close enough for them to see the truth without them killing us first?

Journey smiled and nodded first toward the cockpit and then at the agents sitting across the compartment. *That's what* they're *here for. And they're good at what they do. The best. What you need to focus on is gaining the trust of the two telepaths. They've met you before. You were locked up with one of them. They've seen you do something... unpleasant, it's true, but you can use even that to your advantage. Show them that we're trying to save them from being driven to that same extreme. We're working to make sure that no one—telepath or otherwise—has to do anything like that in self-defense ever again.*

It was true. Theresa didn't regret what she'd done at the Institute—except maybe what she'd done to Simmons—but she did long for a world where people didn't have to do that kind of thing.

In any case, you're hanging back for most of this mission, thought Journey. She gestured at Theresa's injured arm, which was in a sling. *Your time will come when we have neutralized all threats of violence. Then, at that point, you'll be the one in the spotlight. And maybe you can use that arm to get a little sympathy.*

Commander Patel's voice came over the speakers. "Eight minutes out from the farm, UATC-11. I advise you to keep your distance from the main targets. Use long-range weapons, and in any case, do not approach the targets."

While he spoke, Journey unbuckled her safety harness and walked to the Dragonfly's cockpit.

"Like you, Commander Patel," she said to the dashboard microphone, "I am fully aware of the *peculiar* nature of our targets. We can take care of ourselves just fine. If we all follow our orders, we'll be able to help one another out."

There was a pause. For a second, Theresa thought that Patel wasn't going to respond. Finally, his voice crackled over the speaker in a stiff tone. "Understood. I hope that when this is over, you'll have a good report to present to your superiors."

"Do your job," said Journey, "and I'm sure I will."

73

Val

"Okay, everybody," said Val. "Let's head out and get hunkered down before the barbarians arrive."

The small bunker under the El Camino only held four, so it had been decided that Merida would accompany Val's family so that Kim could keep an eye on her arm. That meant she and Jessica would be separated during the coming fight, and they were saying their goodbyes in the front yard while Wallace picked out a weapon for himself from Evan's armory.

He returned with an old Turkish semi-automatic shotgun and held it up high, his eyes wide. "You know, if you had told me a week ago..." He shook his head.

"You'll get used to it," said Val.

Wallace slung the shotgun over his shoulder. "I hope not."

"You look pretty sexy with a gun," said Celina.

Even in the dark, Val could see the clone blush. But he also smiled and straightened his back, drawing himself up to his full height.

"Still," he said, recovering. "It's great that you have such a prepared cousin. He's like the Tom Bombadil of crazy, right-wing preppers, you know?"

"Who?" said Kim.

Wallace's eyes widened. "Tom Bombadil? You know, from..." He shook his head again. "Never mind."

"My sexy nerd," said Celina.

When they returned to the front yard, they found Jessica and Merida sitting on the front porch steps. The two women kissed one last time and then stood to go.

"Got everything?" Jessica said.

"I sure as hell hope so," said Val, glancing around at Kim and Braden, who were loaded down with enough guns to invade Russia. "What a life I've dragged you all into."

"Just so you know, I'm still pissed at you for shooting me," Jessica said, hugging Val. "Never going to forgive you for that."

Val drew back from her sister and looked her in the eyes. "*Sedating* you. And just so you know, I'm sorry."

"But you'd do it over again," said Jessica. She offered a matter-of-fact smile.

"I would,"

The two women looked at one another, unspoken words hanging between them.

"I wish there was more time," said Val finally.

Jessica's eyes glistened in the moonlight. "Maybe when this is all over..." But she didn't finish the thought. Val didn't dare finish it, either.

When they reached the "Home is Where the Heart Is" sign, Val shone her flashlight into the trees. She could just barely make out the El Camino. Just a rusted-out body with no wheels sitting on dirt and accumulated pine needles. It had been sitting there for decades, apparently, and the pine trees had just grown up around it.

"That's it," said Val. "Let's get inside."

She and Kim led the way, stopping to hold branches up for Braden and Merida to pass. When they were close, a pair of raccoons emerged from the El Camino's bed, their beady eyes shining in the flashlight's beam, and then sprinted away. Merida started.

"Never seen a raccoon?" said Braden.

"I'm from Atlanta, Will Robinson," she said. "The wildest animal I ever see is a furry."

"What's a furry?" said Braden. "Oh... That's... Wow..."

Val shone the light into the bed of the El Camino. Pretty clever. From up top, the hatch looked like a piece of plywood lying in the bed. It was even set at an angle to make it look like it had been laid there haphazardly. But when she reached in and lifted the end closest to the tailgate, it swung upward on a pair of spring-loaded hinges to reveal an underside with a rubber seal to keep out rainwater.

"Evan and Tasia, you're my heroes," said Merida.

"Will you two be okay to climb down?" said Val.

"I can do it," said Merida.

"Me, too," said Kim.

"Okay," said Val. "I'm going first. Braden next. Then Kim and Merida. After you're all settled, I'll come back up for the guns."

The shaft descended about ten feet below ground to a bunker that was about twelve-by-twelve. Shelves lined one wall with canned food, MREs, jugs of water, first aid supplies, and stacks of toilet paper. A pair of small vents with fans on one end of the room ventilated the bunker. There were only two cots, but Val didn't think that more than two of them would be resting at any point, anyway.

"I would say that I'm surprised at the paranoia," said Merida when Val returned with the guns.

"Do you think we can just... wait it out here?" said Braden. "Maybe they won't be able to find us, and then..."

He looked at Val hopefully, but she shook her head. There was no point in trying to lie.

"They'll turn over every rock and leaf until they find us," she said. "Our only way off this property is a Dragonfly."

Merida sat down on one of the cots, moving gingerly because of her arm. "What's the brilliant plan?"

"I don't know about *brilliant*," said Val. She looked at Braden, at his not-quite-a-man's face, and let out a slow breath. "Braden and I are going to fight. He's going to fight his way, and I'm going to fight mine. And when we've taken enough of them—"

"Sssshhhh!" Braden hissed, holding up a hand. "Listen."

74

Theresa

Patel's voice crackled over the speaker again. "Truthbringer-9, we have spotted a vehicle on the edge of the property. Looks ready to provide an escape. Break off and disable. We don't want any of our targets making a quick getaway when we aren't looking."

"Acknowledged, Commander," said a second voice.

"Hold that order, Truthbringer-9," said Journey, her tone low and commanding. "Priority override code 8701."

"Acknowledged," said the second voice.

"Please explain, UATC-11," said Patel, clear annoyance in his tone.

Theresa left her seat and joined Journey at the doorway into the cockpit. Even though she could barely see anything real in the darkness beyond the windshield, the HUD displayed graphics that put blue, orange, and green highlighted outlines around geographic and architectural features below them. From here, Theresa could see outlines of the forest, fields, roads and trails, and several buildings. Also highlighted were the outlines of the Dragonfly squadron that flew in a V-shape ahead.

"Commander," said Journey, adding a little more power to her voice, "we are already aware of that vehicle and the plans that our targets have for it. I have agents in place to prevent anyone from using it to escape. That is all you need to know. I repeat: priority override code 8701."

Pause.

Theresa looked at Journey's face, who was frowning up at the overhead speakers, waiting for Patel's response.

If this prick gives me one word of back-talk, said Journey's voice in Theresa's mind, *I'm going to have his ass disappeared faster than you can say—*

"Understood," said Patel. "Truthbringers 1 through 12, make a perimeter around the property. Banshees 1 and 2, proceed to the barn. UATC-11..."

He paused here, and Journey smiled.

Men really can't stand for a woman to tell them what to do.

"...please proceed according to your own orders. We will sweep the property and meet you at the primary residence."

But sometimes they learn.

"Copy that, Commander," said Journey.

Why stop them from disabling the car? thought Theresa.

Journey cast Theresa a knowing glance. *Daniel and I talked this morning. Jessica Brantley is about to try something drastic in an attempt to make sure that people don't dismiss the leak as a hoax. Daniel's got a good plan to discredit both Brantley and the leak. At least in the minds of a lot of people. And 'a lot' is all we need.*

Theresa shook her head. *Sounds like he has plans for everything.*

Journey nodded and offered a matter-of-fact shrug. *You respond to situations as they come up. You make plans, and then the situation changes. You make new plans. That's how you survive in this world.*

Theresa thought of the stunt she'd pulled at the Institute. *Yeah.*

Journey gave the Dragonfly's pilot and co-pilot instructions on how to approach the house, but Theresa paid no attention. Another unwelcome image flashed in her mind. Her parents were standing over the bodies of the senator, the general, and Simmons. Her mother stared down at the corpses and the blood on the pavement, her mouth agape. That hurt enough. What hurt more was her father, who was looking right at her. Tears poured down his face, and his hands were held out at his sides in a gesture of confusion. Maybe despair. How could she have turned into this? his expression asked.

She turned away from the cockpit and focused her attention on the black-clad agents, who had all collected rifles and begun loading them. An idea occurred to her. The beginning of an idea, rather. A suspicion. But she suppressed it. Pushed it as far down in the depths of her thoughts as she could. She would revisit it later, when she was alone.

For now, she busied her mind with the plan that was about to be carried out. Since she was both injured and inexperienced at this kind of mission, she was to stay in the crew area while Journey and the other agents carried out their jobs. She would become important at the end, when the two telepaths and their companions boarded the Dragonfly—willingly, she hoped. If necessary, Theresa would be there to manipulate the non-telepaths.

Journey stood beside Theresa and addressed the agents. "Alright, everyone. We're here with a specific goal in mind, but that goal may evolve as we learn about the willingness of the objectives to come with us. Primary objectives are two telepaths. Best case scenario is that they board this plane willingly. They need to *want* to join us, so let's prove to them that it's in their best interest to join us. Secondary goals include doing the same for their parents and others who accompany them. But if that proves impossible..."

She stepped forward, her arms crossed. *We're here to do good,* said her thought-voice. *But we can't force mercy on those who don't want it.*

"You have your orders," she added aloud. "Good luck. Stick to the plan. But be ready for all contingencies. In any case, we get the two telepaths on this ship. Tranquilize them only as an absolute last resort."

75

Val

She climbed the ladder up the shaft, brushing cobwebs away and batting away a couple of small spiders. The musty smell reminded her of all the times she'd had to crawl under the house and help Kim make plumbing repairs. She stopped about halfway up. Any farther and a Dragonfly pilot would probably be able to detect her heat signature. It was a good spot, though. From here, she could definitely hear the sound of Dragonfly engines.

"Come on up, Braden," she called down the shaft.

The boy climbed slowly and squeezed in next to her. Their bodies barely fit side-by-side in the cramped space. Val could feel Braden's heart pounding through his arm, which was pressed into hers.

"Sense anything?"

Braden closed his eyes. "Maybe. Not sure yet."

Val pressed the button on the Courier. "Celina?"

"I'm here," she said, her voice sounding hollow, which meant that she was positioned in the shaft of the other bunker. Her usual tone—slightly sultry, slightly wised-up and arrogant—was gone. She genuinely sounded nervous. More than likely, she was terrified of being caught and sent to another laboratory for experimentation. The fact that she was also currently squeezed into a shaft that led down to an underground bunker probably didn't help.

"How are things on your end?" said Val. "Can you hear anything? And can you *hear* anything?"

"We can hear the Dragonfly planes," said Celina. "Not sure how close. I'm sensing someone, too, but it's not strong enough for me to do anything interesting with them yet."

"Okay," said Val. "As soon as you're able, see what kind of mischief you can get up to. You remember what we talked about."

"I remember. Out."

Nothing for you? thought Val.

Braden shook his head. *Still listening.*

"You're looking especially for one separated from the others," said Val. "Preferably one of the smaller ones. A UAD-9, though I don't know if you'll be able to tell the model designation by reading minds. You'll know them by how many minds you sense, though. The UAD-9s only carry two people—a pilot and a gunner."

"I know," said Braden. "And if I find them, you're going to kill them, right?"

"I'm sorry," said Val. "Yes. And if all goes as I plan, you're probably going to kill some of them, too. I need you to be okay with that. *They*—" Here, she nodded toward the room at the bottom of the shaft. "—need you to be okay with it. It's what—"

What our lives depend on. I know.

I'm sorry, Braden, she thought. *But we have to play the cards in our hands, not the ones we wish we had.*

"I know," he said. "I'm not complaining."

Celina's voice came through the Courier. "Got a couple of them close by. Is it weird that one of them is thinking about sex right now? I mean, these guys are here to maim and kill a child—sorry, Braden—and they're up against one of the most badass terrorists in the world—sorry, Val—and they're going to have to deal with one of the most dangerous telepaths alive—that's me... sorry, Braden—but one of these guys is flying along in his Butterfly-or-whatever-it's-called and thinking about bending some woman over and—"

"Can you do anything *helpful*?" said Val.

The girl paused. "Sorry. Hi, Braden!"

"Celina..." said Val, anger rising in her throat. *Keep it calm*, she reminded herself.

"Oh, I can always do something *useful*," said Celina. "Hang on."

"Anybody nearby?" said Val to Braden.

He shook his head.

Val climbed up the rest of the shaft, slid the bolt to unlock the hatch, and listened to the night air. She could hear Dragonfly engines in the distance, but nothing close yet.

"Watch this, sister," said Celina through the Courier.

Noise in the distance. A blast of automatic gunfire. A change in the pitch of some of the Dragonflies' engines. Acceleration. An explosion. A second explosion along with the sound of something smashing through trees. More gunfire, and then a third explosion.

"Did she do it?" called Braden up the shaft.

"How was *that*, Missuz Badass Marine Lady?" said Celina.

"Yes!" said Val.

But now she heard something else. The whine of a Dragonfly engine was coming closer. A lump of excitement and fear rising in her throat, Val closed the hatch and hurried down the ladder. Braden moved aside to give her room.

"I hear him," said Braden. "The pilot. *Them*, I mean. They're coming our way."

"Focus on the pilot," said Val. "Make him land in the path that brought us here. One of the UADs ought to fit. And then when they land—"

"Oh, shit," said Celina on the Courier. "That's not good."

"What?" said Val.

Silence.

76

Jessica

Jessica sat quietly on one of the four cots while Celina did her thing up in the shaft. Evan waited at the bottom of the shaft, a rifle in his hand, and Isaiah busied himself with offering everyone food and bottled water.

How's it going? thought Jessica.

Celina heard her. *Piece of cake. Like swatting flies. Give me another twenty minutes, and I'll bring these guys down.*

I'm glad you're so confident, thought Jessica.

You know, making guys 'go down' usually means something different...

Jessica sighed. *Now, Celina?*

Fine, fine. Anyway, I'm going to take care of these guys, and then we'll be on our way to Atlanta for you to give your Gettysburg Address, or whatever it is.

Thank you.

"What happens when this is over?" said Jacob—the *real* Jacob. The boy was sitting beside his mother on the cot across from Jessica, his knees hugged to his chest. He looked exhausted and scared, which she couldn't blame him for—and extremely nauseated, too, which Kim had said was a normal effect of being kept sedated for so long.

"We'll figure that out when the time comes," said Tasia. "Right now, I'm just going to trust in the Lord to..."

She trailed off and looked up at the bunker's ceiling. A roaring like a continuous peal of thunder came down the shaft and reverberated inside the bunker. It started low, but quickly got louder until the walls trembled and years of collected dust rained down from the ceiling and walls.

"It's coming down on top of us!" yelled Celina from the shaft.

Suddenly, an explosion rang out somewhere above them. The shelves that lined the walls shook, rattling cans and other items down onto the floor. One can struck Jessica's foot, sending a jolt of pain all the way up to her knee.

"Get down!" said Evan.

He ran across the bunker toward Tasia and covered her body to shield her, Jacob doing the same from her other side. To her surprise, Wallace and Isaiah rushed her way—both leaning over her in a protective huddle.

Up in the shaft, Celina was screaming.

77

Val

"Are they okay?" said Braden. His arm trembled against Val's.

"Celina's tough," said Val, suppressing the panic that fought to claw its way up from her stomach into her chest. "So are Jessica and the others. They'll be fine. *You* focus on your job. Is that Dragonfly close enough?"

In the darkness of the shaft, Val could just barely see his eyes, which were wide with fear and staring into hers.

"Braden, focus," she said.

Sorry.

He squeezed his eyes shut and turned his face toward the top of the shaft. In the quiet, Val could make out the whining sound of lift engines. It was definitely closer.

I can hear him, said Braden's thought-voice. *Them. They're scared.*

Can you control them? Focus on the pilot.

Braden became very still, his fearful trembling subsiding. *He's...*

In her impatience, Val started to respond with encouragement but decided against it. Better to let him do what he was good at.

The noise of the Dragonfly's engines grew louder. Above them, wind began to faintly rattle the hatch at the top of the shaft. Then, there was the hollow sound of air swirling in the bed of the El Camino. He was doing it.

"Not too close," she whispered. "They can't land here. Has to be the trail."

Braden didn't respond. His body was completely still now, but not relaxed. Val could feel the muscles in his arm. Stiff with tension. Even his chest seemed completely still.

"Breathe," she said, keeping her voice low. "Don't forget to breathe, or you'll pass out before you get them landed."

His arm seemed to relax a little, and he took in a slow breath.

"That's it," she said.

Ten more seconds of stillness. Fifteen. The Dragonfly grew louder and louder. Wind whistled around the hatch above them. Finally, Val heard the soft *thump* of a landing gear hitting the ground.

"Okay," whispered Braden.

"Keep hold on them," said Val. "Can you make them exit the vehicle?"

He nodded, eyes still closed.

"You're doing great," said Val. "I'm proud of you." She squeezed his shoulder. "Whatever happens, don't let go of them until I can take them out. And remember the plan after I'm in the air."

She looked back down the shaft. Kim and Merida stood at the bottom looking up.

"I love you," she called down to Kim.

"I love you, too," he said. He held up the Courier that Val had given him. "Stay in touch."

"Go kick some ass," said Merida.

Hurry, Mom, said Braden.

• • •

Climbing out of the shaft and shutting the hatch, she could see the Dragonfly sitting on the trail, its four insectile wings raised into their vertical positions. The lift engines on the underside of the wings were still idling, so a strong breeze blew in all directions from the craft and made the trees sway back and forth. Two figures, the pilot and the gunner, stood stiffly beside the cockpit, their bodies silhouetted by the Dragonfly's red landing lights.

Okay, Braden, thought Val. *Read the pilot's mind and look for a location transponder.*

Pause. The pilot turned toward the Dragonfly.

Okay, said Braden. *Got it.*

Does he know the deactivation code?

Pause. *Yes.* His thought-voice sounded strained.

Just one more thing and then you're done, thought Val. *Make him turn it off and remove it.*

The pilot climbed onto the Dragonfly and leaned into the space between his seat and the gunner's. After a minute, he turned from the cockpit holding a small box.

Good job, Braden, Val thought. *Now hold what you've got. I'm about to take care of them.*

Hurry, replied Braden.

Val climbed out of the El Camino's bed and ran full speed at the two agents. No point in sneaking while Braden had a hold of their minds. When she reached the edge of the woods, she drew a 9mm from her waistband and put two shots into each of the men's torsos. As they crumpled to the ground, a wave of nausea swept through her, making her head swim for a moment.

Oh, God... came Braden's voice.

Val's stomach lurched. She hadn't even considered what it would be like for him to be in those men's heads when she shot them.

Let go of them now, Braden! she thought, praying that he could hear her.

When she reached the two men, they were both staring up at the sky, their limbs twitching.

"I'm..." she said, but the word *sorry* died on her lips. She wanted to be sorry. Thought that she ought to be. But she couldn't manage it. She put a bullet into both of their brains, and they fell still.

That done, she fired two shots at the transponder box, which lay on the ground beside the pilot. Then she put the pistol back into her waistband and took the Courier out of her pocket.

"Kim," she said.

"I'm here," her husband replied.

"It's done. Getting into the air now. If you can manage it, get up in that shaft and be with Braden."

"Already there," he said. "Don't worry about us. I'm with him, and he's going to do great."

Val felt a pang at this. They should never have had to ask anything like this of him.

Heroes don't kill, he had told her just a few days ago. He wasn't right about that—at least not in every circumstance—but it was cruel that he was having to learn the lesson this way.

"Hopefully, Braden, you won't have to do any more," said Val. "But if you get a chance to bring one down, do it."

Now Merida's voice came through the Courier, a little faint and hollow. "Good luck!"

"Thanks," said Val.

She climbed into the UAD's pilot seat and pressed the button that closed the canopy. A voice was coming through the comm.

"Truthbringer-7," it said. "Where are you? Your transponder has been deactivated."

Truthbringer. Val shook her head, sighing. At least she and her crew had been given an unironic callsign—"Workaholic-5"—and a completely honest nickname—"The Hellhounds." Whoever had named this squadron had either a grim sense of humor or a spectacular belief in his own importance.

She looked over the controls for this Dragonfly. Very similar to the troop carrier that she had been flying. Just more cramped. She found the toggle that switched weapons controls to the pilot. Armed EMPs and rockets. Prepped all machine guns. Set the small turret on the front to target all moving ground targets. Readied the two drones for deployment on automatic search and neutralize mode.

"Val?" said Evan through the Courier.

"Hey," said Val, grateful to hear his voice. "Are y'all okay?"

Merida broke in before he could answer. "Is Jessica okay?"

"We're okay now," Evan said. "Celina's brought down at least two Dragonflies so far. Looks like one of them crashed pretty close to our entrance shaft. Got hairy there for a minute, but we're good now."

"Truthbringer-7," said the voice through the UAD's communicator again. "Please respond."

Val turned down the speaker's volume. Then she drew back on the control yoke, tilted the wings downward, and revved the lift engines. The UAD began to ascend with a whine, and the HUD's graphics turned red as it switched to attack mode.

"Jessica's okay?" she said, killing all of the UAD's exterior lights and turning on the HUD's night vision.

"I'm fine," said Jessica.

"You'd *better* be fine," said Merida.

"I'm fine, babe," said Jessica. "I love you."

"I love you, too," said Merida.

"Let's keep the line clear except for essential communication," Val said. She settled the Dragonfly into a hover just below the tree line. Several more blips appeared on her radar. All within range of weapons.

"Will do," said Evan.

"Things are about to get pretty loud," Val said. "Braden and Celina, stick to the plan. They're going to stay focused on me, so take advantage of that. Just make sure you don't mistake *me* for one of those bastards. When it's all over, everybody who's riding with us into the sunset should meet at the barn. Everybody who isn't, good luck. I love all of you."

"Go get 'em, sister," said Jessica. "Love you."

"Love you, too," said Val.

She set the Courier on the side console and turned her attention to the UAD's instruments. There were Dragonflies about a hundred yards to her right and to her left. The squadron had formed a circle around the farm. It looked like they were going to close the circle and meet at the house.

"Here we go again," she said.

She pulled back on the control yoke and rose above the tree line. The UAD's targeting system could handle four bogeys at a time, so she prepared to lock onto the two Dragonflies to her right and the two to her left. Once missiles were fired, every vehicle in the air would converge on her. She *had* to take these four out immediately. Otherwise, she'd be completely overwhelmed before she had any chance of taking out more.

Stay alert, Braden, she thought, not sure if he would hear her.

I'm right here with you, Mom, he replied. His range was wider than she'd ever guessed.

She pressed the targeting button. Four beeps. Four Dragonflies. Four missiles.

Fire.

78

Celina

Maybe she was wrong about people.

Take Evan. Right now, he was standing at the bottom of the shaft into this Hole in the Ground, thinking about Doing the Right Thing.

He had a gun in his hand, just in case he needed to Defend the others.

It was cute, really—the male instinct to Protect. But his thoughts were continually interrupted by the memory of shooting the Impostor who had drugged his son and hidden him away to use as an information source. He Felt Sorry for killing that guy. Guilty.

But just now, if he had to do it again, he would.

Celina had never known a man she would call "good." The men in her life had been anything but. Bowen had been the culmination of a long series of men who would, if given the chance, use every woman (and sometimes men) they met like a cut of meat wrapped in plastic and sold from a cold container at the local grocery store.

Noise above. A Dragonfly.

She reached out, grasping in the dark for a mind-hold. For a second, she thought she had him, but now the Dragonflies were moving faster. Something had Stirred Them Up. Like little bees. Like bees in a hive.

Then the explosions came.

Boom. Boom. BoomBoom.

Each one sent a little tremor through the earth that surrounded her like a womb. Isaiah—who was actually a pretty skittish kid for someone who had grown up with parents who worked to be Always Prepared, though he did a good job hiding it—let out a little yelp when a *crash* followed one of the explosions. One of the Dragonflies had gone down somewhere nearby.

With one of the explosions, the closest one, she felt a pair of little *blips* as minds winked out like lights. Death had felt momentous and terrifying during that hell-show at the Institute a couple of nights ago. Every time someone got shot, Celina had felt it like a knife in her heart. But the explosions of the Dragonfly-things made death feel small. No different than a birthday candle being blown out by a child.

happybirthdaytoyou

There!

She felt it. Him. A mind somewhere above. Reaching out. Grasping. Looking through his eyes. Windshield. Glowing graphics.

happybirthdaytoyou

STOP.

A rush as he pulled the Dragonfly to a stop. Hovering.

What are you doing? someone wanted to know. Behind. The same question from a speaker in the console.

DOWN.

The ground rushed up. Someone was screaming. Faster. Faster. Treetops. Ground. Blip.

Another crash nearby. A small tremor in the ground around her.

happybirthdaydearceleeeeeeenaaaaa

Evan called from below. Wanted to know if that was Celina.

Oh, you can always count on me.

happybirthday

to

But what had she been thinking about? Right. People. Evan. Good man. Not perfect, but as close to good as you were going to get in this world. Protect the Family. Follow the Rules. The *real* Rules, anyway.

Then there was Tasia, whose thoughts were on what she and her family would do after today. If they even survived today, that was. They'd have to Go on the Run. The farm would be taken away.

She had told Val that she wanted to help—and had meant it—but she couldn't help feeling a tug of Resentment and Anger at the situation. Anger at Evan, who had maybe been *too* eager to help with this fledgling revolution.

Did his—*their*—obligation to Help override his duty to his family? To himself? She even felt anger at her God. Why would He let this kind of thing happen to people who had Resolved to do their Christian Duty? Why were the Good punished for being Good? But then Tasia scolded herself for all this Resentment. Nobody was *really* Good, after all.

Two days ago, Celina would have agreed with this completely. Evan, Tasia, Jessica, Val, Wallace, and Merida—that beautiful, sexy woman most of all—had taught her that this wasn't quite right. There *were* Good People in the world. But the Good People were, ironically, the people who knew that they weren't *Very* Good—but did the best they could, anyway.

Another mind close by.

But there was something different this time. It was moving more slowly than the others. More deliberately. Searching.

No, that wasn't quite right. He had Noticed Something Suspicious. Too many Dragonflies had crashed in this precise spot for it to be a Coincidence.

So he was looking. Zeroing in.

Oh. Oh, I see.

This one had a Weapon. Something that had been brought here especially for Celina and Braden's benefit.

She started down the ladder, hoping that being farther underground would make a difference, but before she had even descended two rungs, she felt it.

First, a high-pitched sound like a dog-whistle.

Then, a vibration.

And then, an ear-splitting scream.

Well, she thought as she fell down the shaft, *they figured out how to get me. Sneaky, sneaky bast—*

79

Val

Val hovered below the tree line, just ten feet above the ground. She eased the yoke back and guided the plane along the dirt trail about a hundred yards from where she'd fired the missiles. Then she set the Dragonfly down on the landing skids.

"That's four," she said into the Courier. "Plus two more that Celina brought down. So about half. Y'all still okay, Evan? Celina?"

No answer.

"They're probably just busy, Val," said Kim.

She looked over the UAD's weapons controls. Six hundred rounds in the minigun. Twelve missiles left. Two EMP rockets. That was plenty. Plus, there was something else called an "SC-12." She could toggle the weapons control to allow it to fire with the trigger on the control yoke, but she had no idea what it was. A laser, maybe? She'd never seen an "SC" designation before.

About fifty yards ahead, another Dragonfly flew across the path, shining a spotlight down on the ground. As it moved to the east, Val lifted off again and moved forward, staying low until she reached the place where the other UAD had passed over the dirt trail. This was a new kind of fighting for her. If she, Braden, and

Celina could avoid an open dogfight and pick off one or two bogeys at a time, then they all stood a better chance of making it off the farm alive.

Suppressing the thought of how much it would cost Evan, Tasia, and their sons to help them, Val turned the Dragonfly toward the east and ascended to the treetops. As the other UAD came into view, it spun around suddenly. It had picked her up on radar. And like a pair of alert eyes, the spotlights turned from the ground and pointed right at Val.

Val switched to the minigun and fired before the other UAD could get its nose all the way around to face her. Bullets clattered into its fuselage, canopy, and wings. The pilot tried to veer away, but his forward left wing splintered and tore free, tumbling toward the trees. With half of the lift engines on that side gone, the Dragonfly's nose suddenly dipped to the left, and the lift engines on the other side flipped the whole craft over into a barrel roll toward the earth.

"Seven down!" Val shouted into the Courier.

Her radar beeped at her. Missiles. Two of them. One east, one west.

Time to see what this thing can do. She accelerated to full, the force slamming her head back against her seat. She dropped between the trees on either side of the trail. That probably wouldn't make the missiles lose their lock on her, but if she played her cards right...

A bloom of flame somewhere behind her. One of the missiles had hit a tree or the ground. Still another one trailing her. Trees raced past her on either side. Very little room to maneuver. Distance between her and the missile closing fast. Fifty yards. Thirty.

She yanked the yoke back and to the right slightly. The UAD, which was much more nimble than the troop carrier she'd been flying, pulled up into an almost vertical climb. The right-side wingtips barely missed the trees as Val curved around in a wide arc. At the same time, she deployed flares, leaving a bright trail behind her.

"Come on," she groaned through her teeth.

Boom. The missile had either struck a tree or been detonated by the countermeasure flares.

"Val," said Kim. "Something's going on. We're hearing something like footsteps—"

Silence.

Still trying to catch her breath, Val picked up the Courier and headed back toward the El Camino and the bunker. "Say again, Kim."

Nothing.

"Kim."

Two bogeys on her radar. Closing fast. Val targeted them and fired four missiles. Then she dropped below the tree line to head back toward the bunker, her heart racing. What had Kim meant by *footsteps*?

"Kim," said Val. "Braden. Anybody."

As she came around a curve in the trail, the radar sounded an alert. There was another UAD ahead, hovering just above the ground.

"You sneaky fucker," said Val. He'd used her own trick against her.

The instruments issued another alarm. Radar lock. Flashes of light from the other UAD as it fired its minigun. Val jerked the control yoke back and flew right over the other Dragonfly. Several bullets struck her underside, but she managed to escape the worst of it. Emerging from the trees, she wheeled the Dragonfly around to face the bogey. But another alarm sent her reeling to the right, and she barely escaped another volley of bullets. The other UAD was just yards ahead. She could just barely see the silhouettes of its pilot and gunner through the canopy.

Using the Dragonfly's lift engines to swing in a wide circle around her opponent while still facing him, Val fired a missile, praying that it would hit—and also that the concussion didn't knock her out of the sky at such close range.

Both prayers were answered. The rocket hit the side of the UAD, blasting off two of its wings and sending the craft hurtling into the woods in a flat spin. The explosion also knocked Val's Dragonfly backwards, but she pulled back on the yoke, throttled up the lift engines, and killed the propulsion engine, regaining control just as she scraped along the tops of the pines.

"Kim!" she gasped into the Courier. "Braden! Evan! Somebody answer me!"

"Val," said Kim, his voice weak. "We're... I don't know what... happened... It was like—"

Kim's next words were drowned out—not on his end, though. Suddenly, the Dragonfly started to shudder and vibrate. As if they were running out of power, the lift engines slowed and nearly stalled. Val's stomach felt sick as the Dragonfly dropped several feet before the lift engines recovered and settled it back into a hover.

Then the same thing happened again. The Dragonfly shook—harder this time—and dropped, the lift engines sputtering and hesitating as if they were stalling out. At the same time, a sickening droning sound filled Val's head. Pressure built in her ears until she thought that her eardrums would rupture. Shrill alarms sounded from the instrument console, but soon even that noise was drowned out by the rumbling, roaring sound that shook Val's whole body. It was like an explosion happening in slow motion.

Struggling just to keep from passing out, Val turned the Dragonfly wildly, hoping to spin away from whatever was causing the sound that threatened to shake the UAD into pieces. As she did, the Dragonfly's flickering HUD graphics highlighted something on the ground below—something shaped like a man, but taller and much bulkier. Then the HUD and instrument console blinked out. The lift engines died completely, and the Dragonfly plummeted. For a few seconds, the ground rushed up, and then everything turned black.

80

Celina

She landed on Evan, who'd been standing at the bottom of the shaft. The two of them tumbled to the floor, Celina on top of him. Their faces were close together.

Another time, she might have taken advantage of this situation to cause some Mischief, but the whole world—the ground, the air, even Celina's *brain*—was vibrating.

It was like listening to death metal music on headphones with the volume at max.

whatinthehell

Evan was rolling her off him.

Crawling away.

Yelling something that she couldn't understand.

Tasia, Isaiah, Jacob, Jessica, and Wallace were all on the ground, their hands over their heads. From here, Celina could see Jessica's face. Tears poured from the woman's eyes, and her cheeks were pulled back from her teeth in a frozen grimace.

Celina's skin and flesh were rippling as vibrations moved through her body. The taste of iron in her mouth. Something on her lips. Blood. She'd bitten her tongue.

it'slikewindandsound

adamnwindandsoundweapon

Then Evan was moving back toward Celina again. Toward the ladder and the shaft. Dragging a rifle by its strap.

you crazy redneck whatthehelldoyouthinkthat'sgoingtodo

His body shaking like someone with a palsy, Evan got to his feet, hung the rifle over his shoulder by the strap, and began to climb the ladder. His shirt and pants flapped against his skin as if whipped by wind.

comethehellbackhereEvanIcan'tsaveyouoranybodyelsethistime

And then, just as quickly as it had started, the thunder and the vibration stopped. Celina's ears rang in the silence. Tasia was mouthing something, but the words sounded like they were coming from underwater.

Using a cot as support, Celina dragged herself onto her knees. A muffled squealing sound from somewhere up the shaft. Had that fool opened the hatch? She reached out with her mind. He was trying to go outside, the idiot.

Stop it, you crazy man!

The sound of gunfire. Muffled by the ringing in her ears. But still loud enough to hurt.

81

Theresa

She had spent most of her life waiting, and now she was having to do it again. She stood by the loading ramp at the back of the troop carrier, leaning her shoulder against a large hydraulic pushrod that raised and lowered the ramp. Journey had gone to the house with two of the armed agents. Two more stood guard at the bottom of the loading ramp, their rifles held at the ready across their chests. A few more had loaded what looked like rocket launchers onto the hoverbikes and flown away down dirt roads that snaked through the woods. The rest had spread out on foot and disappeared into the trees.

Sounds came from other places on the property. Explosions. Gunfire. Crashes. And another sound that she couldn't identify—something like the rumbling of a train.

She reached out with her mind and listened to the two agents at the bottom of the ramp. One of them was thinking that if they managed to pull this mission off without any losses, that might be enough to get him the medal that had eluded him for the last few years. The other had just remembered that tomorrow was his anniversary. His wife had died several years ago.

One of their radios crackled.

"—some kind of sonic weapon," said a voice. "Never seen anything like it before. Looks like they brought those as a deterrence against the telepaths." Static. "—think we might lose this one, ma'am."

There was a pause. The two agents looked at one another. One of them—the one itching for the medal—thought, *Well, fuckaduck.*

Now Journey's voice came through the radio. "'Losing this one' is not acceptable, Lieutenant. Find our objectives, neutralize any threats to their lives, and then get them out. This is exactly the kind of thing I meant when I said that—" Static. "—will deal with any fallout from your actions tonight, as long as we—" Static. "—objectives."

"Roger, ma'am," said the first voice. "Out."

The agent with a dead wife looked up the ramp at Theresa.

"It's best you stay hidden, ma'am," he said. "Looks like Patel's forces have some kind of weapon designed for people like you."

Good thing I have you and him to protect me, she spoke into his mind.

"Yes, ma'am," he said, nodding once.

Soon, Journey came back from the house, her face dark and strained. She carried a small maroon book in her hands.

These cowboys, she said in Theresa's mind. *Playing with their toys. Their guns. Their planes and rockets. And now some kind of sonic cannon. I wanted to do this nice and quiet, but it looks like we're going to have to make a mess of things. The Senator, Silvan, and the others are going to be working overtime tonight to fix the optics of this thing.*

She stopped in the grass a few yards ahead of the loading ramps and the guards, gesturing with her hand for Theresa to come down.

One day soon, very soon, our mission is going to succeed. And there won't be any more need for the toys these children love to play with so much. No more fighting. Just peace and righteousness. The Olympians coming down from their mountain to live among the people. You're going to help us make that happen.

Theresa descended the ramp, passed between the two agents, and joined Journey on the grass.

"Ma'am," said one of the agents, "I don't think that's..." But he trailed off as Journey cast him a glance.

"It's fine," she said.

"Yes, ma'am," said the agent.

Journey handed the book to Theresa. Gold, blocky letters on a vinyl cover. THE BIBLE: NEW REVISED STANDARD VERSION WITH DEUTEROCANON.

You never had a religion, did you?

Still looking down at the book, Theresa shook her head. Her mother had owned a Bible, something she had inherited from Theresa's grandparents. But Theresa's family had never been church-goers. Her parents had believed in God and in doing what was right, and that had been the extent of their religion.

We're going to build the kingdom of heaven, said Journey. *Right here on Earth. The gods will protect the peace, and the people will rejoice and prosper.*

82

Val

Her ears rang, and a faint smell of smoke filled her nostrils.

Braden, she called out wildly with her mind. *Please answer me.*

But even if they were okay, she had flown too far from the bunker for their minds to be able to touch.

Braden!

She unbuckled the safety harness and groped at the side console. Buttons. Gauges. A small touchscreen. Finally, what she was looking for. She lifted the Courier to her mouth. Pressed the button.

"Anybody," she said. "I'm down. Anybody there?"

Pause. Click. A whispered voice.

"We're okay."

Tasia.

"Got to be quiet," she said. "I'll get back to you in a minute. Turning down the volume now. Won't be able to hear you."

Fuck, Val thought. What about Braden and Kim?

Her eyes adjusted to the darkness. The UAD had fallen straight down and landed with its fuselage against a pair of pine trees. Two of its wings must have scraped against the trees on the way down. They were bent into the vertical orientation and pressed against the tree trunks. Bits of bark and pine branches were scattered on the canopy above her. The canopy itself had remained in one piece, but it had shattered so badly that the thousands of small cracks made it look like frosted glass. She couldn't see anything past a few yards except for the dark shapes of trees.

All power was dead. Faint tendrils of smoke rose from the instrument panels in front of Val and on either side of her seat. What the hell had hit her? An EMP would do this to a vehicle's electronics, but that was no EMP. It had been more like a *sound* weapon.

SC-12, she thought. Sonic cannon?

A thudding sound outside. Rhythmic, like footsteps. Heavy. Something else, too. A mechanical sound. Electric motors. The whirring of servos.

Val pulled the pistol from her waistband, checked to see that a round was chambered, and pulled back the hammer. The sound came closer. Then she could feel the *thumps* in the Dragonfly's floorboard and seat. A shape loomed in the darkness outside. Big. Blocky. Had they sent robots after them? Telepaths couldn't affect robots, after all.

One of the thing's big arms reached out and wrenched open the canopy. Much of the glass gave way, raining down on Val like sharp pieces of sleet. Squinting to keep the glass from her eyes, Val raised the pistol and put two rounds into the hulking shape that was bearing down on her, praying that nothing ricocheted at her.

The bullets had no effect. The machine loomed closer, reached out with its other arm, and wrapped a huge hand around her neck and jaw, lifting her out of the seat.

Gasping for air, Val fired more shots into the machine's torso as it dragged her out of the cockpit and held her up in the air. Pressure built in her head until she thought her eyes might bulge right out of their sockets.

"You are one hell of a pain in the ass," said a voice through a speaker.

It was a suit. A mechanized suit. Maybe eight feet tall. The head was a hemisphere of glass reinforced by a metal frame. Inside it, a man's face leered at her from behind an HUD with green and yellow graphic displays.

"*Fuck you,*" Val tried to respond, but the only sound she could make was a strained grunt.

The body of the mech suit was thick with multifaceted armor plating, and there was some kind of device on the chest—a silvery, oval ring surrounding a black concave dish with a half sphere in the middle. It reminded Val of a speaker. There were two more of these on its shoulders.

"Already found where your son and the *other* freak are hiding out," he said. "Now there's just you to take care of."

Twisting at the waist, he swung the arm and upper body of the mech suit and let go of her. Val flew like a doll and landed in the dirt, rolling several yards. Rock and glass dug into her skin as she rolled, and when she came to a stop, her face smacked into the ground. For a few seconds, her vision went completely black.

Heavy footsteps. A series of mechanical clicks and the whirs of turning servos.

There was an explosion somewhere, and then a crash in the trees. Had someone else shot down a Dragonfly? Who could have done that? It had definitely exploded in the air—like it had been hit by a missile. Then came a second explosion and crash. This time, Val was sure that she'd heard the sound of a rocket engine precede the explosion. What was happening?

"Don't let that give you any hope," said the man in the suit, his tone almost matter-of-fact. "You're dead."

Val looked up. The mech suit stood with one arm raised. The barrel of a gun ran the length of its forearm. It was pointed right at her.

83

Celina

These men and their Causes.

These soldiers just Following Their Orders.

Doing Their Duty.

One of those silly men was somewhere up above. Only, he wasn't just silly, was he? He was Devoted. Which meant that he was very dangerous.

And Evan was up there with him.

Her ears still ringing, Celina staggered toward the ladder and started up. Behind her, Jessica was shouting something, but Celina couldn't understand. Telling her to stop, probably.

Then, Jessica was grabbing at her ankles as she climbed into the shaft. Celina reached out with her mind and forced her to let go.

Up the dark shaft.

Toward the darkness above.

Darkness and noise. Evan was yelling something and firing his gun. Other sounds, too. An explosion up in the air somewhere. A crash. Tree trunks splintering and breaking.

And the Minds.

They were *loud.*

Louder than the gunfire and the explosions.

To someone like Celina they were, anyway.

Evan's mind was yelling. Energy radiated off of it. The problem with being Good like Evan and Tasia was that any time you encountered something truly Bad like the people who had come here tonight, it filled you with the kind of rage that could kill a person. Why would God allow it?

There was another Mind nearby. A soldier. The kind of person who thought that he was Good because he was just here to Follow Orders and to Do His Duty.

To Celina, who had been molested by her own drunken stepfather and locked in an underground cell by people who wanted to exploit her power, this was the worst kind of Evil of all—a person who mistakenly thought that he was here to do Good.

The True Believer.

The one who couldn't conceive of the possibility that he might be Wrong.

If you couldn't even imagine that you might be Wrong, then nothing on Earth could stop you from doing all sorts of horrible things in the name of "Good."

She reached the top of the shaft, which opened into an old covered horse trailer. Evan had left the hatch open. She stepped out onto the trailer floor. Evan had stuck the muzzle of his gun out of one of the air slots in the trailer wall and was letting loose on someone.

Spent shells flew from the gun and clattered onto the metal bottom of the trailer. Through the noise, Celina could hear Evan's thoughts.

Come on, you bastard.

He had already taken out two soldiers. There was just one last one crouched behind a fallen tree a dozen yards or so from the trailer. Celina reached out with her mind and found that soldier, that Last Man Standing, and took hold of him.

Up.

He slowly stood from behind the tree, his mind in a panic. He was fighting Celina's control, and it was taking all that Celina had left to keep hold of him.

Dammit, you...

As if something had broken loose, Celina felt her mind give way, like a dam that had finally broken against the weight of the water. The soldier raised his rifle, and two gunshots rang out at the same time. One bullet struck the soldier right in the face. The other hit Evan in the chest right above his heart.

"No!" Celina shouted.

Evan fell backwards against the wall of the trailer and slid down until he was sitting on the floor. With the rifle lying across his lap, he leaned his head back and closed his eyes. Blood poured from the wound in his chest.

Thou shalt not kill, he thought.

"You can't die now!" said Celina. She knelt next to him. "We're too damn close!"

"Listen," he said. "I know... Val said to wait for her signal, but if... you three are going to head out... it might be time."

"Evan!"

Tasia climbed out of the shaft and crawled across the trailer floor to where Celina knelt by Evan. She pushed Celina aside and threw herself on her husband. Her body shuddered as she wept.

"We... we done good," said Evan, his voice gurgling. He put one hand on the back of Tasia's head and stroked her hair.

"Oh, God," said Jessica, as she climbed out of the shaft. "Evan, no..."

"Y'all... get going," said Evan. "Might be the only... chance you'll..."

His hand fell from Tasia's head and thumped onto the trailer floor.

Tasia pressed her face against his. "*Evan!*"

Jacob and Isaiah climbed out of the shaft, their faces blank. Celina moved aside to let them through, but they both just knelt by the shaft opening, staring at their mother and dying father.

"Don't you dare leave me!" shouted Tasia.

Gathering what strength she had left, Celina reached into Evan's mind.

If you're listening, Evan thought, the sound coming from somewhere far away, *tell Tasia I love her. And tell her I'm... I just... I just tried to...*

But the thought went unfinished. Evan's head lolled to one side, and his dead eyes stared at the opposite wall.

Jessica put a hand on Tasia's back. "Tasia, I'm sorry."

"Go," Tasia whispered. "Go do what you need to do. Just get the hell away from me."

84

Val

A whirring sound behind her. A gentle wash of wind over Val's body. The whine of electric motors. And then a *pop* like a grenade gun.

The man in the mech suit looked up in time to see something small and metal fly through the air and stick to his chest with a *clink*.

To Val it looked like a grenade. But instead of exploding, it sent blue jolts of electricity radiating across the mech's torso. The man screamed and stumbled backwards a few steps before falling onto his back. The mech suit shuddered and then fell still.

"Valerie Hara!" shouted someone behind her.

Val turned. A hoverbike was floating several yards behind her, its rider dressed in black tactical armor and holding something like a grenade launcher. "U.S. Special Forces. We're here to rescue you and your family."

Rescue? U.S. Special Forces? Bullshit.

Val got to her feet. Bits of stone and glass were buried in her skin—arms, shoulders, back, face, head, legs. Everywhere. Streamlets of blood dripped down her arms and face like tears. What the hell was this?

"Please trust me, ma'am," said the man. He raised the shield that covered his face. He was young and had earnest eyes. "You're too injured to run, and there are more people coming to kill you. I can get you to safety. If it makes you feel more secure, go and grab the pistol you dropped. Actually, go get it even if it doesn't make you feel safer. I could use a gunner while I drive. Just hurry."

Just a few days ago, Asa had spoken to her in the same way. He'd even handed her a pistol to make her feel safer. And in his selfish way, Asa had honored that trust in the end—after he had already betrayed her, of course.

This guy was a different story from Asa, though. Where Asa was now as jaded, cynical, and opportunistic as a person could get, this guy had all of the duty-bound sincerity that Val had seen in her fellow Marines fresh out of basic.

Knees and elbows shaking, she got to her feet. "If you're here to rescue us, who are the others? Where's my son? My husband? I'm not going anywhere without them."

"I'm not leaving without them, either, ma'am," said the soldier. "I'll explain on the way."

Val walked to the pistol and picked it up. While she did this, the soldier eased the bike toward her. He had closed his face shield and kept glancing in every direction. The tinted plastic of his face shield had a pale glow from its HUD and AR display.

"It's an honor to help you, ma'am," he said. "You've got one hell of a distinguished service record."

Val stared at him—or rather at her own reflection, distorted by the curved plastic of his face shield. For a second, she thought that she should just shoot him and take the bike. Could this whole thing be an elaborate ruse? An act?

Val pointed the gun at the mech suit. "What if I shoot him?"

"Be my guest," said the soldier. He raised his face shield again. "But be quick. We have to go."

Val studied his eyes. She *could* just shoot him and take the bike. Find Kim, Braden, and the others, and get the hell out. They'd taken down most of the Dragonflies at this point. She could clean up the rest with the troop carrier they'd come here in, follow through on Evan's plan to steal fuel, and then leave the country.

"I'll tell you what," said the soldier. He gripped the bike's controls and swung it around Val so that the front end of the bike was pointed at the mech suit. Frowning, he pressed a button on the bike's dash. A gun with a laser sight rose out of the bike's front body panel. The laser targeted the mech's head.

"Wait," said Val.

The soldier looked at her.

"Is he out? Did that EMP you hit him with knock him out?"

The soldier nodded. "Unconscious, at least. Might be dead, actually."

Val glanced at the mech suit. That bastard had meant to kill her. The barrel of the gun on the suit's arm had been aimed right at her face. So why leave him alive? If not for the soldier on the bike, she'd be a headless corpse right now. Thinking of Braden, though, she knew why. You did what you had to do—and *only* what you had to do. Shaking her head, she took a last look at the mech suit and then climbed into the bike's passenger seat.

"Let's go," she said. "Take me to my family."

But the soldier didn't turn the bike around yet. He fired the gun—a single, echoing blast—and shattered the mech's face shield and turned its pilot's head into a bloody pulp.

"Better safe than sorry," said the soldier. Pulling the controls to the left, he turned the bike around and started forward.

Glancing at the shattered glass of the mech's face, Val pulled the pistol from her waistband and held it at her side. Even now, she didn't trust the soldier. Asa had taught her better. But she wanted to at least see where he planned to take her before she decided to act.

"Have your people found my family?" said Val. "Are they safe?"

He touched a button on the bike's dash. "Command, this is Hicks. Have you located the Hara family yet?"

"We have a location," replied a voice through the bike's speaker. "Heading there now. We'll send you the coordinates."

The soldier—whose name was Hicks, apparently—switched off the communicator. "We'll head that way. I hope that you trust me now. It's important that soldiers trust—"

A blast of gunfire from their right. The bike rocked to one side, flinging Val off and into the dirt. This time, she was no rag doll. She pulled her arms in, letting herself roll along the ground and into the grass before springing to her feet.

Immediately, she was firing the pistol at the place in the woods where the fire had come from. Behind her, there was a crash and the sound of clogged propellers as the hoverbike hit the ground. Electric motors whined to a halt. Then Hicks was firing into the woods, too.

Val ran toward the trees to take cover, firing over her shoulder as she went. When she reached the edge of the woods, she crouched behind a large pine trunk and lay down cover fire.

"Come on!" she screamed at Hicks.

Still firing his rifle into the woods, the soldier rushed toward Val and took cover behind a tree a few feet away. Their attacker fired another volley.

"Got you," said Hicks. He raised the rifle and fired a grenade from the under-barrel launcher.

An explosion erupted in the woods where the gunfire had been, and then there was silence.

"Not bad for an old lady," Hicks said. Val couldn't see his face in the shadows of the woods, but she could hear a smile in his voice. "I'm Lieutenant Hicks, by the way."

"I guessed," said Val. She kept watching the tree line across the way. There could well be another attacker. "Think that was the only one?"

"Not sure," said Hicks. "I guess what we do now is—"

But a *thudding* sound cut him off. Then Val heard the distinctive sound of a sharp blade being drawn out of flesh and body armor. The soldier let out a strangled gasp before crumpling to the ground.

"Hicks!" she screamed. She drew her gun and fired into the shadows behind where Hicks had fallen. Nothing.

Before she could react, a foot flew out of the darkness and knocked the gun out of her hand. Instinctively, Val threw up both her arms to block the next blow, and a blade sliced into her forearm. Grimacing at the pain, she dove to one side and rolled, trying to get out of the woods and into the open so that her attacker would have to come into the moonlight and be seen.

She leapt to her feet and spun—just in time to see the next attack coming from her left. A big man with black stripes on his face and arms. At least six feet, probably two-fifty. All muscle. Double-edged tactical knife in his hand. He came on fast, the knife swinging and jabbing.

Her lungs burning, Val dodged several swipes of the blade before blocking his knife arm with her forearm and hooking her fist into his ribcage. This barely had an effect on him.

Val ducked and ran left, hoping to get behind him for a side-kick in the kidney, but the soldier moved fast in spite of his size.

His right leg, thick as a tree trunk, swung high in a crescent kick and crashed right into her temple.

Pain radiated through her skull and down her spine as she fell onto her stomach.

"Fucking bastard," she spat.

Raising her head from the dirt, she spotted it. The pistol. Just out of her reach. All she had to do was lunge, grab the gun, and put a bullet—

But the thought of reaching the gun died as a huge fist struck her in the back—and drove the blade of the tactical knife into her chest, splitting one of her ribs. She gasped. Tried to scream. But between the blade in her left lung and the knee that pressed down on her spine, she could barely draw a breath at all.

85

Kim

The thundering sound seemed to last forever. He and Merida sat against the wall with Braden between them, each trying to shield him as best they could while also protecting themselves.

Kim knew it was futile, though. If the attack continued, their eardrums would pop first. Then what? The capillaries in their fingers and hands would shake apart. Then the same would start happening all over their bodies, including the lungs and brain. Irreparable damage. Death.

But Kim felt something else besides the piercing pain of the vibrations. An electric tingle, like when Braden was having a nightmare. Even now, Braden was still trying. He was still fighting. All his life, Val and Kim had been terrified of something happening to him, had wanted nothing more than to protect him—and here he was, protecting his father right to the end.

Then, just as Kim thought that he might die as blood vessels ruptured throughout his body, the sound and the vibrations stopped. As if a switch had been flipped, the unbearable pressure and pain were gone in an instant. And then Kim realized he was still screaming—Braden and Merida, too. One by one, their voices died, and Kim's ears rang in the silence.

"Oh, God," he said. He didn't so much hear the sound of his own voice as he did *feel* it. It was like yelling while wearing a good set of ear plugs. "Braden..."

He pressed his mouth against the top of the boy's head, breathing him in and kissing him.

I don't know where Mom is, said Braden's thought-voice. Though Kim could hear it clearly, it sounded fainter than usual. Was that just exhaustion? Or had they hurt him somehow? *I can't sense her. But... wait...*

He lifted his head. Tears were streaming down his cheeks. On the other side of him, Merida shifted slowly to one side and then rubbed her face with her good hand. The sound of her clothes shifting against the concrete floor and cinderblock wall sounded muffled, too. They would all be lucky not to have permanent hearing damage.

There's somebody there, Braden said. *Several people. Soldiers and... and a...*

A different voice spoke in Kim's mind now. A woman's voice. Soothing.

I know you're afraid, she said. Looking at Braden and Merida's faces, Kim could see that they heard it, too. *I'm not here to hurt you. I'm about to come down the ladder. Please do not attack me.*

She's telling the truth, said Braden's thought-voice, still faint. *And there's somebody else with her. I know that mind... It's...*

But he trailed off as a pair of feet and legs emerged from the shaft. A woman. She reached the bottom of the ladder and turned to face them. Her dark eyes wore a look of sadness and sympathy. Behind her, another woman came down the ladder. Like Kim and

Merida, one of this woman's arms was in a sling. She was younger than the first woman. And familiar.

86

Val

"Got you, you fucking bitch," growled a mouth right next to Val's ear.

She let out a gasp and a small whine as he drew the knife out of her back. She couldn't see it, but she knew that he was raising it to strike again.

"Gonna fucking kill that husband of yours, too," said the man. "And then that fucking *freak* of a kid."

White dots, dancing in her eyes. Like stars. Far away.

Kim, she thought. *Braden.*

Thunder in the distance. Or was it close? Gunfire? Even the air shook.

And then the weight was gone from her back as her enemy collapsed into the dirt at her right.

"I'm sorry," gasped a voice from somewhere close by.

Val lifted her head to look left.

Another body. Hicks. He lay on his side about eight yards away.

But his arm was reaching toward her now, the rifle in his hand, its barrel slightly raised off the dirt.

Val tried to speak. "Thank..." But the word died in her throat, and then her vision blurred. She lay her head down and closed her eyes, offering up a prayer for her family.

Hicks said something else, but she couldn't understand him. She didn't think he was talking to her, anyway. A beep. A muffled voice. Someone speaking through a communicator. And then silence.

We're going to lose this fight, she had told Kim just days ago.

With a fleeting tug of shame, she realized that it was easier to surrender to the darkness than she had ever expected.

EPILOGUE

Jessica

The dawn sky turned crimson and then orange as Jessica, Wallace, and Celina approached the north side of Atlanta. Ahead, a green sign read GEORGIA CITADEL: EXIT NOW. Jessica turned on her blinker, changed lanes, and exited. Another ten miles and they'd be at the Citadel, where the conference was being held.

Wallace had ridden in the back seat of the car for the whole trip, working on a new set of press corps e-credentials for Jessica. He'd also kept Jessica and Celina updated on the news. Several state senators and representatives had backed out of the conference, but most were still attending. The Governor and Lieutenant Governor would be there. Dozens of Georgia business leaders. And around two thousand citizens were expected to be there to listen to deliberations and clamber for a chance to have their voices heard by the whole world.

"Nothing about what happened at the farm," said Wallace.

"In this case, I think no news really *is* good news," said Jessica.

"Do you think they're okay?"

Jessica didn't answer at first. Evan's dead face, and Tasia's final words to them, a command and a reproach, filled the silence like smoke.

"They have to be," she said after a while, though the dread that had pooled in the pit of her stomach said otherwise.

"I'm not sure that's a logical answer," said Wallace.

Jessica met his eyes in the rearview mirror. It wasn't logical, but logic alone wasn't going to get her through this. She shrugged, putting on a light tone that she didn't at all feel. "These days, pretty much everybody I know thinks that I've completely abandoned logic."

"That thought has occurred to me," said Celina, who sounded groggy. "Once or twice."

"Yeah, me too," said Wallace.

"Well, you should have some hope," said Jessica.

"Oh yeah?" said Wallace. "Okay. I'll make a note and stick it to the bathroom mirror in the house that I can probably never return to. 'Have hope! Because Jessica Brantley says so.'"

"I'm serious."

Wallace snorted. In some ways, he reminded her of Merida. That thought sent a sharp pang through her chest.

"And what makes you so committed to hope, may I ask?" he said.

Jessica didn't answer for a moment. Traipsing through the woods earlier to find the car, she'd almost given up several times. More than once she'd had to stop and put her hand on a tree trunk for support, her legs threatening to give out under her. After seeing Evan's death and hearing the misery and anger in Tasia's voice, she had wondered whether it was better to go back—or to just stop and wait for someone to find her. Despair was so easy. Hope was hard.

But Val was hard, too. And maybe Jessica could be, as well.

Finally, she answered Wallace's question. "If you knew my sister, you'd understand. She and I haven't always been close, but ever since I was a little girl, I always knew something about her."

She thought of Val punching the guy who had tried to drag Jessica into the locker room at school. He had been twice Val's size, and she had still laid him out cold with that punch.

"What's that?" said Wallace.

"Val's stubborn," said Jessica. "And really infuriating sometimes. But she's also *good,* and there is not a damn thing in this world that can stop her."

She glanced in the rearview mirror at Wallace, expecting a skeptical expression. Instead, he was staring at his computer, wide-eyed.

"Oh," he said. "Holy... Oh, my God."

"What is it?" said Jessica, her heart leaping into her throat. "What happened?"

Agora: The Ideas Marketplace

Fox News: BREAKING: Reports indicate a massive explosion in #Moscow. No official statements as of yet.

CNN: BREAKING: Explosion reported in #Moscow. Blackouts happening across #Russia and as far west as #Lithuania, #Belarus, and #Ukraine

Danni254: Oh my God. I was on holo with my husband whos in Moscow! There was a huge noise in the background a bright light and then the holo cut off! I'm so scared I think my husband is dead!!!

Rorschach1987: I exist in Minsk people are insane going in this place please do not loot your neighbors (TRANSLATED FROM TRASYANKA BY AGORA LEARN)

CNN: BREAKING: Apparent nuclear device discovered in #Beijing. Chinese officials say it malfunctioned, failed to detonate.

XavierLovesCarlos: yo chk this vid out looks like people are fkn up #SaintPetersburg stealin holos and shoes don't yall russian fools know the world ending round yall asses???

KarolS: Yoshkin cat! I am in Serpukhov and I can see mushroom cloud over #Moscow area. (TRANSLATED FROM RUSSIAN BY AGORA LEARN)

CNN: BREAKING: President to hold news conference at 10:00 AM ET to address the #MoscowBombing

MSNBC: Georgia, Cascadia secession conferences to move ahead today, security tightened in response to #MoscowBombing. Vice President deletes Shout threatening military action if states follow through on secession.

Fox News: BREAKING: Russian President #Lebedev alive and safe in Saint Petersburg, promises "swift and terrible" action against those responsible for #MoscowBombing.

abcdef1234567: I am a person with access to the Russian government. Russian military leaders and Lebedev discussing military action. General Sokolov advocating strikes against U.S, Germany, France, Britain. He believes American and European "mind-reader spies" responsible for #MoscowBombing.

SHOUTS AREN'T LOADING RIGHT NOW.
PLEASE TRY AGAIN LATER.

THANKS (AND SORRY!) FROM
THE AGORA TEAM.

FORBIDDEN MINDS | BOOK THREE

THE LATE HOUR

COMING 2022

ABOUT THE AUTHOR

Armond Boudreaux is a writer and English professor who lives in Georgia with his wife and children. In addition to the Forbidden Minds series, he also writes nonfiction about pop culture, philosophy, and politics.